"This novel is a strikingly original addition to the rich, burgeoning field of gender studies and is written in a deceptively simple style, never melodramatic but understated, even humble, a plain song as readable and vast as wheat fields grown to the horizon along the great American plains."

Lex Williford, author of *Macauley's Thumb*

"This novel is charming, compelling, and wholly absorbing. The writing is precise, unadorned, and, at times, quietly lyrical. At its heart, this is a story about community, identity, and love. While the novel certainly tackles a subject—gender identity—that has been rightfully getting a lot of traction lately in various media, what draws me into this story is the way Maher writes of friendship and love and daily life in this small town in Indiana, Heaven. The tenderness with which Maher renders these characters and this community is compelling and heartrending."

Chad Simpson, author of *Tell Everyone I Said Hi*

"In *Earth As It Is*, Jan Maher deftly and delicately threads her narrative, the story of a heterosexual cross-dresser seeking a home, through thirty years of American culture. Her novel is deceptively powerful, smooth like the surface of a river that belies the pull beneath it. You slip in, and before you know it you've traveled quite a distance and have no interest in leaving. A very rewarding, and at turns, surprising work."

Steve Adams, 2014 Pushcart Prize Winner for Nonfiction

"This book is an excellent read—the story is so very sweet and poignant. Maher has done a wonderful job showing the nature of true love."

Jan Brown, co-founder of Mid-Hudson Transgender Association

"The luminous story of Charlie/Charlene delves into what it means to be a man or a woman—it wraps the reader up in the warm, loving, gossipy, and sometimes uncomfortable world of women in a small-town beauty salon. Jan Maher captures the essence of complex, memorable characters and reflects both ordinary and extraordinary lives in mid-twentieth-century America."

Julie Weston, author of *Moonshadows*

"Maher has that gift, coveted among writers, of entering fully whatever psyche she touches. At once amusing, sensitive, and articulate, she carries us to surprising places—in this case into the heart of a cross-dressing dentist whose humanity we at once recognize as our own."

Ann Tracy, author of *What Do Cowboys Like?*

"Charlie Bader's love of softness and delicacy should be irrelevant to how he is perceived but that's not the way things are, so Charlie's got a problem. How he resolves it brings him face to face with major ethical questions we all encounter. When and to whom do we reveal truths about our intimate reality? Why and for whose sake do we keep secrets? And how much comfort and strength do we gain when we discover we are not alone? Visit Heaven, Indiana, in Jan Maher's groundbreaking novel and explore these essential questions about identity, authenticity, compromise, and love."

Susan Koppelman, PhD, editor of *Women in the Trees: U.S. Women's Short Stories about Battering and Resistance, 1839–2000* and *Between Mothers and Daughters: Stories across a Generation*

"Gender diversity is, and has always been, all around—in our families, hometowns, places of worship, workplaces, and communities. Maher's *Earth As It Is* takes place in a time in which individual, family, and societal possibilities and expectations collide and combine in unexpected ways while friendship, loyalty, and love prevail."

Luca Maurer, director of the Center for LGBT Education, Outreach & Services, Ithaca College

EARTH AS IT IS

break away books

INDIANA UNIVERSITY PRESS

Bloomington & Indianapolis

EARTH AS IT IS

Jan Maher

This book is a publication of

INDIANA UNIVERSITY PRESS
Office of Scholarly Publishing
Herman B Wells Library 350
1320 East 10th Street
Bloomington, Indiana 47405 USA

iupress.indiana.edu

Manufactured in the
United States of America

*Library of Congress
Cataloging-in-Publication Data*

Names: Maher, Jan, author.
Title: Earth as it is / Jan Maher.
Description: Bloomington :
    Indiana University Press, 2017.
    | Series: Break away books
Identifiers: LCCN 2016024864 | ISBN
    9780253024046 (pb : alk. paper)
    | ISBN 9780253024107 (eb)
Subjects: LCSH:
    Transvestites – Indiana – Fiction.
    | Transvestism – Fiction. |
    Gender identity – Fiction.
    | GSAFD: Love stories.
Classification: LCC PS3613.A34929
    E27 2017 | DDC 813/.6 – dc23
LC record available at https://
    lccn.loc.gov/2016024864

1 2 3 4 5   22 21 20 19 18 17

Somewhere the load is lifted.

JESSIE B. POUNDS

CONTENTS

ACKNOWLEDGMENTS

Thank you to readers who offered valuable feedback and encouragement along the way: Rachelle Ackerman, Steve Adams, Jan Brown, Lonnie Fairchild, Elizabeth Garfield, Allen Lang, Diana Maher, Danny Miller, Sorrel North, Douglas Skopp.

Thank you to writing group colleagues for steadfast support: Elizabeth Garfield and Douglas Skopp (again), Susan Carr, Imelda Daranciang, Susie Irwin, Lorna Lee, Cynthia Newgarden, Laura Palkovic, Ann Tracy, Vera Vivante.

Thank you to Tom Moran and the Institute for Ethics in Public Life at SUNY Plattsburgh for a room of my own and a place at the table, and to Mike Morgan for guidance on voicing techniques.

Thank you to all whose stories, opinions, and insights have guided and inspired me.

Thank you to Sarah Jacobi and Break Away Books for believing in this project.

Thank you to Doug Selwyn for more reasons than I have room to list.

EARTH AS IT IS

HEAVEN, INDIANA, 1964

Helen Breck knew something was wrong. Just knew it. Charlene Bader never missed an appointment with a customer. Not in the nearly nineteen years her shop had been open. The women of Heaven counted on Charlene's Beauty Shop like they counted on social hour at church. She was more dependable than their dependable husbands, more faithful than the US mail. But then, even the US mail had been delayed since Saturday by the awful wave of snow and ice storms that had hit. For six nights and five days Heaven had frozen over. It was beautiful in its way, like a crystal palace in a fairy tale, but treacherous.

Of course, Charlene would have canceled any appointments she had at the beginning of the week when no one could walk or drive safely. The ice and bitter cold made for a deadly combination that anyone with sense would surely know better than to challenge. But now the temperature was climbing, snow was melting, streets and sidewalks were passable, and phones were mostly back in service. No, something was definitely wrong.

Helen knocked once on the beauty shop door, twice, waited a minute, then a third time before picking her way back through the sidewalk ice patches to her car. She sat for a moment trying to take deep breaths, tapping her gloved fingers on the steering wheel. She had come to rely on her monthly visit to Charlene as the one time she could speak her mind more or less freely without fear of hearing her words boomerang back on her through the gossip mill. Today, she'd hoped to discuss a new investment opportunity with the hairdresser. No one else in Heaven, including Helen's husband Lester, even knew she had investments. The strangeness of Charlene's shop being locked up tight made her chest tighten. Settle down, she told herself. *Maybe* ... but try as she might, she could not for the life of her think of a way to end that sentence positively. She put the car in gear and drove the two blocks to Clara's Kitchen where she borrowed the phone. It was an effort to dial with numb shaky hands, but she managed. There was no answer either at Charlene's home or at her shop. Helen's next call was to Harry Hess down at the police station.

Harry tried at first to calm her fears with reason, then thought better of it. Helen was, as everyone knew, a little around the bend. Had been ever since the death of her daughter Melinda a decade earlier. No, it wouldn't do to perturb Helen Breck. Harry swung by Clara's Kitchen in his patrol car and, together, he and Helen drove back up the street to Charlene's Beauty Shop. It remained closed. They drove on to Charlene's house.

Harry noted that the short walkway from the street to the porch was still quite icy, though there was crusty snow piled on both sides, a sure sign that Charlene had at least tried to keep up with the weather that had dumped white stuff on the town and surrounding area for almost a week.

They made their way carefully. He held Helen's elbow and could feel her nervous tension right through the sleeve of the heavy wool coat she wore. It made him nervous, too.

Having safely gained the porch, Harry rang the doorbell, then knocked. After waiting a respectable time for a response and hearing none, he tested the door. It opened easily, but this in itself was not a concern. No one in Heaven locked doors.

Seeing an empty living room and kitchen, he headed down the short hallway to check the bedroom.

Helen's scream brought him back. Rushing to the sound, he found her pale, shaking, standing in the bathroom over the crumpled form of Charlene Bader, who lay face down on the floor by a full tub of water, clad in a baby-blue terrycloth bathrobe.

Harry dropped to his knees and rolled her over. He held a hand to her mouth and another to her neck, feeling for signs of life. Charlene's skin was rough and cold. He felt no breath, no pulse.

Helen shrieked again, and her scream could have been his own. Charlene's bathrobe had fallen open. Charlene was undeniably dead. And Charlene Bader was undeniably a man.

2

DALLAS, TEXAS, 1933

Charlie Bader was alone in his house for the first time since his wedding night. He'd taken such great care these past five months to avoid just this circumstance, but now here he was.

At his office, surrounded by metal drills and enameled pans, sterile hard surfaces and sharp-tipped picks, he could suppress his urges; there was nothing to feed them. Today, though, his last patient had canceled so Charlie was free to lock up and leave early. He might have walked over to Sorgerstrom's to accompany his wife Anne home when she was finished working for the day, but it was too early for that. He had a full hour and a half with nothing to do. So now he was alone, standing in their bedroom.

His mind went in two directions at once. Anne, beautiful Anne, the love of his life. After all these months, Charlie still couldn't believe his luck: that she'd allowed him to court her, to propose, to marry her, to share her bed.

The halo of honey-blonde hair that framed her face was what he'd first noticed, that day a year ago when he'd accepted his landlady Mrs. Hesher's invitation to attend Sunday services at Christ of Calvary Church. Next, it was her golden voice. Her sweet soprano lifting above the others to sing of laying one's burdens at the feet of the Lord gladdened his heart. And when she'd made it a point to smile at his invalid sister Hannah, sat down to chat with the girl in the wheelchair, asked her questions and listened patiently as she struggled to push through her Parkinson's to answer them, Charlie was entirely smitten. Anne was a righteous Christian, warm, caring, and beautiful. Quite simply, he adored her.

At this moment, however, as he stood in the bedroom of their small house, it was Anne's nightgown that won the battle in his mind. This was the burden Charlie Bader was unable to lay down: his need for softness.

He'd discovered that, too, in church, as a child sandwiched in the pew between his father's scratchy wool suit and his mother's Sunday best. At five, he'd begun hiding in the closet where her dress and the faux fox fur she wore in cooler months spent the workweek. There, he could sit on the old steamer trunk, wrap the fox collar around his neck, rest against the cool fabric of the dress, and try to decide which he loved to feel the most. Was it the luxurious strip of fur, or the silkiness of the skirt? Or perhaps the satin lining on the belly of the fox collar?

He'd struggled with this desperately secret and damnable habit all through his childhood, through his move from Kirbyville to Dallas to attend dental school, right up to his honeymoon; but he'd sworn to stop it once he was married, and for five months, he'd succeeded. The scarves he'd bought for Hannah but borrowed while she slept stayed put in her dresser drawer unless she requested one. The cashmere sweater he'd gifted her with lay untouched unless she decided to wear it.

Anne, unwittingly, had made matters more difficult for Charlie by taking over care of Hannah's hair. Before the marriage, it was Charlie who combed it, worked the tangles out, braided and twisted it into the latest styles for his sister to admire in the mirror. After the wedding, Charlie's only opportunity to run his fingers through Hannah's thick tresses was the one evening a week Anne attended the missionary study group at church and Charlie was the one who brushed the braids out and helped her into bed.

Then Hannah's disease worsened, and they'd had to put her in a nursing home. Now, the only softness he had access to was Anne's nightgown and matching robe. When he embraced her, he embraced her robe as well. When they were intimate with one another, he was glad her sense of propriety prompted her to keep the nightgown on. He made love to them both: Anne and her gown.

Every day except Sunday, his angel wife worked for Mr. Sorgerstrom at the five and dime. And every day she worked, she got off when the store closed at six o'clock, then walked twenty minutes to get home. Charlie checked the clock. He had just over an hour. He opened the closet door and reached in to run his fingers along the cool, satiny folds of his wife's robe.

How could he have known that this afternoon, as he stood caressing the sateen, Mr. Sorgerstrom had told Anne to go early? That she'd done a bit of shopping, and would soon be home? She'd have been there already except that, on an impulse, she'd stopped on the way to say hello to her husband's old landlady, Mrs. Hesher.

Mrs. Hesher, the weathered widow who had first introduced them in church, had taken a special interest in them as two orphans of the great influenza epidemic, and considered herself personally responsible for their happiness. While Charlie was stripping off his shirt and pants, Mrs. Hesher was plying Anne with tea and cookies. While Charlie was slipping into the silky gown, Anne was updating Mrs. Hesher on Hannah's move to the nursing home (the doctors say most folks who get the Parkinson's after having sleepy sickness are a lot older; it's so sad, but she needs a level of care we just can't provide any longer) and Charlie's dental practice (doing better than most, thanks to a patient with simply dreadful teeth but excellent luck who struck oil on his land). While Charlie was regarding himself in the mirror, pushing his pectorals into small breast shapes, his wife was inquiring about Mrs. Hesher's son, who, shell-shocked and fragile, had finally come out of two decades of hiding in his room and gotten on with the WPA to help a muralist. While Anne was asking Mrs. Hesher the secret to making a hearty, lump-free sauce so she could surprise Charlie with biscuits and gravy for supper that night, Charlie was sitting at Anne's dressing table, reminiscing about his mother's dress and fox fur. He couldn't know that Mrs. Hesher was dabbing a bit of cologne behind Anne's ears, counseling her with a wink and a twinkle in her eye to woo her husband with the scent. He couldn't know she was sending Anne on her way home at that very moment.

Because it was still well before six o'clock, he allowed himself to tend to his nails. It was one thing he'd found he could do that no one seemed to notice.

* * *

"What . . ." Anne stood in the bedroom doorway, unable to comprehend the scene she'd stumbled onto. All the happy thoughts of how to delight her husband with sweet smells and favorite dishes vanished in the split second it took her to register what she saw there. Her Charlie Bader, the handsome, up-and-coming dentist, her *husband* wearing the peach-colored sateen dressing gown that had been the centerpiece of *her* bridal trousseau.

Charlie jumped up, frantic, from the dressing table, whirled away from her, stripped the robe off, yanked his pants on, and only then dared turn to face her.

"I'm sorry . . . I . . ."

Anne stared, stammering. Her Charlie? "What are you . . . why . . . what does . . . how could . . . ?"

"I'm sorry." Charlie's hands fluttered, trying to give him something to hide behind. "I wanted to tell you. I was afraid you'd . . . you wouldn't understand."

Anne found her voice. It erupted, burned her throat, poured out of her. "Wouldn't understand what? You in my . . . Charlie, how could you? How could you court me and marry me and . . . and . . . and *touch* me when all along you knew you were . . ."

"But I'm not . . ."

"I am not blind, Charlie Bader! I just *saw* you. I saw you . . ." She couldn't bear to give name to the spectacle. Her gown. Him wearing her gown. "You have lied to me. You have lied your way into my life, into my heart, into my bed. I was pure for you, but you have touched my body with your perverted hands and . . . and . . ." She flew into frenetic action, grabbing her clothes, her suitcase from the back of the closet, wrenching open the drawers of her bureau and feeding the clothes into the open maw of the luggage.

"Please, Anne, please don't. What are you doing? Where are you going?"

"That is not one bit of your business!" She yanked her blouses and skirts off the closet rod and folded them, yes folded them. She would have order. She would make something fit. She would make. Things. Fit.

"Please don't leave." He choked on the words. "I can't live without you. Anne, I'll move out till you'll have me back. I'll sleep at the office. Just stay, please stay." Even as he offered this desperate bargain, he felt a pit-of-stomach despair knowing it was hopeless.

She slammed the case shut. "I'll need a day to arrange travel. I will not stay under the same roof with you. I'm going into the kitchen till you leave. Let me know when you're on the way out," she hissed at him, then burst into sobs and ran from the room.

Charlie found her there, hands on the edge of the stove, holding herself up. "I'm going now," he spoke to the back of her head. "I know I have no right to ask you anything, but please, don't tell anyone. It will ruin me."

She refused to turn, to look at him. "Don't worry," she said bitterly. "What do you think people would say about me if they knew I didn't have the sense to recognize a pansy boy? I don't need anyone feeling sorry for me."

"It's not what you think. It really isn't. I'm not one of those . . . I don't . . . It's you I love."

"Just go."

"Will you let me explain?"

"Go."

"I do love you. With all my heart. It's not what you think. It's . . ."

"Get out, please. Now." Though he could not see her face he knew her chin jutted out and he knew from her voice she was crying through her harsh words. That was the last he saw of her. The points of her shoulder blades, the stiffness of her neck, the rigid way she held her arms against the stovetop edge.

Charlie hoped against hope that she'd reconsider. His heart leapt, when he awakened the next morning in his dental chair, at the sight of a note slid under his office door. He rushed to read it, but it only said that he could come back to the house now because she was gone, and not to come after her. She was headed to New Boston, where there was a missionary group that trained people for service in French West Africa. If her husband's soul was irretrievably lost, at least maybe she could save a few savages. He stood for a few moments holding the note, staring at it. Yes, his soul was lost. Gone forever with his beautiful bride. In its place, a hollowing and hopeless thing growing. He tore the note into tiny pieces, took them home to the backyard, and buried them.

* * *

Hannah spoke so softly it was difficult to hear what she asked. Charlie knelt by his sister's wheelchair and cupped his hand to his ear.

"What did you say?"

"Where is Anne?"

"She's gone away for a while."

Hannah's eyes looked like they wanted to say something, but her mouth refused to push any more sound out.

"She asked me to tell you hello for her."

Charlie could feel Hannah staring at him, even as he looked away, avoiding direct eye contact. Oh, he hated this dissembling. He'd never lied to his sister before. She was so fond of Anne, what could he tell her? That he was sorry, but she'd found him wearing her lingerie and left him? That now that she'd found out about this unnatural thing he felt compelled to do, they'd never, neither one of them, see her again?

Maybe someday he could figure out a way to explain. Tell Hannah how it had always been this way, even before she was born. That he'd just get urges and have to do something about it. Maybe she could understand. It was never something he intended to do, not really. More like an itch that would start as a tickle and grow until— every now and then—it just had to be scratched.

Maybe someday Hannah would forgive him for causing the only person in her life she loved besides him to vanish from her pitifully limited world. She asked for so little. As her disease closed in on her, she bore it with stubborn grace. But everyone could tell she was delighted beyond measure when Anne and Charlie visited her. And though Charlie was the one she performed somersaults for when she was three and splashed in the creek with when she was seven, the one who nursed her through her long illnesses and indulged her insistence that he move them to Dallas to become one of Texas's first certified dentists, Anne was the person who brought the world of womanhood to her. The one who made her feel fashionable. The one who shared sisterly secrets with her. The one who could make her feel almost normal. It was Anne who could bring a smile to her face that cut through the disease-imposed mask.

Hannah was trying to talk again. Again, Charlie cupped his hand to his ear and leaned in to hear. "Charlie."

"Yes, Hannah?"

"Will she come to see me next week?"

"I don't know, Hannah. I don't think so. But it's not your fault. It's my fault."

"What did you do?"

"I disappointed her."

"How?"

"I'll tell you someday. I promise. Don't blame Anne."

"Charlie?"

"Yes?"

"You didn't . . . break your vows?"

"No, Hannah. I love Anne too much. I kept the commandents." He attempted a grin, hoping this deliberate use of her childhood mispronunciation would amuse and distract her, but instead he had to swallow hard to stifle grief.

"Charlie?"

"Yes?"

He waited a long time, but Hannah's energy for speaking was gone. She lapsed into silence. Only her hands moved, rhythmically rolling against her thighs. Her face was impassive, save a tear that trickled down her left cheek. Finally, Charlie spoke again.

"Hannah, there's something else I need to tell you. I'm going to move on up to Chicago. Dallas would be too far away for me to visit you more than a couple of times a year, so I've found a place for you to stay in Indianapolis. They have other folks there like you, with the Parkinson's, so they'll know how to care for you better. I'll take you up next week, and I'll come to see you just as often as I can. I'll come every weekend if I can." He paused again, wrestling emotion to maintain his composure.

Hannah stared at the wall.

"I need a fresh start. I need to start over again. I need to go where no one knows me. No one."

"Charlie . . ."

"What?"

"Do braids for me. The kind you used to do right after Mama died."

"Of course." Charlie moved behind her chair and pulled his fingers through her thick blonde hair. He could feel his sister relax as he worked the tangles out, and fashioned two French braids. It comforted him, too.

They sat for another twenty minutes or so, Charlie watching Hannah, Hannah watching the wall. Then the nurse came to get her ready for an afternoon nap.

3

CHICAGO, ILLINOIS, 1933

He arrived in Chicago with his drill, his filling supplies, denture-making materials, and just enough savings to rent a small room in a boarding house on North Halsted Street and buy a few clothes. He determined to give himself just two weeks in which to indulge his urges. Go all the way with it. A full outfit. Safe from discovery in his little closet of a room he would dress to the nines. Get it all out of his system. Then he would quit forever.

It was what they called an Indian summer day, one of those glorious warm fall days that invites, in fact insists on, a stroll through the neighborhood. There was a clothing store a couple of blocks away, and he went in, said he was looking for an outfit to buy his fiancée. He expected to find a skirt-and-sweater combination, but stumbled instead on something much more extraordinary.

Working as a dentist one sees teeth, mouths, lips, and facial skin close up, but also collarbones and necks. A woman's collarbone is shorter, with more curve. A man's collarbone is thicker in the middle. A man's neck has an Adam's apple, a woman's doesn't. Eve's apple stuck in Adam's throat.

That's how he knew. The sales clerk was shorter than Charlie. She had thick brown hair swept up in an elegant twist, beautiful long nails, with bright red polish to match her lipstick. She wore a gray tweed skirt and pink, boat-neck pullover. The tiniest hint of an Adam's apple peeked out. And the collarbones of a man. She was very attentive to Charlie, showed him a number of sweaters, asked him questions about his fiancée. He talked about Anne as if he were courting her all over again. Even though he knew he'd never dare court again. He changed only one detail. Anne was, he told the clerk, tall for a woman.

He caught himself staring at the clerk's neck, and then, to avoid that, her face. Her gracious smile flustered him, so he looked down instead at the countertop and kept his eyes on the items she showed him.

He selected a white cardigan, a broad-collared, black-and-white checked blouse, a rich red silk scarf, and a charcoal gray skirt, paid his money, said thank you, and hurried home. Was he going daft? Or had he really noticed a man under that makeup? No one else in the store—not the other clerk, nor other customers—seemed to think there was anything unusual going on. As he sat with the scarf comforting his neck, stroking the sweater, something that felt very dangerous called to Charlie. Perhaps, rather than hiding in his room, he might venture out. Venture back to the store where he'd found . . . what had he found? He wasn't sure. He wanted to know more. He had to know more.

He located undergarments in the Monkey Ward catalogue he'd picked up in the entry hall to the boarding house addressed to the previous tenant of his room, and a pair of shoes too. He phoned in his order and had the items wrapped and put aside for him, told them at "will call" he was picking up his wife's package for her. On his way back home, he went to a theatrical supply company and told them he was playing the lead in *Charley's Aunt* in a community theater production. The proprietor helped him pick out an ash blonde wig, stage makeup, lipstick, and a jar of Pond's cold cream. You'll want the cold cream, the fellow told him, to get all that off your skin after the show.

This is a wonderful thing about Chicago, thought Charlie. It's not the least bit like Kirbyville, where everybody knows everybody else's business. Here, I am anonymous. Here, I can go one block from my room and no one knows me. The people on Halsted Street hardly notice me going by. Not that people are unfriendly, just that there are so darned many of them you can get lost if you want to. And I do want to get lost. Nobody knows I've just bought myself a wig. Nobody knows I've got a brassiere in this bag. Nobody knows a thing about me.

The next day Charlie checked to make sure his door was locked and made his preparations. He laid everything out on the bed. The look he'd modeled after Joan Crawford, minus low-cut necklines. He shaved his arms and legs and rubbed them with a little of the cold cream. He filed and buffed his nails. He put the undergarments on— brassiere, panties, garter belt, silk stockings—and just sat for twenty minutes or so with his eyes closed, feeling the smooth, cool, silky fabrics against his skin. Next came the eyebrows: careful plucking to shape them, but not so much that he'd look peculiar when it came time to change back into his regular clothing in another few hours. He'd already shaved his face carefully, wanting no nicks to announce his maleness, and now he shaved again. Rubbed more Pond's in. Applied a light touch of the pancake makeup. Stuffed cotton pads into the bra. Positioned the wig, already styled, something he'd stayed up late doing the night before. Stepped into the skirt, slipped on the blouse, buttoned it up. That took a little getting used to. He was accustomed to his shirt buttons being on the right. His fingers fumbled, but the buttons were large and that made it easier. Once buttoned, he added the lipstick. Knotted the scarf loosely around his neck and tucked the ends into the blouse so his Adam's apple was securely and well concealed. Looked, for the first time, at the whole effect in the mirror. Someone who looked like Joan Crawford's cousin looked back at him. Charlie amazed himself.

His room was the closest to the front of the building, with a window that looked out on the stoop so he could see when the coast was clear. It was a small boarding house; the other tenants on his floor were an elderly Polish woman who left her room every afternoon at one o'clock and returned at three, a young fellow who worked at the stockyards and usually didn't come home until he'd had a few pints at McCloskey's, and a Japanese couple who worked twelve-hour days in a dry cleaner on Lincoln Avenue.

Mr. and Mrs. Nakagawa had long since gone to work and wouldn't be back until after seven. Darby Neep would be even later. Charlie watched out the window till Mrs. Kowalsky went out to do her marketing. While he waited, he practiced speaking out loud in a high voice, whatever he could think of to say. A big black bug bit a big black bear. A flea and a fly in a flue. Round the rugged rock the ragged rascal ran. Then he was out and walking up the street, a little unsteady in the black leather pumps. Charlie, out for a careful, thrilling stroll in his new skirt, blouse, sweater, scarf, wig and hat, stockings and pumps; his first full outfit that was indisputably his own, not secretly borrowed from mother or wife, not shared with sister, not a single piece of clothing but the whole nine yards. He could feel the flutter of his heart.

He had guessed at the shoe size, and they were just a bit too small. He hadn't dared practice walking because the tenant below him, a schoolteacher by the name of Lillian Finley, had commented at supper a few nights back that she heard him pace overhead at night. If she hears me pace at night in stocking feet, Charlie worried, she'll certainly hear me pacing overhead in these.

Charlie did his best to stroll casually up Halsted Street to Cott's Clothing Store and went in. The clerk who'd sold him the sweater wasn't in evidence, so he looked through the new-arrivals dress rack. The saleslady on the floor was in her sixties, had small bits of powder in the creases of her crow's feet, smelled like lavender, and kept telling Charlie about a new scent the gentlemen were sure to love. It was a toilet water, not a cologne. Everyone was on a tight budget these days, she pointed out, so the company had introduced a whole line of cosmetics and scented waters that were elegant, but very affordable. And the gentlemen would really go for it. She dabbed a bit on her wrist and offered it to him to smell.

The scent of lavender made him anxious, in spite of its reputation for calming the nerves. Lavender would forever remind him of the looming and critical figure of Miss Willick, his elementary school teacher. He would have happily gone to his grave never smelling the scent of lavender again. He wrinkled his nose reflexively and the saleslady pulled her hand back. "What scents do you prefer?"

Do you have anything to make a lady who's really a gentleman irresistible to a lady with an open mind? No, he couldn't ask that. He shrugged, which seemed to inspire the woman to try to educate him about how to attract men. He was standing at the cologne counter enduring the woman's persistent prattling on about the relative merits of rosewater and geranium when the clerk he was waiting for came out of the back room.

She remembered him immediately. "Good morning," she said. "That's the blouse I sold you yesterday, isn't it? It looks wonderful on you!"

"Thank you," Charlie spluttered. That she'd recognize him in an instant was not something he'd expected. Was he that transparent? His heart was pounding and his voice was threatening to break, so he turned away and pretended to be contemplating items on the new-arrivals rack until he felt a little calmer and, too, until the woman behind the cologne counter gave up on him and drifted to another part of the store. Then he looked back to yesterday's clerk, who now stood near the front counter. He tottered toward her and took the plunge. "You did such a good job of picking this one out, I wonder if you have any other recommendations?" He was shaking so he could barely squeak the words out.

She smiled. "I have a brushed cashmere sweater that is quite beautiful. It just came in." She brought a delicate, pale yellow faux turtleneck from behind the counter and offered it to him. "Feel this," she said. "Isn't it gorgeous?"

Charlie touched the unbelievably soft patch of sweater.

"Are you new around here? I don't believe I've seen you before. Did Luella send you by any chance?"

"I don't know anyone named Luella. I just moved up from Texas." He was trying hard to keep his voice high, but it cracked on "Texas" the way it did when he was fourteen.

"Whereabouts?" the older woman wanted to know from across the store floor. What a busybody, Charlie thought, steeling himself for the task of continuing to sound feminine. He was saved from her curiosity when another customer came in and wanted to try the new scent.

"I know it can be kind of hard to meet people with your interests when you've just come to town. Are you a churchgoer?" The clerk asked it quietly, and in a slightly lower voice, signaling that Charlie could relax his voice a bit too, if he kept it sotto.

"Usually. I haven't found a church yet in Chicago."

"I hope you'll come to my church this Sunday. We have a wonderful pastor, and"—the clerk switched back to a woman's voice as the other customer drifted from the perfume counter, contemplating the rack of new arrivals—"there are several ladies our age," she winked and went on, "who attend regularly."

"It's very kind of you to invite me."

"It's called Grace Chapel. It's just about six blocks up Fullerton on the left side of the street. Now, I would be shirking my responsibilities to my employer if I didn't also invite you to try one of these scarves. I think this one would be particularly attractive with the yellow sweater. Scarves make everything so flexible. And," she smiled and winked again, "they hide all kinds of small faults. I, for example, like to cover a little double-chin that seems to be developing in spite of my efforts to give up sweets."

Charlie paid for the sweater and scarf, and wondered if he dared shop for shoes that really fit. "Do you know of a good shoe store?" he asked.

Two hours later, he was sitting on his bed daubing Mercurochrome on painful blisters, but feeling triumphant, and not only at having acquired a new pair of pumps with sensible heels and sufficient room for his feet. He had made it out and back again without being found out by anyone but the clerk. And wasn't that something? That the clerk was a man in woman's clothing? Who must do this every day, or at least every workday? Charlie would never want to dress up every day. Just one more time. To wear the yellow sweater and his new shoes.

And there was a church where he could dare it? Not like the church of his childhood, where the best he could hope for was a crowded pew that required pressing against his mother's dress. From what the clerk said, this was a church where he could wear his *own* dress. He hoped by Sunday the blisters plaguing his feet would heal over enough to allow him to test his nerve and attend services in his new outfit. To do it one more time. He'd have to practice the voice more. Or figure out how to say less. Then, he told himself, he would stop. He would put the sweaters away. Maybe take them out to feel once in a while if the urge got too strong. He would donate the shoes to charity. The brassiere would go into the garbage chute. He'd take the scarves to Hannah on his next visit. He would get this out of his system and get on with life.

As he pulled the yellow sweater out of its box to put it away, a small piece of paper fluttered out and fell to the floor. Charlie picked it up and read, "You are welcome to join us Saturday evening as well, for dessert and tea. We are a social club of like-minded ladies who call ourselves the Full Self Sisterhood. We meet at my house, 2318 N. Dayton, 5:00 PM. Yours sincerely, Joanne Bailey."

Friday morning Charlie made a long-distance call to Indianapolis, asking the nurse to explain to Hannah that he was still getting settled in Chicago, and would be down the next weekend without doubt. Then he walked by 2318 North Dayton. It was a duplex, with a large front porch. He dared walk up the steps, ready with the story that he was looking for 2318 North Lincoln should anyone ask him what he wanted. He would pretend to be lost, on the wrong street. It would fit with the consternation he felt, and surely be believable.

There were two mailboxes on the porch, by two doorbells. Joseph Bailey was the name on the upstairs bell; Joanne Bailey was downstairs. Charlie hurried home, heart pounding. Would he dare do this? Could he? Should he? Shouldn't he just stop right now? What if Joanne and her friends thought he was what Anne thought he was? But Joanne hadn't seemed—Charlie stood still to consider this thought—effeminate. She hadn't seemed interested in him, other than as a customer, and a kindred spirit and kind of co-conspirator. He hadn't felt any of the thrill he'd felt when he first met Anne, none of the surge of physical interest. The thrill associated with meeting Joanne was that of being recognized but not being caught. It was entirely different. Charlie decided to trust it.

Saturday morning he woke up early. Shaved. Couldn't eat breakfast. Too tense, too wound up. Shaved again. Laid out the skirt, the yellow sweater, the scarf, the undergarments. Shaved his legs. As he leaned over to run the razor up his calves, his heart felt as if it wanted to jump right out through his chest. Pausing to steady his nerves, he caught sight of his fingernails. They were trimmed, clean, and neat, but the cuticles were a little rough. He finished shaving his legs, pulled on his pants, and went to the grocery store to buy peanut oil. Back in his room, he put a bit of the oil in the ashtray that had come with the furnishings in the place, and put it on the windowsill in the sunlight. When it was a little warm to the touch, he rubbed it into his cuticles, pushing them back until they were even and smooth, the way he'd watched his mother do it a quarter century before.

He looked at the clock. It was just noon. Too tense to eat lunch, and not wanting to interrupt his preparations again to go down to the dining room, he examined his eyebrows. Pulled a few stray hairs out by pinching them between his fingernails. 12:20. He rubbed some of the peanut oil on his legs, soothing the skin that was not used to razor blades. 12:30. He lay down, tried to rest. 1:00. Another shave, and a little Pond's on his cheeks and chin.

At 3:30, he put the wig stand on his table and fiddled a little, pulling the hair at the hairline down a bit to hide the edge of the mesh that held it in place. Charlie had a widow's peak, inherited from his father Jarvis; the wig did not. That was the thing that was oddest to him when he actually put the wig on and saw himself in the mirror. His distinctive hairline was gone, replaced by curls. At 3:40, he applied the lipstick, not neatly enough, wiped it off, and tried again. Better. At 4:00, he put the skirt, sweater, and shoes on, and looped the scarf around his neck. Then he sat on the edge of his bed and crossed his ankles. That turned out to be less than comfortable, so he relaxed his posture and worked on his voice, opting for more practical phrases this time. Thank you for inviting me. Your house is beautiful. I really must go now.

Finally, it was time to walk over to Dayton Street. He looked out his window to make sure no one was coming or going at the door downstairs. Then he opened his door, looked to make sure no one was in the hallway upstairs, and listened to make sure no one was out and about in the downstairs hallway. A quick trip down the steps, through the door, off the porch, onto the sidewalk and he was free to fully assume his new persona without fear of a neighbor inside the building recognizing him. Out on the street, the disguise was convincing enough that a young man hurrying by who bumped into him said, "Pardon me, ma'am" and kept right on going.

He walked more steadily in shoes that actually fit him. They felt better, too, for the fact that he'd found a box of bunion pads in the hallway bathroom and taken two to cover his blisters. Later, he'd buy a box at the pharmacy and replace the ones he'd borrowed.

It seemed sudden, his arrival at the house on Dayton. Here he was at a place he'd unconsciously sought much of his life, but never expected to find. Never even dared to dream of. A place where there were people like him. Men like him. A possibility he had never before considered and still wasn't sure he believed.

He walked up the steps and there he stood on the porch, wondering if he dared. Wondering what he had been invited to. Wondering who he was, and what he was doing here. He knew so little about himself and his hungers, even less about others who shared his compulsion. He knew only that he craved the softness of women's clothing, had craved it as long as he could remember. Had spent a lifetime of furtive indulgence, first in his parents' closet with his mother's fox fur, then the room at Mrs. Hesher's boarding house in Dallas after everyone was asleep with scarves he'd gifted to his invalid sister, accompanied always by fear of discovery. The wrenching pain of his wife's scorn swarmed his memory. Suddenly he doubted his instincts of three days before, when he was sure the clerk's friendliness had no sexual overtones. Before he could bolt, though, a taxicab stopped, discharged its two passengers, and drove on. Neither was as tall as Charlie. Both were very elegantly dressed, sporting fur stoles, though there was really no need from a weather standpoint, and alligator shoes and matching handbags. "Isn't she home?" the shorter of the two, a barrel-bodied brunette, asked. "She said five o'clock, didn't she? It's just five right now."

"I didn't ring the bell yet," Charlie confessed, and with his opportunity to flee having passed, he reached to press the button. From far off inside the house, they could hear the doorbell's clarion call, and a moment later they heard Joanne calling, "Just a moment." She opened the door and positively beamed when she saw Charlie in the group.

"I was afraid you wouldn't find the note," she said, "or would find it but not respond. Do come in." She smiled brightly and turned to the others. "Come in, come in. Have you met one another yet? I realize I don't even know your name."

"Charlie," he said.

"Oh, no, dear. Your name for dressing."

"I . . . I don't know."

"How would it be if we call you Charlene? Is that all right with you?"

Charlie blushed. Of course he would need a name to go with the outfit. "It surely is. It's fine."

"Charlene!" she enthused. "Of course you can choose any name you like, any time, but Charlene will do for today till you have a chance to think about it. This is Theresa, and this is Luella." Theresa turned out to be the one who'd already spoken to him. Joanne reached out to touch Theresa's fur. "What a beautiful stole! It must have cost you a fortune." Charlie wanted to follow suit, but held back.

Theresa smiled. "Installments. I'll be eating stale bread crusts for dinner and paying for this a good long time. It was an utterly reckless purchase, but I just had to have it. One gets so tired of looking shabby."

Luella, a dishwater blonde with tight curls who stood slightly taller than her companion, was not to be left out. "It's from Monsieur René's, where I got mine." She held a befurred arm out, inviting Joanne and Charlene to feel, to know that her stole was every bit as authentic as Theresa's.

Charlie touched, tentatively. "It's so beautiful!" he murmured. Luella's stole made his mother's old fox fur from Kirbyville, stored in Charlie's memory, feel like a porcupine pelt in comparison.

"M'sieur René is someone we might want to invite," Luella told the others with a wink.

"Oh, really?" Joanne asked, eyebrows raised.

"Oh yes," Theresa confirmed. "We're sure of it."

Charlie was suddenly lightheaded with the realization that there were indeed others in the world like him. And that he was standing there with some of them just as openly as his parents and their friends used to stand on the porch of their little church in Kirbyville, for all to see, just as normal as the next person.

Joanne urged the trio to come inside. She would stay near the door to wait for Darla, Marie, and Jacquie. "They," Luella confided with a hint of a whine, "are always late."

"Susie isn't coming?"

"No, she has a family obligation today. Her in-laws are in town."

"That's a shame." Theresa turned to Charlie. "This is your first time at Joanne's." It was a statement, not a question. "And how did you find us?"

"Excuse me?"

"How did you and Joanne connect? How did she recognize you as one of us?"

"Oh!" He felt so bumbling, but so fascinated with these two self-assured women—elegant, graceful, yet he knew for a fact, men underneath their jewels and furs. "I bought this sweater from her."

"She has impeccable taste, doesn't she? My wife swears by her advice."

"Your wife?"

"Knows about me? Oh yes, dear. I am one of the luckiest of the lucky. My wife is who first introduced me to Joanne, in fact. She's very discerning."

Luella caught Charlie's eye. "She's lucky indeed. My wife would faint if she ever knew. And then she'd leave me."

"That's what mine did," Charlie said.

"Oh, I'm sorry!" Theresa reached out to touch his hand, and that simple act of kindness, so unexpected, moved him so that tears came unbidden to his eyes.

"It's all right," said Luella. "Here, sit down. You're safe here."

Joanne hung the fur stoles in the coat closet while Luella and Theresa led Charlie into the living room.

The doorbell announced that the first of Joanne's latecomers had arrived. Luella handed Charlie a handkerchief, which he gratefully accepted.

"*Bonjour! Mesdames! Mes amies!*" The willowy figure with a shock of dense black curls, brown eyes, and olive skin who stood in the door grabbed Joanne by the shoulders and planted a kiss on each cheek.

"Hello, Marie."

"Hallo, *toute le monde.*" Marie's smile revealed several missing teeth that contradicted her otherwise youthful appearance.

"Don't mind Marie," Theresa said to Charlie. "She is feeling *française, ne'est-ce-pas?*"

"*Oui,* I am feeling *très française* today."

"Marie was born in France," Luella explained.

"And I miss it still," Marie pouted.

"But she was only five years old when she left," Theresa added.

"Someday I will go back again."

Joanne interrupted with a practiced graciousness that steered the conversation back to introductions. "Marie, this is Charlene, who has just recently moved to Chicago. Charlene," she continued, "this is Marie. Now would everyone like some tea? This is something I learned in a booklet about making ends meet. One tea bag, steeped in boiling hot water. Add one tablespoon of apple jelly. It makes four times as many servings." She poured four cups from her teapot and took the tray around to each of her guests.

"It is delicious," Charlie affirmed.

"My friends, I have *des mauvaises nouvelles.*" Marie paused to sip tea and build suspense, then continued with a pout. "My job application with the CCC is turned down."

"CCC?" Theresa asked.

"Civilian Conservation Corps."

"Oh yes, of course."

"You aren't too old? I thought you had to be under twenty-four." Luella winked at Theresa, put her cup down, and signaled to Joanne that the tea was indeed delicious.

"And don't I look under twenty-four?"

"You look seventeen," Joanne soothed.

"I was only teasing," Luella assured Marie.

"Seventeen is fine. Sixteen is too young. In any case, I am twenty-two. No, that isn't why."

"Why won't they take you?" Theresa took up the questioning.

"I have to have six teeth. Three above, three below. I have only five, and they are all below. *C'est stupide!*" Marie fumed. "What difference does it make how many teeth I have? The CCC will plant trees and build roads. What do my teeth have to do with it?"

"It's the government," Luella said. "They have to have their rules. Otherwise . . ."

"Let's not get into politics, ladies," Joanne begged.

"Luella is not a fan of Mr. Roosevelt," Theresa explained to Charlie.

"Ah, but someday she will need to take a road and it will turn out to be one built by the CCC!" Marie said, as triumphantly as if it had actually already happened, and then fell into a sulk. "But I will not be one of the crew who built it, you see. Because? I will tell you why. *Parce que* there was nothing for my mother to eat when she was raising me up, and nothing for me to eat, so we have bad teeth, both of us. Maybe there are lucky ones who have always had good food."

She fluttered her eyelashes at Luella, a tease verging on bitter. "For us, the Germans..."

"Can't you get false teeth?" Joanne interrupted.

"How can I pay for false teeth?"

"Maybe you could find someone who would be willing to wait until you get paid."

"There is a dentist near my apartment. I asked him and he said, 'I'm sorry, but there is a Depression on. I have to eat too.' Everything is pay at the time of services."

Before he had time to think about it, Charlie's voice had dropped to its normal range and he had blurted out an offer. "I could do it for you."

"Excuse me, you...?"

"I am a dentist too," Charlie explained. "I could make uppers for you."

"*Mais non*, you are joking!"

"Truly. That's what I do. I fix teeth. I can make false teeth for you. I can do it."

"*Dieu est bon!*"

"But I don't have an office set up yet. I just moved up here from Dallas."

Theresa looked at Luella. "Luella, is your little storefront still for rent?"

Luella clapped in approval of Theresa's implied solution. "Of course! It would be perfect. It's on Fullerton. Very near here. Charlene, come by and see what you think. If you like it, I'll give you the first month's rent free."

"Are you sure?"

"No one can afford to open a business these days. It's been vacant since my last tenant moved out in the middle of the night in March of '30. I'm just lucky I paid the mortgage off in '28."

The clang of the doorbell signaled the last of the latecomers. Jacquie and Darla bustled through the door. Jacquie, tall, muscular, brown hair styled in deep-set finger waves, spotted Charlie immediately. "Somebody new? Joanne, introduce us, please! Never mind, I'll do it. I'm Jacquie, this is my dear friend Darla. And you are?"

Charlie glanced at Joanne, who pointed upward to remind him to change his voice, then gave him an encouraging wink.

"I'm . . . Charlene," Charlie warbled.

"Charlene, I am so very pleased to meet you. You sound just a tiny bit like you are from my neck of the woods."

Charlie shook the extended hand, taking his cue from Jacquie's limp wrist to keep it gentle and ladylike.

"Where is that?"

Darla, chubby, rosy, mousy brown, and demure, extended her hand in greeting. "Jacquie is from Texas. Dallas, Texas."

"I just moved here from Dallas."

"I knew it, I knew it!" Jacquie crowed. "I told you I always recognize a Texas accent!"

"Is it that much different from anywhere else in the south?" Joanne was politely skeptical.

"Oh my, yes, to the sensitive ear. And you know I am nothing if not sensitive in every respect."

Jacquie was clearly the most ebullient of the group, even more so than Marie. She was also the youngest, Charlie guessed. Perhaps eighteen or nineteen. The others, aside from Marie, seemed to be in their thirties, near his own age.

As he focused on the struggle to balance tea and cookies on his lap and listened to the chatter and laughter of the Full Self Sisterhood, Charlie wondered. Were there men like these in Dallas? If so, and if he'd found them, could he have managed a double life? A wave of missing Anne hit him so hard that he almost gasped.

His pondering was interrupted by Jacquie's cheerful demand. "And now," she announced, "I want to hear all about how you decided."

"Decided?"

"To dress."

"I don't know. I just wanted to . . ." Charlie found himself unwilling to finish that sentence. To get it out of his system? That would be rude indeed to say to such a group. And maybe he didn't need to be in such a rush to put his urges behind him.

"This is your first time, right? Or nearly first?"

"Is it that obvious?"

"My dear, of course it is, but only to those of us who have been in your place. It takes practice, like everything."

Charlie felt his face flush. Maybe he had not been so convincingly female on the street. Maybe that man who bumped into him was actually . . .

Jacquie was quick to reassure him. "You look magnificent. No one would ever know from that. It's your voice, darling. You have got to relax your voice. Y'all are trying too hard."

"How do I do that?"

Joanne passed the cookie plate and chimed in. "Think of it as singing," she said. "You can make your voice higher if you sing falsetto. Then it's just a matter of speaking in that same range. It's like a very gentle song. Not too many intervals between the individual notes. Just a steady, gentle, melodic voicing."

Jacquie bounced up from her chair and came to sit next to Charlie on the sofa. "Are there songs you used to sing when you were young?"

"Church songs," Charlie said.

"What was your favorite?"

"'The Old Rugged Cross.' A traveling preacher taught it to us the year I turned eleven."

"Oh, that's a beautiful song. One of my favorites too. Good, then. We'll sing 'The Old Rugged Cross.' Sing it for me. Sing it the way you did when you were eleven. Before your voice changed. I'll sing with you."

"On a hill far away stood an old rugged cross," Charlie and Jacquie sang. Joanne urged, "Relax!" and joined in. "The emblem of suffering and shame."

Everyone except Marie added their voices. "And I love that old cross where the dearest and best for a world of lost sinners was slain."

"I don't know this song," Marie said, "but I want to learn it."

Joanne coached her through the chorus, calling each line out before it was sung. "So I'll cherish the old rugged cross, till my trophies at last I lay down. I will cling to the old rugged cross, and exchange it someday for a crown."

By the time the meeting was over, the Full Self Sisterhood had sung "All Things Bright and Beautiful," "Wondrous Love," and "Beautiful Isle of Somewhere." As the final refrain faded—"Somewhere, somewhere, Beautiful Isle of Somewhere! Land of the true, where we live anew, Beautiful Isle of Somewhere!"—Marie was dabbing at her eyes with a handkerchief. "It is so beautiful, *n'est-ce pas?*"

Charlie nodded. His own eyes were brimming. "I believe the proper answer in French would be, '*Oui, oui!*'"

Marie laughed. "*Ça y est,*" she declared.

"And do you hear how you sound now?" Jacquie added.

"*C'est magnifique!*" Marie said.

"*Oui, oui,*" Joanne added. "You have found your voice, Charlene."

For Charlie, hearing the laughter of the Full Self Sisterhood was like coming home, except there had never before been a home to come to.

"*Oui, oui,*" Charlie confirmed, and felt the thrill of truly becoming, in that moment, for that moment, Charlene.

* * *

Charlie's life settled into a routine of sorts. He set up an office in Luella's storefront on Fullerton Street, buying a secondhand chair and installing his drill. As he had in Dallas, he went to his little office and spent the day there whether he had patients scheduled or not. His first customer was Henry, whom he had met as Marie. He made Henry a full set of uppers. Two or three other Full Self Sisters came to him as well. The first two months no one could pay, but since Norbert, whom he had met as Luella, was willing to wait for rent, he was able to scrimp by on his savings while his practice grew. With his new teeth Henry was accepted into the CCC, and was able to send payment. Word of mouth spread, and slowly business built until, even in these Depression times, Charlie had enough work to enable him to send money for Hannah's care down to Indianapolis with a little extra so she could ask the nurses to get her candies or hairpins now and then. He could pay his rooming house and office rent. He could keep himself fed and clothed, and he could, once in a while, indulge in a new item of clothing for Charlene. He didn't need much other than that, except for the train ticket he bought once a month to go to visit Hannah.

He generally took dinner downstairs in his boarding house, where he was cordial with other boarders but reserved. If introduced to a young miss of marriageable age, he retreated into stammering and awkwardness, too terrified to ever risk the dangers of growing close to another woman. These sorts of events would invariably call up a tension for him that he would have to relieve later, in the privacy of his room.

He settled in, happy enough with life on the near north side of Chicago. It was the church services at the Grace Chapel that he liked best—even more than the Full Self Sisterhood meetings. Sitting next to Joanne, singing the hymns, letting the words spoken by the minister flow around him, reminded him of the little church in Kirbyville where, sandwiched between his mother Ilsa's silky dress and his father Jarvis's nubby wool suit, he would listen to Reverend Granger's exhortations. Three weeks out of four he dressed in his—or rather Charlene's—Sunday best, and walked by Joanne's to pick her up on the way. Then the two of them strolled up to the church on Fullerton.

Every fourth week, instead of choosing which dress to wear, he boarded the Hoosier Line bound for Indianapolis to spend the day with Hannah. He'd comb and braid her hair while he told her about the details of life in Chicago: the bakery on Halsted that made such good *kuchen*, like Ilsa used to make when times were good and holidays were near. (The nurse cautioned him not to bring any to Hannah, lest she choke.) He described to her all the neighbors in his rooming house. Mrs. Kowalsky with her thick accent and smells of cabbage forever wafting from her room out into the hallways and beyond; the Nakagawas who were so very pleasant, always saying hello; the Lees who spoke Chinese and kept to themselves; Mrs. Ozick, the Greek widow whose thick black braids didn't match her wrinkled, weathered complexion; the schoolteacher below him who was taller and thinner than the intimidating Miss Willick of their own elementary school years, but just as stern; the muscular Darby Neep who worked at the stockyards and smelled like it too. The landlady, a Mrs. Beaurigard, hailed from Louisiana and wore heavy black dresses no matter what the season or weather, and never said a word to tenants that wasn't of compelling necessity. "She's not a conversationalist like Mrs. Hesher at all," Charlie told Hannah, who clutched at the fabric of her dress and rolled it rhythmically in her twitching fingers.

He confessed to her that in spite of Chicago's charms, he sometimes missed small-town life. He missed being able to walk by the creek, for example, to sit on the overhanging branch watching minnows and tadpoles flit by. The Chicago River just wasn't the same. He missed the songbirds. There were robins near his rooming house in Chicago, but they couldn't hold a candle to the nighttime one-man-band mockingbird. "Remember how we'd lie awake and talk after Mama and Papa were gone, and hear the mockingbird?" he'd ask Hannah, and her eyes would shine with the pleasure of memory. Sometimes he even missed the way everyone knew everyone else back in Kirbyville, though he had to admit he didn't miss their snoopy judgmental neighbor Mrs. Baumgardner. But no matter what he missed, he lived in Chicago now, and had friends there, and work was beginning to pick up. He wasn't complaining. "Like Mama always said, keep on the move. Keep busy. 'Rest makes rust.'" Then he wanted to bite his tongue. What Hannah wouldn't give, he thought, to be able to follow that maternal advice.

As if she'd read his thoughts, she made a supreme effort to speak. "I'm rusting," she managed to say, and it was hard to tell if it was the trace of a smile or a frown that punctuated it.

Sometimes, when he could see Hannah was really feeling glum, he would sing the old church songs to her. Especially the ones that told how beautiful paradise would be, how temporal earthly suffering is. He'd sing to her of her mansion in the sky, or sweet fields arrayed in living green and rivers of delight. He'd bet her that those rivers had the cutest tadpoles of all swimming in them. Cuter even than the ones they used to watch in the Kirbyville creek. And Jesus bugs. You bet there'd have to be Jesus bugs in heaven.

Then it would be time to board the train back to Chicago. Charlie always found that people opened up to him on the way home. It was odd, but true. Other passengers rarely spoke to him on the way down, but after he'd spent the day with Hannah, it was as if she'd caused an invitation to appear on his forehead: "You can talk to me." From Indy to Chicago, he'd hear stories from men out of work, women facing operations, folks who'd lost parents, parents who'd lost children, you name it.

It came into his mind once to wonder, if he'd grown up Catholic like Marie, would he have become a priest and heard people's confessions? And it came into his mind to consider what he'd say to a priest if he were Catholic and had someone to whom he could confess his sins. Most of the commandments he did pretty well with, but he failed utterly when it came to Matthew 5:28. He committed plenty of adultery in his heart, every time he saw a pretty girl walking down the street. And, too, he'd have to confess to telling a lie every time he put on a dress.

For the most part, outside of visiting Hannah, going to church, and having tea with the Full Self Sisterhood, weeks, months, and years went by with Charlie keeping to himself. When the Full Self Sisters came to him as his dental patients, they were just men, and not even men with whom he necessarily had much in common. The only conversation that ever passed between them in which they acknowledged the entirely other world they inhabited together was when once in a while one of them would ask, "Will you be going this weekend?"

Joanne was an exception. It was Joanne—not Joseph—who worked at Cott's Clothing Store, and Joanne—not Joseph—who came for a filling when her sweet tooth developed a cavity. Only when she had to conduct legal business did she divest herself of pads, lipstick, nail polish, and wig to turn into Joseph. As soon as Joseph had fulfilled the task—signing in front of a notary, withdrawing funds from a bank account, putting a paycheck made out to Joanne but endorsed over to Joseph into savings—he headed home to his upstairs apartment. Generally, as soon as the lock was secure and the curtains checked to make sure they were fully closed, he'd leave his men's wear in the upstairs closet, head down the back stairway, and welcome becoming a she again. No one Joseph associated with in his business dealings ever met Joanne, and none of Joanne's friends or coworkers ever met Joseph. The mailman had seen each upon occasion and assumed that they were brother and sister sharing the duplex.

Nevertheless, there were rare times when Joseph had Charlie over for a beer, usually arranged when Joseph was coming home from a business errand and passing Charlie's office on the way. He'd suggest Charlie stop by after work. Charlie would close early if he didn't have any patients on the schedule, stop at the market for sandwich makings, and spend a couple of hours with Joseph before walking back to his room. They split their conversation to go with their identities: in Cott's, wearing dresses, it was all fashion—scents, scarves, skirts, and blouses. In church, it was much the same: small talk about hair management or a good place to shop. In Joseph's apartment they shared an easy release back into maleness. Mostly, they didn't talk at all, but listened to a White Sox game on the radio or played dominoes, though Joseph did tell Charlie where to find prostitutes who were respectable, discreet, and reasonably priced for those times when self-stimulation just wasn't enough. Charlie thanked him for the tip, but never made use of it. He opted instead for suppression, and if that didn't work, he harkened back to the model provided by Skooch and Taylor, boys he'd gone to school with, who'd given him an unasked for lesson in how to masturbate three decades before at the edge of the woods in Kirbyville. That, the boys had taught him, is what a pinup calendar is for.

They never talked about their double life. Charlie thought about that, thought it was strange, but it seemed to Charlie that Joseph needed it that way, so it was all right with Charlie too. He told Joseph about the creek back in Kirbyville, and the river where the fish ran thick the morning after a full moon. Joseph showed him flies he'd tied for trout fishing in Wisconsin. Those were things the Full Self Sisters

4

INDIANAPOLIS, INDIANA, 1938

Charlie knelt by his sister's side. "Hannah, Doctor Marsten told me they've got a new operation they can do that might help you. It might not. He said he talked to you about it and he thinks you might want to try it."

Hannah was motionless except for a rhythmic tremor that moved through her right arm and hand. For years, she'd continued her steady, downward decline. Now she was a statue of a young woman. A monument to beauty, a picture of youth frozen in time, save her expression, which was flat. No discernible emotion on her face, no classic smile, or even Mona Lisa enigma. She hardly even blinked.

Charlie sat facing her, reached out and took her trembling hand in his.

"I have to try to see what you want. Like I say, it's an experimental operation. They go in and cut a little piece of your brain and for some people that makes them able to move again. There's less rigidity and fewer tremors. But there's no guarantee that it will work."

He kept his focus on Hannah's eyes. The only part of her that moved or changed. Her pupils widened and he thought he felt her squeeze his hand.

"Without the operation, the doctor says you'll probably stay like you are now. He's never known anyone to get better and he's never known anyone as young as you to have it so bad. But you need to know, they've only done this a few dozen times, Hannah, and it didn't help everyone, and some people didn't pull through. It's an experiment. It's nothing guaranteed. And there's always a risk with surgery. So maybe you don't want to . . ."

Hannah's pupils constricted.

"You want to try it?" Charlie watched the light come back into her eyes and had his answer. "I'll tell Doctor Marsten."

* * *

Charlie watched the doctor walk down the hallway to the waiting area and could tell the news wasn't going to be good. As practiced as the surgeon was in neutrality, his pace was reluctant and his eyes kept scanning for anywhere to focus except Charlie. There was defeat in his tired shoulders.

"Mr. Bader?"

"Yes."

"I'm so sorry to have to tell you. . . . We lost your sister."

Charlie stared at him. Lost my sister, he thought. It sounds as if they've just misplaced her. Put her in the wrong file drawer. *She's here somewhere, it will just take a minute to find her. Where is she? Where is my sister?* His breath caught, and a wave of nausea enveloped him.

"Mr. Bader?"

The doctor was waiting for a response. An acknowledgment.

"I'm sure you did all you could," Charlie managed to assure him. The doctor's touch of compassion on his arm loosed a torrent of feeling. "She was lost a long time ago." Charlie choked on the words. "When our mama and daddy died and then she got the sleepy sickness. She just got more and more lost." His face was wet with grief. "She used to do cartwheels, did you know? She used to chase butterflies."

"Would you like to see her? I have to warn you, it will be a shock. We had to shave her head you know, to prepare for the surgery."

"She had such pretty hair." Hannah was gone. The doctors had lost her. They even lost her beautiful hair. The odds were against her, they both knew that going into this, but as long as she was still in surgery there was the hope she'd be one of the few who would benefit. Charlie had dared to hope and knew she'd hoped with him, that she'd be able to walk again, and talk fluently, and feed herself, and laugh, and tell Charlie funny stories about the doctors and nurses and other patients, and confide in him her plans for the future. Now she was gone and that hope was gone and Anne was forever gone and his parents were long since gone. Charlie was utterly alone, in that lonesome valley. Facing death alone would have been easier. It was life, his pitiful life, that stared him in the face at this moment. "Dr. Marsten, I wonder if you could do me a favor. It would be something I could remember her by."

"What's that?"

"Did you keep her hair? Could I have it?"

"I'm sorry, we wouldn't be allowed to do something like that."

"Of course not," Charlie nodded, taking a great gulp of air to stifle a sob. "Of course. Never mind."

"I could probably give you a lock of it."

Charlie worked to breathe, to retain a modicum of composure. "Thank you," he said. "Thank you. I would appreciate that so much."

Since neither Charlie nor Hannah had any family, the nursing home provided a generic funeral, presided over by a well-intentioned minister who pretended to know Hannah. He didn't, of course, so his praise of her noted only those qualities that were expected of young women and none that defined Hannah. Her love of insects, her way with broody hens, her quick, questioning mind—these were elements the kindly fellow failed to note. Nor could he imagine how Hannah had once danced around the chinaberry bush, or talked her brother's ear off.

At the graveside, Charlie lingered after the brief ceremony. "Hannah, you used to have so much to say, I never had to do much to keep up my end of the conversation. Then it got so I had to do all the talking and you had to do all the listening. I don't know if you can hear me now or not and I don't know if I'll have much to say from here on out. But I reckon if I do have something to say, you're still the person I'm most likely to say it to. Dear Hannah. Sweet Hannah. I'm sorry. I'm so sorry. I should have . . ." What? Kept his secret better so Anne would never have left him? Visited Hannah more often? Refused the surgery and continued to watch his sister disappear into her disease? Anger rose in him. "It isn't fair what happened to you. It just isn't fair." The sobs came then, consuming him. The memories of Hannah the tagalong. Hannah the chatterbox, Hannah the girl with a thousand curiosities. Then, feeling selfish that he'd forgotten his role as big brother and comforter, he calmed himself and finally managed a determined smile. "You know what I think? Now that you aren't stuck down here in that body that just wouldn't do anything anymore? I think you're up there dancing with the angels. And talking their ears off."

He stayed there, silent now, at her grave until the custodian of the cemetery came to tell him it was time to close the gates.

Back in Chicago at Grace Chapel, the minister asked his congregation to pray for the soul of Hannah, sister of Charlene, a soul gone home to God. "They were close as only sisters can be close," he told his flock, "and we know that Charlene will miss her dearly, but that at least she is no longer suffering. She is in Jesus's embrace now, and nothing can harm her ever again."

"Amen," murmured the members of the congregation, and after the service many of the women made a point of coming over to Charlene and expressing their sympathy.

On the way home, Joanne remarked that it was always the women who understood sorrow. That was as close as she ever came to saying why she preferred her life as a female.

*   *   *

In Chicago, with Hannah gone, Charlie's world was ever more circumscribed and routine. Living in his room, walking to his dental office every day except Saturday and Sunday, dressing up once a month for soirees at Joanne's house, and once a week for church. Perhaps once every couple of months having a beer with Joanne's alter-self Joseph. The sexual urges that had plagued him when he had first headed north were fewer and farther between, satisfied quickly with the help of a pinup picture and his sateen robe. In a word, his life was predictable. He told himself he'd always preferred the predictable to the unexpected. Convinced himself that the safety of the Sisterhood and the economic security of his dental office were all he'd ever wanted. Somewhere in the world, countries were at war. Somewhere in the world, people lost their homes, their lives. Somewhere in the world, societies were cracking and falling apart at the seams. In Chicago, life was secured by routines. It would have been perfect if there'd been a stream nearby, with a hornbeam tree next to it, and someone to share it with, but he dared not even contemplate the foolish notion that he would ever know anyone like Anne again. He knew better than to want the impossible. He wore his mother's admonition like a sequestered housewife's shawl. *Be thankful for what you got.*

5

CHICAGO, 1941

It was a cold crisp day. This Sunday in particular, Charlie was as close to at peace with himself as he ever got. He'd risen early, made a pot of coffee, taken his time over toast and eggs, shaved his face, shaved his legs, plucked his eyebrows, styled his wig, padded his bra, tucked and wrapped his maleness, pulled on his stockings, laid out the new skirt-and-blouse combination that Joanne had sold him the week before. The blouse was a muted cotton beige with a ruffled collar that continued down the front to cover the buttons in a soft cascade of folds. The skirt a brown and beige herringbone. Brown leather pumps and handbag, and a single choker strand of pearls completed the outfit.

After breakfast, he completed dressing. From now until he returned after church, he would be Charlene.

Charlene pulled on her coat, quickly and quietly headed downstairs, slipped out the door, and walked the short distance to Dayton Street where she rang Joanne's doorbell. The two of them walked together to church, chatting the way friends do about a mix of inconsequential and profoundly important things. They shared enthusiasm about the nylon stockings that came out in '40 as an alternative to silk, which was in such short supply. Joanne worried about having gained five pounds over Thanksgiving and about her grandparents in London. They were too stubborn to leave, she said. Bombs had destroyed half their house and most of the houses in their neighborhood, but they'd stayed and survived. She didn't know when there would be another attack that might not find them as lucky. Charlene chatted about a broken nail, a new store that carried size twelve women's shoes, and how Hannah could always get eggs from under irritable hens without being pecked.

Charlie missed his sister so very much. On his loneliest days he'd think about how his parents never mentioned any other relatives: not grandparents, nor aunts, uncles, or cousins. The most he'd ever gotten out of his mother Ilsa was that her parents had lived in Germany but died before their daughter sailed for Galveston in 1898. His father wasn't one to question about anything, let alone personal particulars such as family, and why he didn't seem to have any to speak of. So once Ilsa and Jarvis succumbed to influenza, Hannah had been his only family. When he worked at the sawmill to keep the rent paid on their little house, it was for Hannah. When he learned to cook it was to put food on the table for her. When he studied May's medicines and brewed them up, it was to nurse his sister through the lethargy that threatened to claim her. When he moved them to Dallas so he could study dentistry at Baylor, it was because it was what she wanted him to do. Alone in his Chicago room, Charlie tended to torment himself with the memories of her antics and incessant questions.

Being Charlene gave a bit of blessed distance. Charlene could recall these stories as if they'd happened to someone else. Someone close, but someone else. She could tell Joanne about Hannah's wide-eyed wonder contemplating tiny legs beginning to show on the tadpoles that frequented the stream near their house. She could recount the way Hannah chided her brother for catching butterflies, and insisted they be released. She could brag about Hannah's brightness and determination, and reminisce fondly about the way she could talk circles around a person before she got sick.

The sermon was about neutrality. It made a lot of sense—until Joanne and Charlene stepped back out on the street to find that while they'd been singing "Rock of Ages," the Japanese had been bombing Pearl Harbor. Within days, the United States was officially at war, not only with Japan but also Italy and Germany.

*   *   *

US entry into the war wrenched the Full Self Sisterhood from fashion, recipes, and hairdos into the arena of combat and patriotism. By the time their January meeting rolled around, Jacquie had enlisted in the marines, Marie in the navy, and Helena, who had only recently joined the soirees, in the air force. "I heard they really need doctors and dentists," Jacquie told Charlene, "and they'll pay you to bring your own equipment, too."

"I'm too old to fight," Charlene protested.

"You wouldn't be fighting. Just fixing teeth for the boys who do," Joanne prodded. "I wish I had some skill that would help."

Susie agreed. "I'm volunteering at the Red Cross, but I'd much rather take on Mr. Hitler over there."

"You can't dress in the army, you know," Charlene reminded her.

"You don't think dressing is more important than getting rid of that monster, do you? As much as I enjoy the company of you all, I'd give it up in a heartbeat if I could get my hands around Adolf's throat." Susie's vehemence cut through the appearances. Her voice dropped, and she was clearly Sam, wearing a dress and ready to kill.

Charlie was appalled at himself. Of course there were more important causes in the world than putting on wigs and women's clothing. How could he be so selfish and shallow?

Was it the shame he felt at being admonished by Susie? The single-minded war fever of the Full Self Sisterhood? Or perhaps a long-ago promise he had made to Hannah? Way back during the Great War, she'd come to him full of worry that the Huns might breach the border of Texas. He'd vowed to her he'd never let it happen. Now the

Huns were led by a powerful new tyrant determined to destroy the country he loved so much. That night as he lay in bed the idea took sudden hold of him and wouldn't let go. He'd do it. Tomorrow he'd go to the recruiting office. Not only that. He'd leave his shadow self behind. He'd be a man. Just a man. A man fighting for his country as any man should in whatever way he could. It crossed his mind that if he died in the war, at least he would go respectably.

They had a bit of a formal ceremony for all the Full Self Sisters who were going off to war. It was Joanne's idea to create a fashion time capsule. She provided the cedar chest, and everyone, whether headed overseas or staying at the home front, contributed one outfit. "After the war," Joanne promised, "we'll open the chest and see how much fashions have changed. I'll make a prediction," she added. "Keep your knees looking pretty, ladies. We're bound to have shortages as a result of the war, and that means hemlines are going nowhere but up."

"*Mon Dieu!*" Marie pulled her hem above her knees and stared at them in horror. "They already look *terrible!*"

"Marie, your knees are fine," Luella pronounced. "Just don't get them full of shrapnel and you'll be all right."

Jacquie raised a cup of tea for a toast. "Here's to a quick end to a necessary war."

"Hear, hear," Joanne chimed in. "And a quick end to Hitler."

"And Tojo," Theresa added.

Luella fought back a catch in her throat. "May all you brave and able ones come back soon and without so much as a scratch."

Even Charlene, normally a listener, felt moved to add a thought. "And may all you on the home front know it will be thinking of you that will keep us going." She contributed her most recent purchases to the time capsule. The next day, Charlie dropped off the rest of Charlene's ensembles at Joanne's with instructions to let the others who would still be gathering have their pick. Any items they didn't want should go to the Salvation Army.

6

PARIS, FRANCE, 1944

"Hey, listen, I found a nice little place. The girls are pretty, clean look-ing, don't charge that much, but not too cheap either, you know what I mean? It's low key, no rowdy parties, no messy-mess with the *gen-darmes*. You, me, Benny, Ed, howsabout it? We need a little break, a little nookie nook. We can drive in to pick up the drills and stop on our way back."

Paris was liberated, and with it, the libido of men who'd been on the front lines without a break for too long. Charlie's assistant Tommy had a sweetheart back home in Keokuk, but Tommy was a realist. Guys have needs, pure and simple. They'd be heading out to the Belgian front tomorrow, he and Charlie sharing a mobile dental unit, and it was now or never for some real rest and recreation.

* * *

Genevieve stiffened and pulled away. "*Ah, non! Pas encore!* You will—" But it was too late. Her silken panties were covered with se-men. Charlie lay next to her, his face buried in the pillow.

"You could have *un peu de considération*," she fumed. "Now how do I dress for more clients?" And she let go a torrent of French that needed no translation, though Charlie, in his mortification, was able to make out enough to know that she was mentioning the matter of lost income due to soiled work clothes.

"*Je m'excuse, s'il vous plait, je . . .*" He searched for words and stammered, but his minimal French failed him. Genevieve softened.

"*Ecoute*, GI. *C'est bien.*" It's okay."

"No." Charlie pulled himself together. "*Combien?*"

"*Comment?*"

"*Combien coûtent les . . .*" His pathetic grasp of French made the negotiation even more humiliating. "*Je vous payer. Ici.*" He sat up and reached over to pull a wad of franc notes from the pocket of his pants, which lay draped over an imitation Louis Quatorze side chair. Genevieve's eyes widened. "*Je vous donner pour le temps,*" Charlie said, "*et pour . . . les pantalons.*" He had no idea if *pantalons* was the right word, but it was the only article of clothing Genevieve was still wearing, so he trusted the meaning was clear.

Genevieve's look told him he was disgracing himself. He didn't care now. He wanted to close the deal: buy her time, her panties, and her silence about his initial inability to perform followed by his sudden uncontrolled ejaculation. He wanted, desperately, simply to get back to the war, where it felt safer.

Between Charlie's pitiful French and Genevieve's business acumen, he left ten minutes later with the sperm-soaked panties deep in his pocket and she had enough money to take the rest of the night off, truly celebrate her city's freedom from Nazi occupation, and treat herself not just to new lacy underwear, but to a new dress as well.

In the lobby, Charlie's buddies were happily, drunkenly comparing notes on the repertoire of French whores. He fell in beside them as they tumbled into the street in pursuit of further Parisian adventure.

"Charlie, you going with us to La Plume?"

"You're awfully quiet, Charlie. Wasn't your girl any good?"

"Oh, she was fine."

"Hey, lay off the old man."

They liked to kid Charlie about his advanced age. He was in his forties, the rest of his company, even the captain, in their mid-twenties at most.

Charlie went along with their fun. Anything to get away, be alone. "This old man is going back to the hotel," he said. "I'll see you all in the morning."

"You okay?"

"No problem. Just tired. You'll see when you get as old as me," he kidded them, and when they reached the entrance to the dance hall that was next on their itinerary, he slipped down the street and turned at the corner to go back to their hotel.

He didn't go there yet, though. Not likely they'd be back soon, but he didn't dare risk it. He had tried so hard to bury his need, but it had nagged at him, grown monstrously large and insistent. He couldn't ignore it any longer, and he didn't dare get caught.

On Rue de Chanson he stopped at l'Hôtel Minuit. *"Avez vous une chambre pour un person?"* he asked, and for a few francs in advance he got a closet-sized bedroom space. Though the toilet was down the hall, there was a sink with a mirror in the room itself. Safely inside, he bolted the door and wedged the chair against the doorknob. It is ridiculous, Charlie said to himself, that I am far more terrified to be found out by my own friends than to be killed by Nazi goons. Nothing he had yet experienced as Company D's chief dental officer had made his heart pound the way it was now pounding.

Dear God, please don't let me have a heart attack, he prayed. Don't let me be caught dead in women's underwear. The thought sobered him, and he pulled the panties from his pocket and threw them on the bed. He sat on the edge, and it moaned and sagged precipitously under his weight. He let himself sink down into the soggy, worn mattress and took a deep breath. A few more careful inhalations and exhalations helped to center him in his purpose. He stood, undressed quickly, and picked up the panties. They were sticky and wet. He turned back the comforter on the bed and pulled a bit of the sheet loose, catching out of the corner of his eye the mad dash of a bedbug for the safety of darkness. He wiped off as much of the stickiness as he could with the loosened sheet. When the panties were as dry as he could get them, Charlie sat down again on the bed's edge and drew them on. The silkiness felt exquisite and forbidden, soothing and terrible, comforting and dangerously damning. He stood, stepped in front of the mirror, and contemplated the image: a middle-aged dentist in women's underwear in a fleabag Parisian hotel in the middle of a war. What terrible affliction is this, Charlie begged his reflection to tell him. Why can't you give this up?

It's not that he hadn't wanted the sex with Genevieve. After years of suppressing, sublimating, redirecting, and finally just ignoring any such urges, he was ready. Not just ready, but eager for sexual release that didn't carry with it the risk of relationship.

There, though, face to face with the opportunity, no matter how willing his head, his body was simply, maddeningly unresponsive. Then unbidden, at the moment Genevieve took charge and he felt the silkiness of her underwear rubbing against his skin, came a tangled rush of memories. Anne in her dressing gown on their wedding night and the closet he'd hid in as a child to wear his mother's fox fur and secret mud baths in the little creek behind the Kirbyville house and adolescent sex in Crazy May's little house, herbs hanging overhead, and his childhood nemeses Skootch and Taylor taunting him as they wagged themselves at a cheesecake picture in the crook of a tree branch. He worked so hard, had always worked so hard, to control it all. In this moment, sick of the harshness of war and weary to the bone of a life that denied his soft side, he had lost that control.

He tore the panties off, tossed them in the trash can, pulled his army drabs back on, and hurried to the hotel where his buddies found him ostensibly sound asleep when they came in hours later.

7

BELGIUM, 1944

Ordinarily they would have had a driver, but the one assigned to their mobile lab had fallen ill at the last minute and been hospitalized with a gall bladder attack, so Charlie was at the wheel. He was thankful that Tommy was a talker. As the convoy headed out and they drove to the eastern front, Charlie was happy to drive and let Tommy talk. Talking had never been his favorite part of dentistry, though it was something you had to do to pass the time while the patient couldn't say a word. Tommy was far from skilled in drilling, fashioning a filling, or creating a denture but he could keep the chatter going. In that respect, he reminded Charlie of Hannah, and for that matter, of his mother Ilsa.

"Hey, Charlie, you know something?"

"Mmmm."

"You know what I was thinking?"

"Mmmm?"

"It's nuts."

Charlie waited. Not long. Never long.

"We bust our asses out here in this godforsaken place to fix a guy's teeth so he can go out and maybe get his whole damn face shot off. And if we're lucky, or maybe I should say if he's lucky, he goes out there and shoots some other kid's face off, maybe some kid just got his own teeth fixed by a Kraut dentist. What are we doing? It's fuckin' nuts. I mean it isn't really nuts. I mean, I know we gotta stop Hitler and Tojo or we're gonna have to stop 'em back home. But it just feels nuts sometimes to patch up a guy's mouth so's he can get his whole damn head blown off. Or even his arm or leg. What if he gets his arms blown off? How's he gonna brush his teeth after that, you know?"

"Well, they say the Krauts are on the ropes now. It's just a matter of time."

"You believe that?"

"Might as well."

*   *   *

The third night out their rations and sundries packets were waiting for them. Four cans of baked beans, a small can of peaches, a couple of cookies, a bar of waxy chocolate, a bit of hard candy, five small, round biscuits, three cigarettes, a pencil, a pad of ten pages, and two envelopes. Charlie ate the chocolate, and the cookies, before turning his attention to the dollop of butterscotch, a small dab on a not-much-larger square of grayish-brown thin cardboard. He sucked on the hard candy with an infantile satisfaction. The sweetness made him wild with longing for everything this place didn't have: warmth, safety, the company of like-minded friends. When the candy itself was gone, he licked the cardboard, and when it began to disintegrate he chewed it, looking for one more molecule of taste, one more tiny memory of sweetness, one last vestige of a different life. Tommy came back from the latrine and Charlie nodded at his package. It had taken a massive effort simply to not rip Tommy's open and eat a second piece of butterscotch.

Tommy was a smoker.

"Care to trade?"

"What for what?"

"The cigs for the candy."

"You're on."

Tommy took Charlie's three Lucky Strikes and tucked them with two of his own into the inside pocket of the thick flannel sleeveless vest he'd found in the hallway of a school they'd bunked in two days before and layered under his jacket.

Charlie tore the candy off the paper and resisted the temptation to crunch it in his teeth. Instead, he tucked it into his cheek to let it dissolve slowly.

"You going to write to Emily?"

"I might."

"She'll want to hear from you."

"I dunno, Charlie. I never know what to say. Sometimes I'm afraid I won't know how to be with her when I get back. You know what I mean?"

"Not sure I do."

"I mean she's never left Keokuk, never wanted to leave it. Never seen guys get their arms and legs and heads blown off. Never wondered if she's gonna live past Tuesday, never wondered if she's gonna freeze to death before morning. I seen so much ugliness out here. I sure as hell don't want to put it on her. I don't know if I can ever wipe it out of my mind."

"You will, Tommy. Sure you will."

"What if she wants kids? Hell, I know she wants kids. I don't know if I want to bring kids into this fucked-up world. You know what they always say. You can't go home again."

"You'll pick up where you left off, Tommy."

"You think so?"

"I know so."

"Izzat what you're gonna do? Pick up where you left off?"

"I expect so."

"Where did you leave off?"

Where indeed? A routine life of loneliness and deception. At the time, Charlie had thought he enjoyed it. In retrospect, it just seemed empty and sad to him. "Nowhere in particular."

"See what I'm saying? You don't know. I don't know."

"No, you did leave somewhere in particular. You'll go back. You'll go back to Keokuk."

Charlie thought of warm places. Here in the mobile unit in the frozen forest, where he practiced as refined a dentistry as he could with his stiff fingers, foot-pedaled drill of the kind he hadn't had to use for decades, and inadequate supplies, he never thought of Chicago winters, but searing Texas summers entertained him. The thoughts came to him unbidden. They whispered to him of the burbling creek in Kirbyville, of tadpoles and Jesus bugs and dragonflies, and sun-dappled water. They murmured of fox fur in warm, dark, clothing-lined closets. They reminded him of blazing, baking days so hot you really could fry eggs on the sidewalk, if you lived in a part of town that had sidewalks and could afford to waste eggs.

* * *

"Hey listen, do me a favor, will you?" Driving through the impenetrable frozen fog, Charlie and Tommy had gotten separated from their company when the engine broke down. Now they were hopelessly lost, setting up camp somewhere in the vicinity of St. Vith in an abandoned country house that had been stripped of all but a couple of benches, a broken table, and one frozen-solid head of cabbage on the floor in the kitchen lying near the door. Charlie was getting a fire started in the fireplace with the few dry sticks of wood they'd found. Tommy was rolling out their bedrolls. "If I don't make it out of here and you do, will you go to my folks' house? There's a sycamore tree in the front yard that has my initials carved in it and my birth year, 1918. Could you carve 1945 under that? And then on the other side, finish the dates for the heart I carved and let Emily know. Tommy and Emily, April 4, 1941, to . . . whatever. Just if I don't make it, you know? I used to live in the damn tree. I ran away from home once and you know what I did? I climbed that tree, sat up in the branches, and my mom and dad came out on the porch, must've known right off I'd be up there. They just stood on the porch and talked about what my mom was going to make for dinner."

Charlie struck a match and lit the kindling. Tommy held his hands as close to the fire as he dared.

"Then they went inside."

"Yeah? What'd you do?" That would keep Tommy going for another chunk of time. Charlie would use that time to remember the hard candies his mother used to hide in her pockets and dispense during church and the way he sweated in the summertime, sandwiched between his parents in the pew.

"I got stuck up in the tree. Couldn't get down. They must have figured that out because my dad came back out, went out to the garage, and my mom followed him to ask what he was doing. 'There's a branch up in that tree needs trimming,' he said, 'so I aim to do just that first thing tomorrow. I'm just gonna set the ladder up tonight to be ready for it. And maybe while I'm at it I might nail some little boards up to make climbing steps, in case Tommy comes back, you know. I think he might like a tree house. You know, just in case he comes back.'

"And he nailed steps up the trunk of the tree and left the big fruit picker there too. So I had two ways to get down. Then they went back into the house again and I had my way back without losing face, you know. I went back in the house and there were my mom and dad at the dinner table and my mom looked up and said, 'Are you hungry? I can put a plate out for you.' And I just nodded and sat down at my place."

"So you can go home again."

"Maybe. Maybe. I sure as hell hope so."

In the jagged black cold of midnight, Charlie pulled his wool blanket closer around him while they waited for the fire to temper the room's frigidity enough to allow them to sleep. "Yeah," he said. "I know. Maybe I will someday, too. Maybe."

"Back to Chicago?"

"I don't know. I don't think so. I used to love it there, but now I think I'd like someplace quieter. More peaceful. Maybe I still haven't found where home really is. Maybe it doesn't really exist."

"Sure it does, Charlie. You just said so yourself."

By three in the morning the fire had died down to a few pale embers.

"Charlie, you awake? I'm shivering too hard to sleep."

Charlie mumbled agreement.

"Wish I was back in Keokuk. It gets cold there but I never felt cold like this before."

"Burn the table." Charlie could barely say the words, his teeth chattering like castanets.

Tommy pulled the table to him. He slammed it against the hearth, splintering the wood, layered the smallest pieces on the fading memory of fire, and lit his last cigarette on the kindled bits.

"I was just thinking . . ."

"About what?"

"I had a grandmom grew up somewhere around here."

"Yeah? Where?"

Tommy placed the rest of the table pieces on the fire and watched the flames reach up, lick, then seize them. "Somewhere in France near the Belgium border. She met my granddad in the last war and came back to Iowa with him. Died before I was born."

"My mom was born in Bremen."

"Where's that?"

"Germany."

"No kidding. Your folks were Krauts?"

"Just my mom. I don't know as I ever heard what my dad was. He was born in Texas."

"And that doesn't bother you, that your mom was a Kraut?"

"She got her citizenship."

"Did your dad fight in the Great War?"

"He was too old by the time it broke out. And he had a bad arm. Got smashed by a tree branch during a hurricane. He tried, but they wouldn't take him. He died, though, same as if he'd gone. Died in the flu epidemic. Both my mom and dad."

"That's rough."

"Mmmm."

Tommy pinched the burning top off his vanishing cigarette and tucked the butt away for one last drag in the morning. "My dad was in the war, before I was born. I don't remember much about him till I was about three. There was a big Armistice Day parade, and they had all the guys who'd fought marching in it together, or in wheel-chairs or whatever. Anyways, they had a float with girls on it and the high school marching band and a cannon at the head of it, then a convertible with my dad and the one other guy who got decorated for something or other, I don't know what, and they let me ride in the convertible next to my dad and I was scared out of my fuckin' wits."

"Of being in a parade?"

"Hell, no. I loved that part. What was terrifying was the way my dad acted. His name was John. They played 'When Johnny Comes Marching Home' and everybody along the parade route sang along. Okay so far. But at the end of the song they shot off the cannon and my dad went a little crazy. Tried to push me down off the seat and cover me with his body. Like he thought the Krauts were back, gunning for us. The mayor was riding in the front seat and he had been in the Mexican-American War with Teddy Roosevelt. That's the story he told anyway. And he whipped around and yelled, 'Ten hut!' and saluted my dad and that snapped him out of it. He saluted back and the crowd went wild and I wet my pants. He looked, well, he didn't look real to me. He didn't look like my dad. But there was something real powerful in having everybody yelling for us like that. And I never forgot the way he just snapped to attention. But yeah, that scared the crap out of me, seeing him like that."

"We better burn the benches."

"Cold as a witch's tit, innit?"

"Yep."

"Ever see one?"

"A witch's tit?"

"I saw one once."

"How'd you know it wasn't just some ordinary tit?"

"I thought everyone knew. A witch's got three tits. Two just like any babe has and an extra one down below the others."

"And you saw one? How'd you come to do that?"

"My brother took me to the carnival once and they had a dancing girl in it was a witch. She had a little whaddya call them things they stir their frogs and blood and stuff in?"

"Cauldrons?"

"That's it. She had a cauldron and she kept taking off stuff she was wearing and dropping it into the cauldron. First she took off her robe. And she had some black nightgown kind of thing on under it, and then she took that off, and she had a kind of sash around her middle and her underwear was black. Then she took the brassiere off and she had pasties and tassels and she shimmied while she stirred the cauldron, and then she took the sash off and there was another goddamn tit with a pasty on it, and she shimmied that one too. It was the damnedest thing I ever seen."

"Was it the same size as the others?"

"Was a little smaller, and over to the middle, not exact middle, but closer than not. Then she took the hat off and held it in front of her snatch while she took her panties off and flung them into the cauldron, and she danced around a little and showed us her butt. Then she danced behind the cauldron so it hid her snatch and tossed the hat in, and there was a big poof of smoke come out of the cauldron and when it cleared, she was gone, tits and all. In't that something?"

"Yes, it sure is."

"You ever see anything like that?"

"Never did."

"Sure would like to see some tits again. That Monique had a nice set. In Paris. Did your girl have good ones?"

"They were all right."

"Remember the first time you saw tits? I mean real ones, not in a carny act."

"It's not something you forget." Charlie conjured up the warm summer afternoon of that long-ago time, and a barefoot woman with a ready laugh in a house full of herbs.

"No, that's for sure. What was her name?"

"They called her Crazy May. She wasn't really crazy, but she did some crazy things."

"Like?"

"Just things. Things teenaged fellas loved to learn about."

"Like what?"

"Let's get some sleep, Tommy."

"Charlie, do you think we're going to get home? Are we ever going to see home again?" Tommy's voice cracked. Charlie felt that look Jarvis used to give him cross his own face: the men-don't-cry look. He was glad Tommy couldn't see him in the dark.

"Right about now, I'd settle for another good wool blanket."

"You ever in the Boy Scouts?"

"They didn't have Scouts where I grew up. They had 4-H."

"You know it's tricky when you're this cold," Tommy warned. "First sign of freezing to death is you get sleepy."

"I'd go to sleep if I could."

"You know what they say in the Survival Manual."

"No, I wasn't a Boy Scout."

"Oh, right. You just said that. I think my brain's froze solid."

"I know whatcha mean."

"They say you should buddy up, get next to someone else, conserve body heat."

"Yeah?"

"We should probably do that, so's we don't freeze our nuts off."

"Come over here if you want. I don't mind."

"Okay, here's what we gotta do." Tommy pulled himself along the floor and positioned himself parallel to Charlie. "We need one blanket under us and the other one on top. It'll work better if we take our clothes off."

"You nuts?"

"No, really. We just use 'em like extra blankets but we need skin to skin to save our body heat."

"How 'bout we leave our shorts on."

"Sure. Just hurry."

They fumbled their way into as awkward a position as Charlie had ever experienced.

Tommy couldn't stop shivering. "Jesus, I think my hand is froze."

"Here, let me rub it."

"Sure never thought I'd end up like this. Freezing my ass off, hugging a guy twenty years older'n me."

"Fifteen."

"Twenty, fifteen. The point is I was working in construction, making decent-enough dough and getting ready to settle down with my sweetheart. No offense, but I'd sure rather be cozying up with her."

"No offense taken. Give me your other hand. Put this one between your legs. Keep it warm."

"Jesus! Damn, it's cold." Suddenly, Tommy was bawling like a baby. "Shit, Charlie, what if we die here? What if we just freeze solid in this godforsaken place? Will they even find us? Or will the Krauts just grind us up for dog food?"

"Christ, Tommy, I dunno. Let's not think about that now. Pull yourself together." Charlie was remembering rubbing Hannah's arms, the day Miss Willick had accused her of pretending weakness. Hannah had cried, in frustration at not being believed, in fear at not understanding what was happening to her body.

"I don't want to die, Charlie."

"No one does, Tommy. No one does. Tuck this hand in. Let's just go to sleep. We don't know what's gonna happen tomorrow. We gotta be ready."

"Shit, yeah, Charlie. You're a good friend. I hope you get outta here alive."

"You too, Tommy."

Charlie thought of the hornbeam tree. Of sitting under it, rubbing mud from the creek bank over his arms and legs, letting it dry in the oven of Texas summer heat, then wading into the creek to let the water dissolve the dirt again. He thought of casting his fishhook into the river and pulling out sunnies for dinner. He thought of May, and the way she led him inside her mint-scented hut to initiate him into the wonders of sex, laughing and teasing and making him feel like a child and a man all at the same time. He thought of Hannah, her chatter and somersaults, and Ilsa heating the iron over the fireplace coals and Jarvis teaching him how to drive a nail straight and true on the scorching day they built the chicken coop.

"Charlie?"

"Mmmm?"

"Do you pray?"

"Mmmm?"

"You know, to God?"

"I do."

"D'you remember the Lord's Prayer?"

"Yeah."

"How does it go?"

"Our Father, who art in heaven, hallowed be thy name. Thy kingdom come, thy will be done, on earth as it is in heaven. Give us this day our daily bread, and forgive us our trespasses, as we forgive those who trespass against us. Lead us not into temptation, but deliver us from evil, for thine is the kingdom, and the power, and the glory, forever and ever, amen."

"You say trespasses."

"Huh?"

"You say trespasses. That was the only difference between the way I remember it and the way you said it."

"I thought you didn't remember it."

"Yeah, but when you said it I did. As soon as you started to say it I remembered it. 'Cept we said debts and debtors. 'Forgive us our debts as we forgive our debtors.'"

Somehow they made it through the night. In the morning, they hacked at the woodwork to kindle the fire again, burned the benches, melted snow to drink, and ate the cabbage, thawing its leaves one by one, chewing them slowly, like communion wafers. The sun made an effort to penetrate the fog, then gave up on it.

"Hell's gone and done it," Tommy said, feeding bandages from the first aid kit to the diminishing flames. "Hell's gone and froze over and here we are in the fuckin' middle of it. Fuckin' froze and fuckin' lost." Then he stopped talking and stared. They had a visitor.

He couldn't have been more than sixteen, this fellow who stood in the doorway of the house aiming a Mauser and screaming at them. A good-looking kid. Nice, straight teeth. The sallow complexion of someone who'd had too little sun, the frame of a fellow who'd eaten too few meals, and military ones at that. Charlie and Tommy held their hands high, in the universal signal of surrender, and tried to figure out what they were being ordered to do. The German boy pointed the gun at Charlie's neck and jerked his chin.

"I think he wants the dog tags." Charlie pointed to his tag, keeping his hand held high. The boy nodded.

"Fuck him."

"I'd rather give him my dog tags."

Charlie slowly, deliberately lowered one hand, grabbed the chain, and pulled it over his head. He tossed the tags across the room to the boy, who barked another order. Something in Charlie's long-ago memories stirred, and he remembered a few words from the bedtime routine of his childhood, when his mother would tell him it was time to get into his nightshirt. The boy wanted his uniform. He unbuttoned his coat.

"What the hell are you doing?"

"He wants my clothes."

"And you're going to give them to him?"

"Don't think I have a lot of choice in that matter right now."

The German boy shouted at them.

"He wants us to shut up," Charlie explained.

"How do you know?"

"I remember my mother saying something like that to my father when she got mad."

The German boy crouched to pick up the tags, keeping the rifle aimed as he slipped them on, then stepped into the room. He shouted again.

Charlie nodded, and kept stepping out of his clothes. His body shook till he thought his bones would shatter.

"You're fucking crazy," Tommy said.

"Shut up, Tommy. Don't make him mad."

The boy loosed a screaming torrent in German and Tommy snapped. "Crazy fucking Kraut! Why you want to look like an American? You're fuckin' crazy!"

The word hung briefly, then froze and shattered in the arctic air. Could have been meant for the whole world out there. The whole crazy world that sent its youngest, strongest, most promising young men to shoot at each other until they died or went home maimed, physically or mentally, or too often both. The whole crazy setup. The whole crazy deal where people thought they had to murder other people by the dozens, the hundreds, the thousands. The tens of thousands. The millions. Forgive us our trespasses. Our debts. Forgive us, Father, we know not what we do. The first shot went a little wild. Tommy spun from the force, staggered, then lunged at their captor, who dodged to the side. Tommy lurched past, through the door to the outside. The next shot pinned him. He sagged and fell, his hot blood seeping out to melt the snow for a second before it hardened again in an icy red halo, Tommy silent and still at the center of a ghastly bloom.

The third shot, near Charlie's head, forced him into action. He tossed the crumpled olive drabs. The boy struggled out of his own uniform and into Charlie's. Charlie was beginning to understand. It meant the Americans were nearby. He watched the boy run off into the woods, pulled the enemy uniform on, wrapped the blankets around himself to stave off freezing and to keep from being misidentified, and prayed to be rescued. *Thy will be done, on earth as it is in heaven. Deliver me from evil. Deliver me.*

8

HEAVEN, 1945

"Anybody home?"

Minnie rested against the porch railing while she waited for a response and inventoried the items in the basket she carried. A dozen farm fresh eggs from Helen and Lester's hens, a pound of home-churned butter, a loaf of unsliced whole wheat from the ovens of Heaven's Bread, a package of cinnamon rolls from same, a sour cream rhubarb pie that Stella had baked, a bag of shell peas from Thelma's garden, a quart jar of beef noodle soup from Clara's Kitchen, a pint of Ida's wild strawberry jam, and a bouquet of dahlias—tight-petaled maroons and delicate starburst whites—from Alma Porter's flower beds.

Minnie hoped she wasn't being too forward. Heaven, Indiana, didn't really have an official Welcome Wagon, so she'd taken it upon herself to create and represent an ad hoc one.

She was tickled pink, she'd told all contributors, that there was going to be a new beauty shop in Heaven. She figured they'd all heard by now that a Miss Charlene Bader had just moved to town (the movers had been there all yesterday afternoon), made a down payment on the little house on Elm back of the bakery, rented out the front of Tilda Lewis's house on Main Street, and taken out an advertisement in *Heaven's Sentinel* announcing that she would be open for business in two weeks. People didn't too often move to Heaven to start businesses. And they almost never came looking to buy a house. More often, they came to work at Hoosier Chemicals when they were hiring, then moved away again when they got laid off.

They had indeed heard, and the news had set her friends to speculating. Maybe this will be the start of a renaissance for Heaven. Lord knows the town can use a good beauty shop. With the war in Europe finally over, a bunch of fellows coming back (and what a blessing that we only lost one so far when you think of how many from Hartford City died), and now Hoosier Chemicals hiring a night shift, the women will have a little more disposable income and a little more reason to spend it making themselves pretty for their husbands and boyfriends. Not to mention the fact that Agnes Siebold just doesn't have the energy or the eyesight to cut hair anymore, but she's been keeping at it just to give folks a local option. Now she can finally retire before something terrible happens with those scissors.

More than one of them considered the possibility that she might treat herself to the ministrations of a real hair professional. Minnie topped the list.

"Hello?" Charlene's statuesque frame outlined by the door edge and jamb caught Minnie a bit by surprise. She'd had no idea what an attractive woman Charlene was. Tall, ash blonde hair in a careful arrangement that made the most of a distinctive widow's peak, precisely shaped eyebrows, startling blue eyes, perfectly shaped lips, a willowy and well-proportioned body. The pale blue silk blouse set off her hair color perfectly, and the navy blue skirt was cut to make the most of her long, slender legs.

Minnie blurted out, "You look like a model!" Then she blushed at the inappropriateness of her remark. "Excuse me for saying that. I don't know where my manners went. It's just that most women in Heaven look so plain compared to you."

Charlene rescued her with a gracious smile. "You don't need to apologize for giving a compliment. What can I do for you?"

Minnie thrust the basket of goodies at Charlene. "Welcome Wagon!" she chirped, urgent and cheery. "We put together a few things to help you feel at home and let you know how pleased everyone is that you've decided to open your shop here in Heaven. I'm Minnie Kelso, and I want the honor of making the very first appointment."

"Why, thank you so much." Charlene accepted the basket. "I would be delighted to have you be my first customer. You know I'm not quite ready to open. It'll be two weeks yet."

"Oh yes, I know. I saw your ad."

"But I'll put you down in the appointment book to be the very first one in the chair, which I'm hoping they'll be delivering tomorrow. Would you like to come in?"

"Oh, you probably don't have the time . . ."

"It's Sunday afternoon. I don't have a place to be in the world until tomorrow morning to meet my chair."

"Well, maybe just for a minute."

"Come on in and make yourself at home while I get these beautiful flowers into some water so they don't wilt. Would you like some iced tea?"

Minnie surveyed the living room as she moved to the sofa and sat down. "That would be very nice, thank you. If it's not too much trouble."

"No trouble at all. I just made a pitcher," Charlene called from the kitchen, where she'd suddenly noticed she could see, in the odd set of mirrors formed by cabinet glass panes and windows, the image of her unexpected guest waiting in the living room. Minnie was sitting primly, her hands folded in her lap, her ankles tightly together. Her eyes, though, were in motion: sweeping the room, noting the details. She was taking in the wallpaper, a strip around the top with intertwined dusty roses accenting a creamy white expanse of wall, then the hall tree by the door, with its oaken seat softened by a needlepoint pillow in greens and grays, then the dining table by the front window, and its two chairs, the curve of the chair backs, the rosette pattern carved in the top crosspiece.

A moment later, as Charlene was returning bearing a vase of dahlias and a glass of iced tea, Minnie was looking at a faded photograph that stood in a frame on the end table. A man and woman stood in front of a small chapel. The woman's hair was piled atop her head; her dress was high-collared, puff-sleeved, ruffle-bosomed, full-skirted, and low-hemmed. The man wore a dark suit with a single button closing the jacket over a high-collared white shirt and vest. "Are these your folks?"

"Yes, they are. That's their wedding day. The one picture I think they ever had taken."

"Still living?"

"No. They went in the flu epidemic just after the Great War."

"Oh, I'm sorry."

Charlene saved Minnie from having to ask about a second picture: a young girl, her blonde hair in braids, holding a basket of flowers. "That's my sister Hannah. She lived through the flu, but got the sleepy sickness and then Parkinson's. She would have been thirty-four next month."

"That's so young to go!"

"Yes, they said it was very rare to show up in such a young person. They tried a new operation on her and it didn't work."

"I'm so sorry. How terrible for you to lose both your parents, and then your sister like that."

Minnie looked at Charlene with such a guileless expression of compassion that it threatened Charlene's composure. "Thank you," she managed to say, fighting her memories back with her manners. She handed Minnie the glass of iced tea, put the vase of flowers on the mantel, and took a steadying breath. "Please do let me know if it's too sugary."

Minnie, aware she'd inadvertently upset Charlene and at a momentary loss for words, was glad for the opportunity to sip iced tea and think about what to say next. "It's just right. The tea."

"Good. I like it sweet. Sometimes it's too sweet for others."

"Oh no, it's delicious. I have a bit of a sweet tooth myself."

They sat for a minute, Minnie focused on emptying her glass, Charlene watching Minnie.

"Let me cut you a piece of this pie. It looks so delicious."

"Mercy, no. That's for you."

"Can I refresh your tea?"

"Oh no, thank you. I really shouldn't stay. I know you must have a lot of work to do setting up a new house."

"At least tell me about all the things you brought before you go, would you? Beginning with the flowers. Who grows these beautiful flowers?"

Minnie, released from awkwardness by Charlene's redirection of the topic of conversation, found her voice. "Well, those are from Alma Porter's garden. Alma has been our postmistress for many years. They live over on Church Street right by the post office. We call it Church Street because that's where three of our four churches are: First Christian, Mount Olive Presbyterian, and Prince of Peace Lutheran. Alma goes to Prince of Peace, but her husband Caleb goes to Mount Olive."

Charlene nodded.

"Now the eggs are from Helen and Lester Breck. They live out on Millstone Road, just east of town. They go to First Christian like I do. I surely hope you'll come by Sunday for our service. It's at ten A M. The bread and rolls are from Heaven's Bread. That's the bakery right across the alley behind your house. But the pie is homemade. Stella Wingate baked it from her own rhubarb. She won first place at the fair last year for that pie recipe. Her husband Walter works at Hoosier Chemicals, and Stella helps Clara out in the restaurant in the afternoons. June Wade is there in the mornings, but she didn't contribute anything to the basket. Well, not because she didn't choose to, I just didn't get a chance to ask her."

Charlene inhaled deeply. She felt a little short of breath just listening to Minnie. Hannah could talk like that too, back when she could talk, except she specialized in questions. Best not to think about Hannah right now, though. Best to stay focused on the barrage of information about her newly adopted neighbors.

"Clara Rudaker owns Clara's Kitchen," Minnie continued. "I guess that's pretty obvious from the name. The soup is from there, and you can't beat it. Every day Clara has a different soup on the menu, and then sometimes she makes the beef noodle with her homemade noodles as a special. Have you eaten at Clara's Kitchen yet?"

"No, I haven't really had time to explore much. I just got here yesterday afternoon, and I was only here once before, a couple of months ago, to look at the house and the shop."

"Oh, you're in for a treat. She's the best cook in Hutter County."

What a treat already, thought Charlene, stifling an urge to laugh outright. She certainly didn't want her guest to think she was mocking her. Minnie's torrent of words was just such a friendly and welcome change of pace from the terse exchanges she'd had in her business transactions. The yeps, nopes, and mebbes.

"Now Thelma Mueller grew the beans. Ida, that's Thelma's sister-in-law, married to Thelma's brother Hiram, made the jam. She goes out every June and picks those wild strawberries herself. The butter is from our dairy farm. Just churned it this morning. I know I shouldn'ta worked on Sunday, but I wanted it to be fresh. And of course on a dairy farm the cows work on Sunday whether you want them to or not."

"It's really quite wonderful of you all to make me feel so welcome."

"Well, it's not too often folks move to Heaven, but when they do, we always like to let them know we're glad they're here." Minnie felt herself redden just a little. Truth be known, the only other families she'd ever welcomed to Heaven were those of the pastors or other folks who came to First Christian. What if Charlene was Catholic? Minnie hadn't mentioned St. Sebastian, over on Jefferson, where the papists went. Charlene didn't look Catholic. If anything, perhaps Lutheran. But sometimes people could be Catholic and not look it. They weren't all like the Bickles and Flynns, with their large freckled broods of unruly children.

While Minnie stewed in her private thoughts, Charlene excused herself to put the butter and other perishables into the refrigerator, and while she was in the kitchen, she took advantage of the opportunity to watch a bit more without being noticed. Minnie had changed her position only slightly, now sitting with her ankles crossed. Her folded hands revealed a tension: she was rhythmically rubbing one thumb with the other. A slight furrow in her brow corroborated the impression. Though she'd only just met this woman, the sudden silence of Minnie's voice made Charlene feel like she was missing something she'd always cherished.

"I'm going to have to ask you to tell me again who sent everything over, so I can take notes and send thank-you cards."

Minnie startled out of her reverie, realizing Charlene was back in the room. "Oh, you don't have to do that. I can make up a little list for you with all the names and addresses. I could bring it to you tomorrow."

"I don't want you to go to any more trouble. I can look the addresses up in the phone book if you just tell me the names again."

"It's no trouble. No trouble at all. I come right by Mrs. Lewis's every Monday on my way to trade with Helen. Helen Breck. The eggs. I always get eggs from Helen and she gets her milk and butter from me. It's usually easier for me to get out to her because she's got Melinda to look after. I don't have any children yet. Well, that's good, because I'm not married yet! Melinda's the sweetest thing. You couldn't want a nicer child. It's a shame she's slow. And Helen is so smart. Well, Lester is too, but Helen's the real brains of the operation. The cord was wrapped around her neck when she was born, Melinda's, you know, and they say it cut off the oxygen to her brain and set her back a little." Registering Charlene's look of concern, she hastened to add, "Oh, listen to me! I'm making her sound like she can hardly tie her shoes for herself, and she's not like that at all. She's just a little behind in school. But anyone will tell you she's the sweetest child a person could hope to meet. And, oh, they dote on her, Lester and Helen do."

"I can see I'll learn a lot about my new town if I listen to you."

"Am I talking too much? I am. You must think I'm nothing but a gossip."

"No, I meant no criticism! I really want to hear you tell me about all my new neighbors. It will help me get to know them."

"I don't know all your new neighbors," Minnie confessed. "More the ones that go to First Christian. Mrs. Lewis, for example, she goes to Prince of Peace. But I hear she's a fair landlady. The folks that rented out her front rooms before you always spoke highly of her. They came in '42 to work for Hoosier Chemicals. He was a chemist, and couldn't go to war because of his vision. Was almost blind in one eye. The wife worked there too, in the front office. But then last May he got a job offer over in Ohio he said he couldn't really refuse. Teaching there at the university."

"Have you lived here all your life?"

"Oh yes. All my life. I was born in the same house my mother was born in. Only thing that's changed over the years is the trains. The tracks run right through the middle of our land, you see. The house sits back from the road, so the trains go by pretty much right outside my bedroom window. There're more freight trains than there used to be. I guess what with the war effort, there've been a lot more shipments of raw materials and whatnot to factories in Ohio and Pennsylvania. But I'm afraid I'm talking your ear off. I should go."

"Are you sure I can't freshen your tea? I'd love to hear more."

"Oh, no. I really have to go." Minnie stood and picked up her purse. "But I'll stop by tomorrow with that list. Will you be here or over at Mrs. Lewis's?"

"I'll be over there setting up."

"Of course. To meet the chair."

"And I'll bring my appointment book so we can sign you up to be my very first customer."

"I'll be by around ten, then."

Minnie handed her empty glass to Charlene and thanked her again for the iced tea. She decided to stop at Ida's on her way home to report on Miss Charlene Bader, clearly the most interesting person to have moved to Heaven in a long time. Then she thought about how Ida would ask to know what she'd found out about the newcomer and realized she knew very little. She'd done all the talking! What had she learned? That Charlene's parents had died, her sister too, and that Charlene was a good listener who made perfect iced tea. That wasn't quite enough to merit a report to Ida, so Minnie drove home instead and thought about how to get her hair done in two weeks when she would be the inaugural customer of Charlene's Beauty Shop.

Meanwhile, Charlene brewed herself a cup of mint tea to settle her stomach. Her first full-fledged social conversation in Heaven, demanding not only her best voice and mannerisms, but also considerable emotional control, had taken a toll. *If I'm going to do this every day*, she thought, *I'd best not give myself ulcers over it.*

* * *

Each day, her adopted town grew a bit more familiar. Charlene took little excursions. She met the grocer Herman Hess, and learned from him to buy her chickens on Tuesdays, when they were freshest. She met his brother, Harry, half of Heaven's police force.

She met Clara, the proprietress of Clara's Kitchen, her morning waitress June Wade, and her afternoon helper Stella Wingate. She sampled another of Clara's famous soups, her legendary creamy tomato. (She noted that virtually everything on Clara's menu seemed to be legendary, as everyone she encountered seemed to have a favorite dish at Clara's Kitchen to recommend to her.) She met Evelyn Wasmuth, who worked in the pharmacy at the corner of First and Main and whose husband was the up-and-coming young funeral director in Heaven. She had a cup of tea with her landlady Mrs. Lewis, and learned, then promptly forgot, the names of seven grandchildren who lived in Kentucky. She took walks by the little river that ran through town, and met a couple of the fellows, Bobby and Maurice, who fished every chance they got. Bobby was just starting up an auto repair business; she didn't catch what Maurice did for a living, just that he lived a couple blocks up the alley from Clara's Kitchen. She chatted with Alma Porter, who presided over Heaven's post office, and her daughter Wilma, a towheaded toddler of two.

Most of the time, though, she worked on readying her shop for its grand opening: receiving packages and furniture; overseeing the installation of two sinks, both pink, one for general purposes, another with a dip in the edge for shampoos, a hair dryer chair, the swivel chair, and three chairs for the waiting area; organizing her brushes, combs, shampoos, curling chemicals, scissors, bibs, and towels. She bought copies of *Better Homes and Gardens*, *Reader's Digest*, and the *Saturday Evening Post* for her waiting area. She bought bags of penny candies—root beer barrels, butterscotch discs, and peppermints—to put in a dish by her shop's front door so that everyone who stopped in would have something sweet to remember her by.

But if it was Heaven by day, it was Hell by night. No amount of attention to Charlene's daytime details could keep nocturnal Charlie from the regular reliving of the awful foot-pedaled drill,

the insufficient light, the unrelenting cold, Tommy's constant pa-
laver, and inevitably, the crimson snow so cruelly realistic that he
screamed himself awake. Dreams being dreams, it was not always
Tommy he saw slaughtered in the frigid fog but often Hannah, Anne,
his mother Ilsa, his father Jarvis, even May sometimes. Each on a bier
of bloody ice.

He'd wake up in a sweat of suffocating memory.

The trip to the tree in Iowa haunted him too. Carving the dates
in that tree for Tommy when he first came back. Sometimes he would
sit bolt upright in the bed and cry out because the old sycamore in
Keokuk had changed to the shagbark hickory of his childhood gone
malevolent, wanting to entangle and smother him.

"He talked about you all the time," Charlie had told Tommy's
sweetheart. "It's what kept him going. He wanted me to come back
to the old sycamore tree in his yard where he carved your initials and
complete it. 'Till death do us part. April 4, 1941–January 29, 1945.'
That's where I came from just now. He wanted me to tell you."

Charlie saw it through the sorrow in her eyes: not quite three
years, and for two-thirds of them, Tommy had been gone. That's the
way war was. You vowed to marry as soon as things were over, you
waited, you wrote letters every day, on paper the shade of dusty roses.
You dabbed them with the perfume you wore the last night you saw
him. He told you in his letters that the fellows teased him, calling
them Stinky Pinkies. He told you they were just jealous: that no one
else in the battalion got such beautiful, sweet-smelling words from
their gals. And you survived, somehow, when the news ripped your
heart out. When you learned the person you'd expected to live your
life with was in a foreign graveyard and you wouldn't even get the
release of providing a proper burial. Then, after the official visit, just
when you'd begun to think you were getting over it, or even hoping
against hope that the army made a mistake, comes the awful irrefut-
able proof. The man who saw him die.

She'd looked at first like she wasn't even going to cry. Just stood there, motionless. Almost like she didn't comprehend what he was saying. And then she'd crumbled, sobbed, and beat her fists on the floor. Charlie stood above her, awkward, wondering what to do, then finally knelt down to be able to speak to her. "I'm sorry," he said. "I'm so very sorry." He wanted to comfort her, but didn't dare touch her. Charlene could have stroked her hair, put a sisterly arm around her shoulders, shared her grief. Charlie could only stand there helpless, wishing suddenly that he'd ignored Tommy's request and not carved the final date, not come to report it, not torn the scab off her wounded heart. On the way back home, he rolled down the car window and threw the knife as far from the car as he could.

Charlene took to having a shot of scotch, just one, in a cup of warm milk, in order to get to sleep at night and stay asleep. It seemed to help. She vowed to herself and her dead mother to stop just as soon as she could.

*   *   *

Minnie was giddy with anticipation. Charlene was leading her to the sink at the back of the shop where she was about to get the works: shampoo, trim, set, comb out. "You know, I do believe this is one of life's true luxuries. To have someone fix your hair for you. Did you go to school to learn how to fix hair, or is it just something that came naturally to you?"

"Some of each, I suppose. I went to beauty college in Chicago but I used to do my sister's hair, too."

"Is that where you grew up? Chicago?"

"No, we grew up in Texas. But . . ." The specter of Anne still haunted Charlene, and she had to consciously banish her from the memory. "I moved Hannah to Indianapolis when she needed better care than I could find in Dallas. To a nursing home there."

"So you lived in Indy for a while?"

"No, I moved on up to Chicago."

"Of course. To go to beauty school."

Charlene allowed the misunderstanding. It was far easier, far safer, far simpler that way.

"Did you see her much?"

"As much as I could."

"Was she close in age?"

"She was eight years younger than me."

"I bet she worshipped her older sister."

"She was a little tagalong," Charlene acknowledged with a smile.

"So you're originally from Dallas, then?"

"No, I grew up in Kirbyville. That's in Texas too."

"I don't believe I've ever heard of Kirbyville. Now where is that?"

"It's not too far from Galveston."

"Oh, well, Galveston I've heard of. Storm of the Century. Now, how did you get from Kirbyville to Dallas? And from Chicago to Heaven?"

"It's a long story. Can you put your head back for me? And let me know if the water's too hot."

When Minnie felt the stream of warm water wash over her scalp, and the strong fingers of the new hairdresser massaging the shampoo into a lather, she felt like she'd died and gone to heaven, never mind that was where she was in the first place. It was a pleasure Minnie had never before known. All during the Depression, shampoo was a luxury and hot water was something you got by pumping it cold and heating it on the wood stove. Her mother's touch was brusque and efficient. This was entirely different. Minnie felt like a queen, or better yet, a princess, being readied for her royal wedding to her Prince Charming who would be riding back into town any day now. She hated for the delightful sensations to end, but also hoped for more of Charlene's story once the water was turned off, the towel wrapped around her head, and she was installed in the chair in front of the big mirror. "You were telling me how you got to Dallas," Minnie reminded Charlene, but the little bell over the door jangled, announcing the arrival of Charlene Bader's second customer.

"Are you open for business?"

"Yes, ma'am."

"And I see Minnie has beat me to it. Would you have time to do a perm today?"

"I believe I would, yes."

"I can wait till you're done with Minnie, if you don't have anyone else on your schedule."

Minnie allowed herself a silent sigh. She wanted to be the first to find out Charlene's entire life story, and she didn't want Ida to be there when she did. Ida always got things confused, and besides, she had been showing up getting in Minnie's way ever since they'd started first grade at Hutter Elementary. She'd wait till another time to tease out the remaining details of Charlene's circuitous route to Heaven. "Morning, Ida."

"Morning, Minnie. I ought to have known you'd be the first one here. I should have called for an appointment yesterday!"

"I made mine two weeks ago." Minnie tried not to sound smug.

"I do have two other people on the schedule for today," Charlene said. "We could do something after two thirty or tomorrow. Tomorrow is fairly open."

Cueing yet another entrance, the bell over the door jingled again, and Elizabeth Tipton made her way through. "I know I'm early," she said. "I got my shopping done and decided it doesn't make sense to go home and come back, so I'll just wait till you're ready for me."

"Morning, Elizabeth."

"Morning, Minnie."

"Hello, Elizabeth. You ladies are way ahead of me. Here I thought I was going to be the first one. And instead I'm going to be number four."

"Who's number three? I only see two of us here waiting."

Charlene shook out the towel she'd been drying Minnie's hair with. Watching her shop fill with the women, listening to their easy chat, she felt a disconcerting happiness rising up from her belly. It caught in her throat, and she had to clear it before she spoke. "I believe it's a lady named Eunice Switzer. She's scheduled at one thirty."

"That makes sense," Ida said. "Eunice wouldn't want to miss out on anything. I'm surprised she isn't here already, just to keep an eye on things."

"Well, you ladies make yourself at home. There's some magazines there if you want to look through them." Charlene turned her attention back to Minnie. A bit of hymn drifted through her head from a long-ago gathering. *Somewhere, somewhere. Beautiful isle of somewhere.* "How do you want it to look? How short do you want it?"

"Oh, not too short. I don't fancy these haircuts that make you look halfway to a man. Something that softens my cheekbones a little. Something a little fancy but that'll comb into everyday too."

"Special occasion?"

"I suppose you could say so. My fiancé is due home." Minnie loved the word "fiancé." Such a fancy-sounding word. And to celebrate with a bit of fanciness beyond her usual routines, she was treating herself to this extravagance. To pay for it, she'd sold her sugar rations to Evelyn Wasmuth. Evelyn's husband Herb had the funeral parlor. His was the one business that would never go under. Whether depression, war, or peacetime, people in Heaven were always dying at a sure, steady pace, just like babies were born pretty much no matter what happened out there in the world into which they emerged. So

Evelyn could afford a little extra sugar, and that meant Minnie could afford to be Miss Charlene Bader's very first customer.

"Ahhh. That is definitely a special occasion. Where has he been?"

"Somewhere in France is all I know. He wasn't allowed to ever say exactly where. He was injured. Not too seriously, but enough to be in a hospital over there for a few weeks. I know I shouldn't say it, but I'm glad he was hurt, because otherwise he'd have been sent on to the Pacific."

"How long has he been gone?" Charlene asked.

"Since March '42. Three years, five months, and seven days."

"And now he is coming home. That's wonderful. So what do you think? What hairstyle will celebrate?"

"What do you think, Charlene? Bangs? Or does my face look better with the hair back off my forehead? I want something that's young-looking, but not too young. I'm not trying to be eighteen again, but I don't want to look like a fuddy-duddy."

"I think you'd look adorable in bangs, Minnie," Elizabeth offered. "With a little curl. And curls tucked behind your ears so you can show off your earrings."

Elizabeth Tipton had a way of complimenting you, Minnie thought, that almost made you feel like she didn't take you seriously. *And besides, I didn't ask your opinion, I asked Charlene.*

"I agree," said Charlene, then noticed a flicker of annoyance dance across Minnie's features and just as swiftly disappear. The hairdresser continued, watching both the women in her large mirror to confirm that she was successfully negotiating a compromise. "Not quite a curl, really. Just a slight flip under in the front. That's the way a lot of young ladies are wearing their hair these days." Minnie nodded approval of the plan. Charlene relaxed. How easy it was to talk about hair. *Somewhere, somewhere.*

"When is Warren due back then, Minnie?" Elizabeth paged idly through *Life*, but kept her eye on Charlene at work.

"The last letter I got said he'll be in the States tomorrow. He has to spend a few days at the base, then he'll take the train home and be here a week from Sunday."

"I bet you can't wait to see him."

Minnie nodded. "That's for sure. It's been so long I have to think sometimes to remember what he looks like. The other day, I realized I couldn't remember what color his eyes are."

"Will you be setting a wedding date soon?"

"It's set already. January nineteenth."

"He's going to work with your dad on the farm, isn't he?" Ida piped up. Charlene caught the hint of anxiety in her voice. Funny how you could tell so quickly the social hierarchy and who was at the bottom near the edge.

"That's the plan."

Elizabeth closed the magazine on her lap. "I think that's wonderful, that he and your dad get on so well. And that he's interested in the family business. You're so lucky he's coming back all in one piece, too."

"Yes, I am."

For a few seconds, the shop was silent save for the click of the scissors. Charlene refocused, putting all her attention on giving Minnie the very best haircut possible. Elizabeth returned to reading *Life*, Ida browsed *Better Homes and Gardens*, and Minnie enjoyed the tingling sensations of having locks of hair lifted and clipped. Then Elizabeth looked up from the article she was reading. "If you ask me," she said, "we should have dropped one of those bombs on the Russians, too."

"The Russians are on our side," Minnie reminded her.

"Frederick says you can't trust them. He says they're communists, and communists will stab you in the back if it suits them. Didn't they pull out on us in the Great War? He says there's a lot of people in this country who'd better wake up and smell the coffee."

Minnie decided not to respond. Once again, she hadn't asked Elizabeth, as a matter of fact, in spite of Elizabeth's penchant for that phrase. And she didn't want to make Charlene's work more difficult by moving her head or talking.

Charlene was relieved to hear the little bell ring again, derailing this particular conversational train. She didn't think talk about politics was good for business. It made people too tense. A beauty shop should be a place of respite from the ugliness in the world. This time it was Helen Breck, followed by her daughter Melinda. Charlene glanced up at them. "Good morning, ladies."

Melinda giggled. "I'm not a lady. I'm a girl. Ladies are grown up." She skipped a lopsided skip to the chairs in the little waiting area and hopped into the one closest to the door. "Hello, Mrs. Mueller. Hello, Mrs. Tipton."

Ida smiled. "Hello, Melinda. Is your mama going to get her hair done?"

"I'm getting mine done, too."

"Oh, you are?"

"Yes. But not today. Today she's just going to make the 'pointment. Hello, Miss Kelso."

"Hello, Melinda. Can you say hello to Miss Bader, too?"

"Hello, Miss Bader."

"Hello." Charlene looked up from her focus on Minnie's newly forming bangs. "When would you like to come in?"

"Do you have time on Friday?" Helen was standing by the door, ready to leave. This many people in one place made her vaguely uncomfortable, so even though Minnie was her best friend, she was anxious to get on with the day's errands and get back to the comfort of her own kitchen.

"I believe I do. Morning or afternoon?"

"We can come first thing in the morning."

"All right, then."

"I'm getting my new clothes for school today." Melinda announced the non sequitur proudly.

"Let's go, Melinda." Helen held her hand out, and Melinda jumped up to take it. "Goodbye, Miss Kelso. Goodbye, Mrs. Mueller. Goodbye, Mrs. Tipton. Goodbye, Miss . . ."

"Bader." Charlene smiled at her.

"Goodbye, Miss Bader," Melinda chanted, waving with her free hand.

"See you Friday," Helen said.

"See you Friday," Melinda echoed, as they were ushered out by the jingle of the door bell.

"She's such a well-behaved child," Ida said, once Helen and Melinda were gone.

"She's a charming little girl," Charlene affirmed.

Elizabeth, for once, volunteered no opinion. She hadn't told anyone yet—not even her husband—that she was pregnant, and she was having a moment of fear. What if her baby turned out to be like Melinda? Slow? Elizabeth had been the salutatorian in her high school graduating class, and Frederick had been valedictorian in his, one year ahead of her. She wanted a smart child. Helen and Lester were smart enough themselves, but here they had a daughter who, sweet tempered though she was, would probably never really be able to make anything of herself. Elizabeth felt a wave of nausea pass over her and closed her eyes to steady her wits.

On her way home, Minnie stopped in at the Brecks' to show Helen how her new hairdo had turned out. Minnie, Warren, Lester, and Helen had been half of the graduating class of 1937. Lester and Warren had enlisted together, gone through basic training together. Minnie and Helen had held things together in their absence, like hundreds of thousands of other sisters, daughters, wives, and sweethearts. Pops,

Helen's father-in-law, was out mending fence along the road when Minnie drove up. His granddaughter was holding tools for him.

"Well, well, well, look at that. Don't tell me Warren's home already!"

"No, but he should be here any day now."

"Helen's in the summer kitchen, putting up some pickle relish. Melinda, give me them pliers and run in and tell your mother Minnie's here."

Melinda was staring in fascination at the transformation. "What happened to your hair?"

Minnie laughed. She knew Melinda meant no offense. Not bright enough to tell a lie, even a white one.

"That's what Miss Bader was doing when you saw me earlier today. She was fixing it for me."

"How?"

"She was styling it. So it isn't too curly."

"My hair's naturally curly. That's what Grandpop says. My mommy says it's wavy."

"Run along, Melinda," Pops reminded her, and Melinda skipped off across the lawn to report the news to her mother. "This the new Chevy I've been hearing about?" He gave the auto an approving once-over.

"Well, it's not new. It's a '38."

"New enough. No one buys a brand-new car."

"Herb Wasmuth got a new hearse."

"Well, that's different. That's business."

"And Ernie Ellis got a Ford that's just a year old. Got a deal on a bank repossession over in Marion."

By now, they figured Helen had been alerted to Minnie's presence. Both Pops and Minnie knew well that she didn't appreciate folks, even best friends, just dropping in without warning, so Minnie always stayed in her car and let Helen come out to her when she was ready.

Helen came down the driveway drying her hands on her apron while Melinda tugged at her skirts to go faster. "Melinda, behave yourself," Helen admonished. Melinda ran ahead and pointed to Minnie.

"See, Mommy? The lady fixed her hair."

"Well, look at you!" Helen surveyed the hairdo while Minnie beamed.

"Do you think Warren will like it?"

"If he has any sense he will. It looks wonderful. Do you have time for a cup of coffee?"

"To tell you the truth, I've had too much coffee already today, but would love just a plain glass of water."

If Minnie were really telling the truth, she'd have said Helen was the only woman she knew who could ruin Maxwell House. Helen got straight As in business math, but struggled for a C in home economics. It was funny how some people just never could learn to cook. With other friends, Minnie talked about new recipes and patterns. With Helen, she talked about farming and finances.

"You'll enjoy it," she told Helen. "You'd be surprised how inexpensive it is to get the whole works: shampoo, cut, set. And it's not much more for a permanent wave."

"Maybe when Lester comes home I'll do that. For now I'll just get the ends trimmed and have her cut Melinda's hair."

"What have you heard from him?" Minnie felt a little embarrassed that she'd almost forgotten to ask, so preoccupied was she with preparations for her own sweetheart's imminent arrival.

"He's still in India," Helen said. "He said I could tell people now that the war is over. He's been there all along."

"India! Were they fighting in India too?"

"Some general found out he knows how to play bridge. So he was safe there at the base so long as he and the general kept winning."

"Good for him. To tell you the truth," Minnie said for the second time, but this time it was indeed the truth, "I never could picture Lester killing anyone. He's just too good-natured." As she said it, she wondered what that meant about Warren. Could she imagine him killing? She could, though she preferred to imagine him milking the cows. "Well," she said aloud, "I don't want to keep you from your canning. I'll see you at church."

On the way home, she couldn't help running her fingers through her hair and thinking about what Warren might say when he stepped off the train.

Back at the beauty shop, Charlene swept up stray bits of hair. She'd handled the matter of Minnie's hairstyle well, she felt, if she did say so herself. She tucked the issue of *Life* into her handbag to take with her. No sense in having reading matter around that got people to thinking about war. Then she sterilized combs and brushes, sorted curlers, and laid out her scissors and clips for the next morning's business while she reviewed what she'd learned that day about her new neighbors. Minnie's fiancé, she thought, was a lucky man.

*   *   *

"Minnie says you're from Chicago?"

"That's where I lived before I came here."

"What made you decide to become a Hoosier?"

"Well, I wanted to get back to a quieter way of life."

"You're originally from Indiana?"

"No, I grew up in Texas."

"You don't sound southern."

"I lived in Chicago for quite a while."

"Is it different having a shop in a big city?"

"People are people wherever they are."

"The styles aren't different?"

"Not really."

"I imagine you heard a lot of interesting stories from your customers there. Big-city goings-on."

"Like I said, people are people."

It was a skill, fielding questions but not really answering them. She learned that if she kept her focus closely on the head of hair in front of her, the customers didn't want to break her concentration. There wasn't much she actually had to say, aside from asking how much to take off and whether to set a tight or loose curl. While she focused on hair, information passed from one customer to the next as they came and went. Charlene worked, and Charlene listened.

She was getting to know the women directly, and the men through the eyes and stories of the women.

Minnie, the ebullient young woman with the earthy beauty of a farm girl, waiting for her sweetheart to return from overseas, was her first informant.

Ida was a bit of a hanger-on. She reminded Charlene of Luella back in Chicago, not just because of her tendency to imagine worst-case scenarios, but also because of her loyalty, even to those whom she clearly envied. Ida had no children, and a husband who was reputedly a bit of a cold fish, and Charlene wasn't sure whether Ida's self-pity and deep loneliness were the cause or the effect or both.

Helen was at the other end of the spectrum from Minnie in the gab department. She rarely had something to say, and when she did it was to the point. Friendly enough, but very reserved. Unlike Ida, Helen never seemed to complain.

From the other ladies who came to Charlene's shop, she learned that Helen had a dashingly handsome and even-tempered husband named Lester, also not back from the war yet. Helen and their daughter Melinda lived with Lester's dad Omar, known to all as Pops, on the Breck family farm.

Elizabeth Tipton's husband was Frederick, which distinguished him from Frieda Thompson's husband Fred. Elizabeth didn't approve of Fred, so this was important to remember. Elizabeth was related in some distant way through her husband Frederick to Helen Breck, though Charlene had not followed the tortuous path of first and second cousins once or twice removed and in-laws who forged the relationship. Since Elizabeth and Helen didn't act related, Charlene didn't feel a need to master that particular bit of information.

*   *   *

"Pretty short," Alma Porter directed. "I don't like to fuss with it so I just want a basic haircut. To tell you the truth, this is the first time I've had my hair cut professionally. I've always done it myself. But Minnie said I just had to come in and get a shampoo and haircut so I decided why not? You surely do have an enthusiastic supporter in Minnie."

"Yes," Charlene agreed with Alma. "She's been a tremendous help to me just teaching me about the town."

"You won't find better'n Minnie. That Warren Ressler doesn't know what he's doing, throwing her over for some French woman. Minnie deserves better."

The postmistress registered Charlene's surprise and realized this was news Charlene hadn't heard yet. "She didn't tell you? Poor soul. Here she was all dolled up last Sunday, ready to go meet the train, and the phone rings. Can you imagine, it's a call coming all the way from Paris, of all places. And darned if it isn't Mr. Ressler"—Alma managed to make "Mister" sound like a curse word—"calling to say he'd married a French girl and wasn't coming home after all. Met her in the hospital. She was his nurse. He was going to run the farm, you know. Minnie's dad Paul has a bad back and the brother Gabriel, he's another one went off and didn't come back."

Charlene felt a sharp pang. "Killed in action?"

"Oh, no. He came back in that sense. He just didn't come back to Heaven. Married a girl from California he met out there before he shipped out. They'll be here for Christmas, but her family is all out west and she didn't want to leave. I don't blame her, to tell the truth. I hear it's beautiful out there along the California coast. But isn't that a lump of coal in Minnie's stocking? If you don't mind, I'd rather you didn't tell her I told you. I don't usually talk about people but I just assumed you would have known already."

"I haven't seen her since she came in on my opening day. Should I feather your bangs a little bit?"

"Please." Alma closed her eyes as Charlene stepped in front of her to clip some style into her blunt-cut bangs. "Poor soul. She deserves better. I don't know what gets into a fellow would make him turn his back on everything like that. Leave everything familiar behind."

Charlene stepped to the side so Alma could see herself in the mirror. "Short enough?"

It was short enough, but Alma was loving the sensations of having her hair done so much she considered telling Charlene to take a little more off the back.

Charlene read her mind. "Maybe just a little higher at the neckline?"

"Yes, I think so."

The little bell over the door jingled the news of a newcomer. "Well, look at you!" Clara shook out her umbrella and put it half-open by the door to dry. "That's the perfect 'do for a professional woman."

"Afternoon, Clara. I'll just be about two minutes more and then I'll be ready for you."

Alma checked the mirror again and nodded her approval of the haircut. "How'd you get away from the restaurant, Clara?"

"Oh, I've got Stella watching things. It gets kind of slow this time of day anyway. And what about you? Who's watching Wilma?"

"Mom's with her till I get back."

"Your mom's feeling better, then?"

"Oh yes. She'll be back to full speed in no time."

"You be sure to tell her she's in our prayers."

"I will. Between your prayers and Dr. Brubecker's penicillin, her pneumonia didn't stand a chance."

Charlene finished brushing the hair from Alma's shoulders and doing one last comb-through of her new hairdo. Clara hung her jacket on the coat tree, taking care not to get rain on Alma's.

Alma nodded and changed the subject. "Well, I must say Minnie was right. It's a very pleasant way to spend a bit of time relaxing. Maybe I'll bring my mother in for a shampoo and perm. She used to go to Agnes, but you know Agnes has cut way back."

"Cut way back," Clara laughed. "I guess that's appropriate for someone who makes her living with scissors!" Her tone changed, became solicitous and somber. "Speaking of Minnie, poor thing, I suppose you heard about Warren Ressler. They say she'd already made all but one payment on the dress, and now to have to call up and cancel the order! It's a shame, that's what it is."

"Yes, it surely is," Alma concurred, and Charlene echoed the sentiment with a nod.

While Alma settled her bill with Charlene, Clara slipped into the shampooing chair. "I think I'll make a cream of mushroom soup for tomorrow's special," she said. "That'll give me a reason to call Minnie for more milk, and see how she's doing."

* * *

At Thanksgiving, Charlene eased her Ford, usually allowed to rest in the garage, out of storage and drove the eighty miles to the cemetery in Indy. She knelt by the small gray granite square that marked her sister's resting place. Above Hannah's name, a single rose was chiseled in the stone: the affordable embellishment that, as Charlie, he'd chosen to symbolize his sister's love of nature. Now Charlene traced the shape with her fingers, then traced the letters of Hannah's name. She placed a small pine wreath against the stone, purchased earlier that week from Melinda, who was selling them to help earn money for a class field trip to the winter circus headquarters in Peru, Indiana.

Charlene let her voice drop to its normal register, and without consciously intending it, allowed a trace of a Kirbyville, Texas, accent to reassert itself. "Hello, Hannah. Do you recognize me? Don't let the outside fool you. It's Charlie." She paused, as if to let this information sink in, perhaps for herself as well as for her sister, then, suddenly feeling Hannah's presence, questioning and a bit accusing, continued. The words tumbled out in a flustered hurry. "I'm still your brother, but I'm also Charlene now. That's a long story and maybe someday I'll tell it all to you," she pushed on. "Right now I just want you to know I'm doing fine. I'm not a woman, but I'm . . . I'm living like a woman. Dressing like a woman. I guess you can probably figure out now why Anne left me. She caught me one day. She couldn't understand it. I don't understand it much myself. It's just something I've always had to do from time to time. Now I'm doing it pretty much all the time. That's how everyone knows me where I live now."

She could hear Hannah's admonition. Not about her clothing. About her three-year absence.

"I know I haven't been to see you for a long time. There was a war. Remember how I promised we'd keep the Huns out? I went to help and was overseas for quite a while, not fightin', but fixin' teeth for

Uncle Sam. I came through it all right, 'cept a German boy stole my tags and uniform, then got himself shot, so when I got rescued and came back, well, the army got things all mixed up and decided I was the dead one. Don't bother arguing with the army, Hannah. It gets you absolutely nowhere. Look, I'll make it short and sweet. It was a sign, pure and simple. I decided just to go on and let Charlie be dead and live as Charlene."

She paused. A tiny burst of breeze blew a stray leaf against Hannah's tombstone where it lodged next to the wreath. Its presence calmed Charlene. The sense that she was being judged passed, and in its place she settled into her childhood role of the big brother who could do no wrong, at least as far as his little sister was concerned.

"I'm not a dentist anymore. I hope that's all right with you. You worked right hard to get me into that line of work. And it was good work, too, up until the war. But you know what? I'm in another line of work that you got me into. I'm fixing hair for people, just like I used to comb yours out and braid it.

"I got a nice little house. You'd like it. It's a darn sight nicer than the one we grew up in, but not as big as Mrs. Hesher's house in Dallas. Just the right size for one person. I've got my own little shop, too, where I give people shampoos and sets and sometimes permanent waves. And guess the name of the town I live in. Heaven. I think I decided to move there when I heard the name because I thought for sure that's where you are. The folks are nice as can be. I guess maybe you know that if you are there. In heaven. I miss you like the dickens, Hannah, I won't lie."

A stream of tears made its way down Charlene's face. In the middistance, she could see a man and a woman coming toward her, carrying flowers, clearly headed to a nearby grave.

She blew her nose on a tissue, tucked it into her purse, and hurried to wrap up the visit. "Hannah, speaking of heaven, give Mama and Papa my love."

Charlene rose, shook the kink out of her right knee, and decided, as she walked away past the newly arrived mourners, that she'd do her visiting with Hannah in the privacy of her own home from here on out. "I'll talk to your picture," she whispered as she got to her car. "It's too cold and too crowded out here. We'll talk where it's safe."

9

HEAVEN, 1950

"I don't know what the world's coming to," Elizabeth announced in place of a good-morning-how-are-you sort of greeting as she entered Charlene's shop. She put her purse and sweater on a waiting-area chair and headed to the shampooing sink. "Did you see the paper today?"

"What's the news?"

"They arrested a con man working the area, and it's business-women like you he preys on."

"Like me?"

"You know. Single women. Of course the fellow they have in custody claims he's innocent, but that's exactly what a con man would do, isn't it? I surely hope he hasn't been to see you."

Charlene offered a noncommittal shrug, but Elizabeth had her attention. While Charlene tested the water temperature, Elizabeth recapped the story for her. "They say he starts by sending out mailers advertising life and disability insurance with prices too good to be true. Then he stops by at a woman's place of business to make sure she's received it, takes her out for coffee, talks her into a policy, and takes her application and first payment. A few days later he pops in again, right at the end of the day, with more paperwork to do, and says to make up for the inconvenience, he wants to take her to dinner. They say he just keeps at it as long as it takes, building the trust, you know, with dinner dates and phone calls, till he's buttered her up to the point where she hands over her life savings to him to invest for her."

Elizabeth suspended her story as she scooted down in the chair, rested her head in the cool porcelain cradle, closed her eyes, and gave herself over to the scalp massage, sudsing, and hot water rinse. It gave Charlene time to compose herself. She had indeed gotten the mailer, the visit, the invitations to dinner, and finally the friendly phone call.

"You know," the insurance salesman had said when he'd called, "I can't stop thinking about you. About what would happen if . . . well . . . if something happened. I hate to tell you how many gals like you I've known of who worked their fingers to the bone, built up a little something for themselves and their loved ones, and then got wiped clean out by a spate of bad luck or some other unexpected circumstance that disability just doesn't cover. And then bingo, out of the blue, I get a call this morning from my broker. He's got two thousand shares of a sure deal for me, says it's gonna quadruple as soon as some big news hits the papers early next week. He'll get me in at fifty cents a share and by Tuesday next I can sell for two bucks or more. Only thing is I gotta take the whole lot, two K or nothing. I got most of my cash tied up in another venture right now so I can't take advantage of this, but I'll be honest with you, I gotta keep my foot in the door with this broker. I don't have to tell you that these deals you don't turn down or they don't come your way again. So like I said I'm thinking, who do I know who could really use a little windfall like this? Who really deserves it? And I'm thinking, Charlene Bader, that's who."

And when Charlene had allowed herself to sound a tiny bit interested, he'd hit it home. "Tell you what. I know your cash flow is tight. It's gotta be, with this here recession we're in. I'll stake you to fifty percent. I can get that much together. And you pay me back when you sell. You give me five hundred, and next week when we sell for four grand, you repay me double and take the rest. So your five hundred gets you three grand, mine gets me one. Not bad for one week's . . . I was gonna say 'work' but there's really no work involved. Two phone calls, and I do them for you. One to say 'buy' and one to say 'sell.'"

The details of Elizabeth's story were alarmingly close to Charlene's experience, and in point of fact, just a few mornings prior she had handed her nest egg to the man who promised her she'd increase it manyfold by the week's end. Charlene set her face to a determinedly neutral expression as she finished rinsing Elizabeth's hair and turned the water off.

"Just a little off the ends," Elizabeth instructed as she settled into the big swivel chair, and then continued her narrative. "Isn't that something? And of course not a one of them ever gets their money back. They say even the insurance is bogus."

"Really?" Charlene studied Elizabeth's split ends with fierce concentration.

"Can you imagine thinking you're covered and come to find out some crook has snookered you out of your hard-earned dollars and there you are in an accident with nothing to fall back on?"

"Mmmm."

"Clara mentioned a few weeks ago that you'd had dinner with some fellow. When I saw this, I just thought, well, I don't want to stick my nose in where it doesn't belong, but I sure hope it wasn't this man," Elizabeth said, intensely curious to know then just who Charlene had been seen with in Clara's Kitchen.

"So he's been arrested?" It was increasingly difficult for Charlene to keep her voice steady.

"Yes ma'am. Alexander Cheeley's his name. He's in the Huntington County Jail where he belongs."

"Hmmm," said Charlene.

"They're asking for any more victims out there to contact the Huntington County sheriff."

"Hmmm."

"It makes you wonder," said Elizabeth.

"Uh humm," said Charlene.

The rest of the appointment passed with less momentous news from Elizabeth: David had learned all his colors already, Frederick was going to be away on a business trip for a few days, and the pastor at Prince of Peace Lutheran had announced that he'd be retiring in another year. But as she left, she couldn't help reprising her initial theme. "So you never ran across this con man?"

"I can't say that I have."

"They say he had different companies he claimed to represent, but none of 'em was real."

"Hmmm."

"It just makes you wonder."

"It surely does."

"The way some people will take advantage."

Charlene was glad Elizabeth was her last appointment of the day. She needed to walk home and consider this news.

Her nest egg. Her savings toward a down payment on not just renting from Mrs. Lewis, but owning her own shop. The possibility of being able to make that move immediately had been too alluring to ignore.

She hadn't really lied to Elizabeth about it. "Can't say that I have" meant exactly that: she didn't dare say that she had met the fellow. Word would get around. The police would investigate. People would want to hear her tell the story. It just wouldn't do to be the center of anyone's attention.

As soon as she got home, she pulled out the policy papers and read through them, hoping at least the insurance was real. There was an address for Assurance Ltd., in Indianapolis, but no telephone number. How could she not have noticed? Not had questions? She dialed the operator, asked for long-distance information. No, the Indianapolis operator told her, there was no such business listed. Could it be under another name? No, there was no listing for Alexander

Cheeley, either in business or residential. Charlene felt stricken. Everything. All gone. That five hundred dollars had taken her four years to save. Now she'd have to start back at square one.

Sick at heart, she began the careful unlayering, the de-Charlening for the night. Dress off, falsies out and brassiere off, girdle off, cold cream to soften and restore the skin that would be subjected to depilatories the next morning. The jangle of the phone caught her with lotion on her fingertips. She grabbed a tissue and answered.

"Charlene?"

"Who is it, please?"

"Alexander."

The con man. "Alexander, what a surprise." Her head felt light and she reached out to hold on to the back of her chair.

"How is every little thing? How are you this evening?"

"Fine. Just fine." Charlene took a deep breath. "And you?"

"Well, to tell you the God's honest truth, I'm in a bit of a tight spot."

"Oh?"

"It's a little case of mistaken identity. I'm over here in Huntington, and they've got me locked up here."

"Locked up?"

"Seems there's some fella going around talking single ladies into an investment scheme, taking their money. Can you imagine what sort of lowdown devil would do something like that?"

"I . . . Well, I . . ."

"They got me confused with this here fella, on accounta he sells insurance too."

"Oh my goodness."

"Could you tell them I never tried to sell you stock? Mebbe they'll understand then they got the wrong man. I can see how it happens. Not everyone's what they seem, if you know what I mean." He paused briefly, then continued pointedly. "Like that fella I told you about I had dinner with, thinking he was a lady. Lucky I figured that one out in time!" He laughed. "The fingers, doncha know? I learned how to see if people are healthy enough to sell a policy to by looking at their hands. That's how I knew I had me an imposter. This so-called lady"—his voice dripped contempt—"had a ring finger way longer'n the index. Now that's a con man for sure, if you ask me, and one as deserves whatever happens if a real man comes to find out and be disappointed. Am I right? Of course I'm right. A man passing himself off as a woman? I heard tell of a fella from Louisville once who got caught in a dress and ended up hanging by it with his private ... well, I better just stop there because I know I'm talking to a real lady."

He paused to let the threat sink in. Charlene went cold to her very core. "Anyways, can you just let these folks know I couldn't be the one they're looking for because I was with you the evening this lowlife was taking money from a poor soul in Otterbein? Tell 'em they got the wrong man?"

"Well, I ... I'd be happy to tell them what I know," she managed to squeak out.

"You know, you are one high-class lady and a true friend and I thank you from the bottom of my heart. Say, Charlene, while I've got you on the phone, I'm sorry we won't be able to get together this Thursday after all. Turns out I have to tend to some business down near Vincennes."

They'd had no plans for Thursday, but before she could say anything Alexander thanked her and asked her to hold on. Charlene could hear muffled conversation. Then a different voice came on the phone.

"Miss Charlene Bader?"

She could barely force herself to answer yes.

"This Alexander Cheeley says you're a friend of his?"

Her voice shook. "Well, acquaintance, you could say. I bought a disability insurance policy from him."

"He says he had dinner with you recently."

"Yes . . ."

"What day was that?"

"Well now, that would be . . ." She swallowed and paused, then realized she'd been given her cue. She forged on. " . . . last Thursday."

"What is your relationship, if you don't mind my asking?"

"As I said, we're acquaintances. Friends. We're just friends."

"Did he ever suggest anything beyond friendship?"

"Not really," Charlene replied. Her heart was pounding so loudly she thought surely it must be thumping right through the phone line, but the officer proceeded with his questions as if he heard nothing suspicious.

"Miss Bader, did Mr. Cheeley ever offer to let you in on any money-making schemes? Any stock deals? Anything like that?"

"No . . ." Charlene thought she would faint. Lying outright to an officer of the law. But the truth would ruin her. Alexander Cheeley had made it clear he knew how to do that.

"Did he ever express concern about your financial future?"

"Well, you know, he was selling me an insurance policy. But it was one I wanted," she stammered.

"And you're satisfied with the product he sold you?"

"The product?"

"The insurance policy."

"Oh yes. Yes, I suppose I am."

"You're not sure?"

"Well, it's a disability policy and I'm not disabled yet. Not that I expect to be disabled, but . . . I have a business and if something happened that I couldn't work—"

"Have you read the policy, Miss Bader?"

"Why yes, I have."

"Is it issued by any of the following: Assurance Limited, Life Care, Rural Surety, or Hoosier Security?"

"Yes. No. I don't know. I don't think so."

"All right, Miss Bader. I thank you for your time. If I were you, I'd take a careful look at that policy. And if it says it's issued by any of those companies, would you call us back, please?"

"I'll do that. Thank you."

She hung up the phone and wept. A shot of scotch with milk at bedtime, a habit she'd abandoned some three years earlier, did little to help. Her dreams were of cowering in the back of a dark closet in Kirbyville, strangling in her mother's fur neckpiece, struggling to breathe, her father's gruff voice demanding to know where Charlie had gone. If the door to the closet opened, Charlie would be found out, humiliated, and most certainly whipped. Subsequent nights brought variations: Charlie escaped to hide in his bed, only to have Jarvis throw off the sheets and drag him out by the scruff of his neck; Charlie ran from the closet to the one-room schoolhouse and curled up under his school desk, only to hear the formidable schoolmarm Miss Willick clomping his way in her thick-heeled black shoes, yardstick in hand; Charlie dashed from his hiding spot across the field and road to plunge naked into the creek, only to hear Scooch and Taylor find his clothes by the bank and steal them.

She didn't begin to relax until the *Sentinel* ran a follow-up, noting that Cheeley had apparently been released on bail and had disappeared from the area. The sheriff was quoted as saying he doubted they'd ever see the fellow again. Though she felt guilty about it, Charlene was relieved that in this case, justice might never be done. She promised Hannah, when she told her the whole story, that she would never again be tempted to risk so much on what was basically gambling. "One sweepstakes ticket a year," she vowed. "If I'm meant to be rich, it'll have to be from that."

10

HEAVEN, 1952

The kitchen window faced east. Every morning, she sat at her table savoring her first and then second cup of coffee and looking out this window. Half the year she watched the sun rise, half the year she watched the sky begin to lighten before doing one last check to make sure all her layers were firmly in place, and that no detail would betray her. Then she left her house, leaving the door unlocked, and walked the three blocks to her shop. This was her favorite time of day, the new day. Most people were up. Heaven was an early-rising town. But few of them were out and about yet. As she walked, she saw lights in windows, evidence of others sitting at their own kitchen tables. Waking up and smelling the coffee. Passing Thelma's house, she heard the farm report on WOWO. Thelma's husband Jim was hard of hearing, so his radio was always turned up top volume.

Spring was her favorite season. The songbirds were courting, robins and sparrows and finches all calling to their sweethearts. Audacious cardinals darting through the lime green of the trees with their infant leaves opening to another year of possibilities. Fall was a close second. Painted maple leaves crunching underfoot, releasing their spicy odors. Children's voices in the air again as they passed her house on their way to school.

On Sundays she'd go to church. Every Friday evening when she got home from work, she'd sit for a bit with Hannah's picture, and tell her about how her week had gone.

It might have continued like that for years more. For the rest of her days. A pleasant life. Ordered, predictable, untroubled. That was her plan.

She'd worked harder than ever these past two years, and lived more frugally. That, combined with a small loan from Joanne, gave her enough to replenish the savings she'd lost to the con man and finally to buy her second property in Heaven, Agnes Siebold's old shop. She'd told everyone at church the previous Sunday, and Hannah's picture on Friday, about the imminent grand opening of her new location. She'd hired Amy Lassner to help out part-time with shampoos. That would give Charlene time to add manicures to the services she offered.

Yes, she'd had it all planned. And now it had come to pass. Complimentary coffee and donuts. Balloons. A "Grand Opening" banner painted in red letters by Auld Lang's Signs. Free manicures for the first five ladies in line. Ida was at the head, followed by Melinda (though her mother Helen was much too sensible to join in such self-indulgence, she couldn't deny her fourteen-year-old the pleasure), Katie, Elizabeth, and Minnie. Just as she'd hoped, the manicures were a big hit. Ida was thrilled to be the very first one; she'd talk about that for weeks at First Christian. Melinda was delighted too, marveling at the way Charlene could paint small moon shapes around the cuticles when she applied Powderpuff Pink polish to her nails. Melinda would show the effect off to her friends at school, and they would plead with their mothers to bring them in. Katie would spread the word at St. Sebastian, Elizabeth at Mount Olive, and Minnie would add to Ida's report at First Christian. Charlene's gambit would pay off: ladies at three of Heaven's four churches would be talking about the affordable luxury of manicures after services in the morning. She'd figure out some other way to reach the congregants at Prince of Peace.

What she hadn't planned on was the effect of sitting there with Minnie, taking Minnie's hand in her own. All these years, she'd stood behind, distanced by the plate glass mirror and a focus on follicles. She'd listened to tales of unsuitable suitors, commiserated and comforted, able to keep feelings hidden not only from her best customer, but from herself. But now, feeling her hand touch Minnie's, skin to skin, looking into Minnie's eyes, face to face, she felt, to her horror, a surge of emotion and a wave of pain as an unbidden erection asserted itself against the wraps that kept her contours female. Minnie was oblivious, telling her it was the first manicure she'd ever had in her life, and apologizing for her calluses and bluntly cut nails. Charlene could barely speak. Finally, she excused herself and left Minnie with her hands soaking while she went to the back of the shop to regain her composure. A few deep breaths and the memory of Anne's scathing contempt as she declared her preference for a life of missionary service over that of being the wife of a pansy boy calmed Charlene down barely enough for her to be able to return to the front of the shop and finish the task.

She decided she'd have Amy do the manicures.

That Sunday, she headed up to Chicago to ring the Bailey doorbell, bringing a change of clothing and a tight-fitting cap to hide long hair. Her friend Joanne obliged her need for some man talk. They went upstairs, where they both changed clothes. Then Joe and Charlie opened a couple of beers and sat in the upstairs apartment half listening to a sportscast about the upcoming Salas-Carter rubber match. Charlie mentioned the awkward moment.

"Sounds like she's a little more than just a regular customer," Joe said, properly focused on the beer bottle.

"I can't let it happen again," was Charlie's response.

"You could stay here tonight if you want. Give you time to go over to Wells Street."

"It's not about that."

"Sure. I just thought . . ."

"No."

They drank beer and listened to a man on the radio predict a Salas victory. Joe differed in opinion, saying Carter would definitely win, before returning to the more difficult battle being waged in his friend's heart. "You've got a problem, then. If it's not just about that."

"Yep."

"I don't suppose you could talk to her about . . ."

"I can't."

"Yeah."

"Ever."

Joe nodded.

They made roast beef sandwiches. Joe invited Charlie to stay long enough to watch *The Red Skelton Show*, but Charlie said he had to get back, as it was a long drive. Charlie excused himself to head to the bathroom, while Joe went to the bedroom. Charlene came out and said a fond thank you and goodbye to Joanne, who walked her friend downstairs and to the front door.

"If you ever need to come back to Chicago," Joanne said, "you know you can. You can stay here."

Charlene shook her head. "Thank you, but no."

"Good luck, then."

Charlene nodded her appreciation, and drove back through the Indiana night determined to keep her feelings as much in wraps as the rest of her.

HEAVEN, 1954

Baby Sue Ellen Sue sat on a blanket, sucking a corner of the fabric in her mouth; Ida waited her turn and paged through *Better Homes and Gardens*. Charlene was fastening the protective cape around Elizabeth's neck, while Elizabeth bragged about her baby.

"Seven months and she's already pulling herself around on the furniture. Frederick swears she said 'dada' the other day, and he may be right. She's definitely a daddy's girl. Well, you know they're going to take a picture this weekend for the centennial yearbook, with Frederick and me and Sue Ellen Sue and Katie and Robert Denson and their new baby. So I want to get my split ends trimmed a little and I thought this would be a perfect time for Sue Ellen Sue to experience her very first haircut. Just to even up her baby fuzz a bit so when I put a ribbon in her hair it isn't sticking out at every which length."

"How is Katie doing?"

"As well as can be expected, I guess. Frederick says he hopes they can get the photograph taken while Robert is still sober. It's scheduled for one thirty, so he should be up by then but not yet warming a stool at Pete's Gate." Elizabeth shook her head. "It's just a shame the way he drinks. And with that baby only two months old."

Ida closed the magazine and joined in the conversation. "Well, he never was quite the same after he came back from Korea."

"Frederick says he was like that in high school, too, even on the basketball team. Never really had the gumption to fight. He said they played one game where they were down to four first stringers on the court and the coach still didn't send Robert in."

"Now Frederick didn't go to Korea, did he?" Ida already knew the answer to that question. She just wanted to make the point.

"No, he was needed here in the States because he had special skills."

"Oh, I didn't know he served at all."

"Oh yes. He was in the National Guard. But his job at Hoosier Chemicals was what they wanted him to stay with. He had the highest security clearance. He was working on the home front so men like Robert could get their jobs done and come home too."

"Well, I'm not saying he's lucky, but I'm sure glad women don't get drafted. Sometimes ignorance is bliss, isn't it?"

"If you ask me," Elizabeth sniffed, "ignorance is just ignorance. And, too, there's more than one kind of ignorance. Anybody can be a soldier. It takes someone with brains and vision to figure out how best to equip that soldier."

Charlene broke in. Talk of war made her uncomfortable, and besides, it wouldn't do to have a flat-out argument between customers. "What are the must-sees at the fair?" she asked. "I'm planning to go after work this afternoon."

"There's a palm reader this year," Ida said. "They say she told Evelyn Wasmuth exactly where to find the wedding ring she lost. Right behind her bureau."

"I don't believe in that nonsense," Elizabeth said. "Do you?"

"And Alma Porter has a beautiful quilt on display," Ida continued, refusing the bait. "I believe it'll take the blue ribbon."

"She does exquisite work, doesn't she?" Charlene handed Elizabeth the mirror so she could see and pass judgment on the back.

"Yes, she certainly does," Ida agreed.

"David won a green ribbon for his woodworking project," Elizabeth said, nodding her approval to Charlene for the trim.

"What's a green ribbon for?" Ida asked. "I've never heard of a green ribbon."

"It means he's not old enough to get a regular ribbon. The judge was all set to give it the purple when someone said, 'He's just a junior member and 4-H doesn't give anything but green ribbons to junior members.' So David lost his championship ribbon because he's too young. Can you beat that?"

"What was his project?" Charlene dusted the stray hairs off Elizabeth. "Sue Ellen Sue's turn."

Elizabeth picked up the baby and returned to the chair. "He made the cutest birdhouse. He made a jewelry box for me, too, but Frederick thought it would be better for him to enter the birdhouse."

"Did Thelma enter her limas?" Charlene didn't care much for limas, but she had to admit Thelma's were the best. Clara served them at lunch two weeks a year when they were at their peak.

"She did. And her beefsteak tomatoes, too. I've never known anyone with more of a green thumb," Ida said.

"Well, she has the time." Elizabeth held the mirror so baby Sue Ellen Sue could see herself in it.

"No more than anyone else," Ida protested.

"I just mean with Jim gone on business so much she probably likes to keep busy. Not that he's much company when he's home."

"He got a promotion."

"Did he?"

"He's the regional manager for Floyd's now. He still has to travel, but not as often. More to train the sales crew. He just has to drive to Marion now most of the time instead of all over east central Indiana. He must be good at what he does, to get promoted like that in spite of being a little deaf."

The baby was staring in fascination at the shiny silver scissors Charlene held in her hand. "Look at her!" Elizabeth enthused. "She wants to cut hair too!"

It was difficult for Charlene to cut the fine little wisps at the ends of her wavy locks because Sue Ellen Sue kept looking up or around, always keeping the scissors in sight.

"Tell you what. You hold this." Charlene gave the baby a huge plastic comb to hold, which Sue Ellen Sue promptly put into her mouth and her mother immediately tried to take from her. "It's been sterilized," Charlene assured Elizabeth. One-eighth inch of pure silken baby hair came off and mingled with her mother's somewhat larger pile of split hairs on the floor around the base of the chair. While Sue Ellen Sue got her first real taste of a comb, she got her very first haircut.

* * *

The carnival fortune-teller Madame Gajikanes kept her head bent over the hand she held, and traced a line. "You have something very interesting here. See here, this little break? That usually means a major illness. Something that nearly killed you. But that's not what I see here. I see a change. It's like a death, but not a death. Some part of you, some aspect of you died."

Charlene reddened and shifted her weight back in the chair. "I believe the question was about my sweepstakes ticket."

"Yes, of course," the fortune-teller soothed. "I'm getting to that." She loosened her hand to allow a little reserve into the space between them and traced another line. "This is your wealth line. It doesn't show a lot of money, just enough. You will always have enough, but here, you see, it strongly crosses your work line and that tells me work will always be your source of income."

"You're saying I shouldn't waste my money on games of chance?"

"As long as you can afford them and understand the odds," Madame Gajikanes smiled, "there's no harm done. You don't need me to tell you it would be imprudent to count any sweepstakes chickens before they hatch." She let go of the woman's hand and nodded to indicate the reading was over.

Charlene looked into her eyes and felt a deep plush safety in the palm reader's care. Impulsively, she thrust her hand out again. "Tell me more about the death. The part of me that died."

The fortune-teller took her offer, holding the hand as lightly and carefully as if it had been a hummingbird egg. She traced several more lines, reading their pathways, their crossroads, their tiny breaks. "Let me see your other hand."

Charlene held out her left hand. "What do you see?"

"You really have made something of yourself, haven't you? The lines of your left hand tell one story, your right quite another." Madame Gajikanes glanced into the woman's eyes, smiled gently, then dropped her gaze again to the hands. Touching each palm lightly with all five of her fingers, she softened her voice and said, "No sweepstakes wins in either hand, I'm sorry to say. But you wanted to know about the part that died. And what I see here is that you already know yourself and are testing me. Would you like me to go on?"

"I don't think so. But thank you anyway." She hastened to take three dollar bills from her purse and placed them in the offering basket.

"There is one other thing I noticed," the fortune-teller volunteered. "There is love in your life."

"Love?"

"Yes."

Charlene stood as if she'd been slapped and turned to leave the tent. As she reached the door, Madame Gajikanes spoke again.

"And it will last. That's usually what people really want to know."

Charlene stood statue-still. After a moment she asked, without turning back, her voice cracking, "Can you tell me how it will turn out?"

"No. I can only say your love line is as long as your life line. I see that for certain."

Back outside on the midway, where the August sun had no canvas standing in its way, the heat was even more intense than it had been inside the fortune-teller's tent. Charlene stopped for a lemonade, nodded hello to Ida, Helen, and Lester standing nearby, and then listened in on their conversation.

"Hot 'nough for you?"

"Oh yeah."

"What do you hear from Melinda? Is she still visiting your Aunt Doris?"

"Why, we just got a letter about a week ago, and she says she's enjoying herself."

"And your aunt?"

"She has her ups and downs."

"I guess we all do."

"You can say that again."

"I'll bet she's happy to have Melinda giving her a hand around the house, though."

"Oh my, yes."

"I bet you miss her, though. Four months is a long time for a child her age to be away from home."

"Sixteen is grown enough." Helen's voice was tight. She never had cared for Ida's incessant need to know all the news, whether it was worth knowing or not. "Well, if you'll excuse me now, I promised I'd go see Thelma's prize limas." Helen looked to her husband, who squinted in the sun while he scratched a little patch of skin at the middle of his forehead.

"I'll catch up with you later, Mother." As Helen walked away, Lester confided, "I never did see any reason to get excited about lima beans."

"Don't you like succotash?"

"Why, yes, I do, but that's because it has corn in it. I'd just as soon have the corn and be done with it. Promise me you won't tell your sister-in-law."

"What Thelma doesn't know can't hurt her."

Charlene watched them drift down the midway. She scanned the crowd, hoping yet fearing that she might see Minnie. Most of the people she didn't recognize at all. They came from all corners of Hutter County and beyond to the carnival, especially this year of the centennial celebration. After a couple of minutes, she decided a good walk might quiet her nerves and headed home. Neither corn nor lima beans interested her, truth be known. She didn't get excited about quilts or canning either. She hadn't liked looking at calves since she'd had to help render her 4-H project, a veal calf she'd named Publican, into cuts of meat all those years ago; and she certainly had no desire to make herself sick on carnival rides. She'd mostly come down because it would be hard not to spend at least a little time joining in the festivities, celebrating a hundred years of Heaven, right here on the fertile earth of Indiana. She had to be able to maintain her end of conversations with customers in her beauty shop, all of whom would have come to the carnival at least once and would want to talk about the blue-ribbon exhibits and purple-ribbon champs.

On her way home, Charlene detoured along the river where it meandered away from town and headed out past the cornfields, her heart still racing from the effect of the fortune-teller's words. The tiny bit of breeze that came off the surface was welcome, though the mosquitoes that had bred in the shallow side pools were not. Charlene kept a brisk pace, and waved an envelope from her purse as she went, every now and again using it to slap an insect but more often to keep the still, oven-like air stirred a bit.

She wondered how someone could see something like that by just looking at the lines in her hands. The fortune-teller had challenged her, shaken her from her unquestioning acceptance of exceptionally limited options. She'd worked hard to make her peace with a relationship circumscribed by hair. She could touch Minnie when she shampooed her hair, or set it or combed it out. She could smile at her when her eyes were closed for shampoos and rinses, watch her in the mirror while she chatted, perhaps sneak a stare at her while she sat under the dryer absorbed in *Woman's Day*. That had to be enough. That she had gradually lengthened the time for Minnie's appointments was as much as could be done: more time to work the suds through Minnie's curls, more time to wind her hair on rollers, more time to style it as she combed it out. If Minnie had ever noticed, she hadn't let on. Her appointments took well over an hour, and as often as she dared, Charlene scheduled a break of fifteen minutes between Minnie's appointment and the next one, to increase the possibility she'd have a spate of time alone with her. The tactic generally worked, unless Ida or Eunice was next on the calendar. They always came early.

The fortune-teller's words pushed persistently into her conflicted mind. Could she ever dare tell Minnie the truth? Buoyed by the woman's assurance, she decided yes, she could. She would do it. The next second brought dark doubt. She could never do it. Then back to resolve. She had to do it. Then anxiety. She didn't dare do it. One step brought determination, the next dread. If she did, it would certainly mean loss. She'd most likely be run out of town, back to Chicago to blend in—as a hairdresser, as a dentist, it wouldn't matter. She'd never see her beloved again.

Still the fortune-teller's words tugged. If the love was lasting, did that mean it could withstand the truth? That was the sixty-four-dollar question. Or did it simply mean she would go to her grave never confessing it to Minnie? If I'm going to do it, she thought, I'm going to have to do it soon. Before I lose my nerve. Minnie will be in tomorrow morning. Maybe then. Maybe.

* * *

"I'm so glad you open early." Minnie carried a fan with her that advertised Wasmuth's Funeral Home. "They say it's going to be a record-breaker today. Might even hit a hundred."

Charlene was perspiring too, stewing about her visit to the carnival the evening before and the fortune-teller's unsettling insights. This would be her chance to tell Minnie how she felt about her. She'd been awake half the night, not solely due to the scorching heat, but mostly trying to decide what words to use, how much to say, and how best to say it. Her hands shook as she arranged her scissors, combs, and clips.

Minnie went straight to the shampooing chair and put her head back into the sink indentation. "Oh my, that cold enamel feels good this morning! Don't make the water too hot, Charlene. Just lukewarm."

The knot of anxiety in Charlene's stomach nearly immobilized her. She forced herself to go to the sink, turn the water on. As she worked the lather through Minnie's hair, she worked opening lines through her mind, silently addressing each to the top of Minnie's head, testing its imagined impact. *Minnie, there's something I need to tell you, but . . . Minnie, I have something to say which will undoubtedly surprise you and . . . Minnie, if I were to tell you a secret, a very important one . . . Minnie, this will sound odd to you, perhaps even preposterous, but . . .*

Try as she might, Charlene could not imagine how to end any of her potential beginnings. In each case, she imagined Minnie turning to look at her with a curiosity that would surely turn to disgust and contempt as soon as Charlene finished her sentence.

"That feels wonderful." Minnie's voice penetrated the fog of irresolution that had engulfed Charlene, bringing her to a sudden realization that it was time to rinse. Minnie sighed with exaggerated pleasure. "Ah, yes!"

It was worse when Minnie sat in the big swivel chair in front of the mirror. As Charlene twirled her locks into pin curls and secured them, she dared not look up lest she catch Minnie's eye in reflection, and then what? She was so agitated she dropped two pins in a row on the floor.

Minnie kept up her end of the conversation by commenting on the quilts. It seems a newcomer to the annual competition, a Mrs. Woolsey from over near Montpelier, had almost taken the top prize away from Alma, but at the last minute the judges found a whole corner, the lower left, on the Woolsey quilt that had been machine stitched. "They asked her right out," Minnie recounted, "if she'd hurried to finish in time for the fair and she said yes, she'd been up all night. Can you imagine? It was a beautiful quilt, but Alma's was perfect in every regard and every stitch of it by hand. Have you ever quilted?"

"No, I never have." Charlene could feel her resolve slipping away. Maybe she'd write a letter. Maybe an anonymous one. *Now that is just a ridiculous idea. What good would that do?*

"I went to a quilting bee a time or two," Minnie said, "but I just don't like the feeling of a thimble and without it I stick myself so often I could have joined the carnival as a human pincushion. Did you see the size of the tomatoes this year? I suppose it must have been something to do with all this heat we've been getting. Even out in our garden, I picked one that came close to a pound and a half."

I love you, but it's okay because I'm really a man. Charlene fumbled another bobby pin.

"Say, if you haven't ever tried it, this is a good year to make tomato preserves. Some people don't like 'em, but I think they're delicious. It sounds a little odd, I know, but I like the yellow ones best for that. They don't have as much acid as the red ones."

If you think yellow tomato preserves sounds odd, what would you think if you knew the person pinning your hair up right now is a man who is desperately in love with you? Acid rose in Charlene's throat.

"To tell you the truth, I never could make 'em right myself."

To tell you the truth, I don't care in the least who makes what kind of preserves but I love to hear you talk about it.

"I trade milk and butter with Stella for my supply. Her recipe is the best, and they always come out just the right consistency for spreading. Helen makes them too, but Stella's got the blue-ribbon touch. Not too runny, not too thick. Did you hear Clara is thinking of retiring?"

"Yes, I believe someone was talking about that a few days ago."

"I don't think she's going to."

"Why not?"

"I just can't imagine her not being there."

I can't imagine you not being here. Charlene positioned the drying helmet over Minnie's head and hit the on switch. The noise of the dryer made conversation impossible, but it allowed Charlene to dare say softly, aloud, while Minnie busied herself with a copy of *Prevention* magazine, "I love you."

Charlene retreated to neaten up the clips and scissors. In the mirror, she could see Minnie's reflection, see the little waiting area, see the door with the bell atop, see the picture window that gave her a view of the street in front of the shop. Helen Breck passed by, waved to Minnie. Minnie waved back. Charlene felt a pang of envy for those who simply moved through the world in an uncomplicated fashion. They were who they were. No alternate identities, no dangerous truths lurking beneath their midwestern exteriors threatening them always with the disaster of discovery.

How will I know if I don't say something? What, exactly, should I say? Minnie, what if I told you I'm a man? Could you grow to love me? Minnie, oblivious, picked up *Woman's Day* and paged through recipes for chocolate cake. Each one, the magazine promised her, was the way to a man's heart. Charlene opened her mouth to speak.

Then the gnawingly awful memory of Anne's astonishment, her horror, her back, her shoulder blades, the hiss and venom in her voice overtook Charlene and struck her dumb. Seconds later, one of the carnival performers popped her head through the door and asked if she had time for a walk-in. The humidity was wreaking havoc with her curly hair and she needed it tamed before her daily performances began. By the time Minnie's hair was dry there were two more customers waiting. Charlene's chance had passed.

"See you Sunday," Minnie said, taking a last satisfied look at herself in the big mirror before she headed back out into the scorching Saturday heat.

"Goodbye," Charlene answered. And she knew that she couldn't risk it being that: goodbye. Couldn't. Just couldn't.

At church the next day, Helen was aflutter, announcing that Melinda was finally back from visiting her great-aunt in Sioux City; she had taken the long bus ride home—at least as far as the Marion Greyhound station, where they'd driven over to pick her up—and was so tuckered out she was sleeping in rather than coming to church.

Tuckered, thought Charlene, is an odd word. Tuckered out. She'd been tuckered out a time or two, and it would have been sweet at those times to have come home to loving parents who never seemed to be out of sorts with each other. Not that Helen and Lester hadn't had their challenges. Lester's dad Omar going in such a gruesome way, pulled right into the combine and literally torn apart. What a dreadful shock. That couldn't have been easy. And Melinda. Such a sweet girl. In a way, Melinda reminded Charlene of Crazy May back in Kirbyville. The way May always said exactly what was on her mind and did whatever she felt like doing.

Ilsa used to say May had a bird in the head. Charlene had never understood that image until she'd gone to Europe and seen a cuckoo clock, and later overheard a captain remarking that General Patton seemed a little cuckoo.

These wisps of thoughts and memories drifted through the sky of Charlene's mind as she joined in the chorus of First Christian congregants congratulating Lester and Helen on Melinda's return, and asking after Helen's aunt.

"Now did Melinda finish up her high school there?" Ida wanted to know.

"She was too busy helping Aunt Doris," Helen said. "She needed a constant companion for a while there."

"What was she sick with?" Evelyn Wasmuth asked. Evelyn, clerk at the pharmacy and wife of Herb who ran the funeral home, was always interested in people's life-threatening ailments.

"She's better now," was all she could get by way of details from Helen. "Melinda says she's fit as a fiddle."

Lester took control of the conversation, saying that Melinda would undoubtedly go back to Hutter High for her last semester, and that the new principal seemed like a pretty nice fellow. He'd met the man one morning when he stopped in at Clara's Kitchen for breakfast on his way to the seed store.

Minnie was ebullient, echoing the grapevine's opinion that the new principal promised to be a keeper. "You ain't sweet on him, are you?" Lester teased her, and Minnie blushed. Charlene was struck by a sudden pang of jealousy, only partly mitigated by Minnie's protestations.

"Lester Breck, you know perfectly well he's too young for me!"

When Lester and Helen broke away from the cluster of post-church conversation, Charlene left too, needing time to be alone with her ache. She walked a few blocks out of her way to go home by the river. It was better than chamomile tea for calming her nerves. When she got home, she paused at her front door. *Every day since I moved to this town, I've locked this door when I'm inside; but not once since that*

day Minnie first came by has anyone but me ever crossed the threshold.
I am in this town, but not of it. No one will ever come into this house but
me. At least I can relax about that.

*   *   *

The very next morning, fresh and ghastly news about Melinda
spread like wildfire, jumping from household to household, leaping
from office to shop. Maurice brought it to Clara's Kitchen, and from
there it just exploded outward till the whole male half of the town
knew. Did you hear? Oh, it's just terrible news. Terrible. Melinda.
Yes, that's right, Lester and Helen's Melinda. What about her? Why,
she's dead, that's what. Yes, dead. No, she came home. Saturday night,
they say. They picked her up in Marion and put her to bed. Well, she
was tired from all the traveling, but they say she didn't complain or
feel bad. Just tired. Then Sunday she just kept sleeping all day and
all night and Monday morning she was dead. Just like that. Come to
think of it, I'm not sure who found her. It was Lester called for Doc
Brubecker, but you know he's on his annual fishing trip up in Min-
nesota so they hadda call the fellow over in Hartford City. Yes. Well, I
heard it from Bobby, 'cause I stopped for gas on my way into town and
I guess he heard it from Herb's wife Evelyn who stopped right before
me and she knew it 'cause they called up there to get Herb to bring
the hearse to take her for an autopsy. Yes, an autopsy. Well, they say
the doc said—not Doc Brubecker but the one came from Hartford
City—he said she'd been in a family way. No. No, she wasn't still. Had
been. That's what I'm saying. The doc said she'd had a baby, couldn'ta
been more than a coupla days ago.

Well, you can imagine. Helen's hysterical. Now you know that's
something, when Helen goes like that. Bobby said Evelyn told him
Sheriff Johnson told Herb that Helen thinks there must be a baby in
a bus station somewhere. No, not in Marion. They woulda known

already if it was in Marion. She had to change buses in Chicago. You know, anything can happen up there before a body would know about it. Yes. They've got the search on. It sure makes you think, don't it? I mean, you just never know. Here they thought she was just back home after taking care of Helen's aunt . . . oh, that's the other thing. Seems the aunt says she never was there in Sioux City. Nope. Nope, not even for a day. Ain't that something? Now where she was and how she got along all those months nobody knows. Seems like it must've been Sioux City. Bobby said Evelyn said Helen had a letter from her just the other day from Sioux City, saying how everything was going just fine. Nah, I ain't seen Lester yet. It's a dirty shame, is what it is.

The primary news route for the women of Heaven ran right through the beauty shop. Charlene was still stuck in her self-pitying mood while she shampooed and cut Frieda Thompson's hair that morning. As she brushed the clippings from Frieda's shoulders, Charlene saw in the mirror the reflection of Evelyn Wasmuth hurrying up the street. Evelyn burst into the shop. "Frieda, I'm so sorry to interrupt you. They said you'd be here." Evelyn delivered the terrible news to Frieda and Charlene, asking Frieda to cover for her at the pharmacy so she could help Herb with Melinda's body. She rattled off the names of those on the network who knew already: Thelma had been in buying aspirin when Herb had called, and she said she'd let Ida and Eunice know on her way home. Elizabeth had heard from Frederick. Elizabeth had called Evelyn just seconds after Herb did, and said she'd already phoned Alma and Stella and Minnie. Minnie's mother Laura had said Minnie already knew because she was the one person in the world that Helen would want to see at a time like this, so Lester had called her right away. Minnie was already out at the Breck farm, sitting with Helen.

"Oh my word," Frieda lamented. "This is just going to kill Helen and Lester. Oh my word, the way they dote on that girl! And after that awful way Pops went."

Charlene felt sick to her stomach. To think she'd been feeling sorry for herself, envying Helen, and now to hear this. Be thankful, she told herself in her mother's best voice, for what you got. All the rest of the day, all that week, all through the funeral service and beyond, she couldn't shake her guilty feeling that she had no right to ask for more than she already had. She was lucky. She had a profession that brought her pleasure, she had two sets of friends, she had a cozy little house. She was able to see her beloved Minnie on a regular basis, even if she didn't dare tell her the truth. Poor Helen. Frieda was so right. Helen had doted on her daughter. She was heartbroken, hysterical. Helen, who never showed emotion. Charlene resolved to give Helen the only thing she knew how to give her: a little extra time on her schedule. She'd noticed how in her monthly visits, Helen scooted out as soon as possible whenever anyone else came in, so the next time she made an appointment, Charlene would make sure there was a half-hour buffer between Helen and the next customer.

* * *

It was December before Helen took advantage of Charlene's unstated offer of additional undivided attention. As Charlene finished returning Helen's hair to a French twist one day, and handed her the hand mirror to take a look at the back, Helen suddenly said, "I remember how Melinda used to love to step up in this chair and get twirled around to look at the back of her haircut. She loved coming into town if it meant she could come sit in this chair and get twirled."

"I bet you miss her."

"There's not a day goes by that I don't think about her. And that baby."

"Did they ever get any leads?"

"No. They never found out anything about her."

12

HEAVEN, 1957

Stella watched herself in the mirror while Charlene toweled her hair dry. "Thank you again for loaning me your sign and fitting me into your schedule. I wasn't going to do anything special, but then Walter said, 'How many grand openings does a person expect to have in a lifetime?' 'Only one,' I said, and he said, 'Doncha think it deserves at least as much of a party as your birthday?' He's usually the frugal one in the family, but he insisted I splurge and get a little gussied up. Will you come by and enjoy a piece of my rhubarb coffee cake tomorrow? Free cake and coffee for everyone who stops by on my opening day. I learned from your opening what goodwill free food can get you."

"It certainly is tempting."

"I know you don't like to leave the shop, but it's only a two-minute walk. You could just put a sign up."

"Would you like me to put a little height up here?" Charlene lifted her fingers through Stella's hair.

"Just a little. Can I ask you a question?"

"Of course."

"As a businesswoman to another businesswoman. Do you think I should change the menu?"

"Folks seem to like everything Clara's been serving. I'd stick with that for a while if I were you. People don't like change too much. Give them a chance to just get used to you being the owner before you ask them to give up what they came there for or to accept something new. Except for your rhubarb coffee cake, of course." Charlene grinned and winked at Stella's reflection. "What is Clara going to do now that she's finally retiring?"

"She says she wants to volunteer—can you imagine?—in the school lunchroom!"

"Well, I'm sure they can use the help. How does this look?" Charlene stepped back so Stella could see the effect-in-progress better.

"I like it."

"I think it's a good compromise between casual and professional," Charlene said. "You don't want anything too stuffy and formal."

"No."

"But you do want something with a little style. You want your restaurant to look like you run it, not like it runs you."

"That's a good way to put it."

"Just a minute." Charlene disappeared into the back room and returned a few seconds later with a hairstyling magazine, open to a page showing several hairdos that featured slightly asymmetrical styles. "Do you like any of these?"

"This one."

"That's just what I was thinking. Just a little turn under here and the tiniest flip up here . . ." As Charlene spoke, she teased and shaped and combed Stella's hair to look like the style sported by the model in the magazine. "There. A new hairdo for the new owner of . . . what are you going to call it?"

"I thought I'd keep the name. Seems disrespectful to take Clara's name off when she's still so much alive. I think she retired more because Chester and James were pressuring her. James has been wanting his folks to come to Baltimore to take care of the kids while he and that highfalutin' wife of his go on a cruise, but Clara never wanted to leave the restaurant. This way she and Chester can at least take a vacation and see their grandkids and the ocean once in a while."

"So it's still going to be Clara's Kitchen."

"Yes, for the meantime, anyway. And there's a piece of that rhubarb coffee cake with your name on it anytime you want. If you don't have time to stop in tomorrow, come on in sometime next week."

"I just might. I know your coffee cake is awfully good."

"It's the best, if I do say so myself."

"Amen to that." Elizabeth Tipton had bustled through the door just in time to pronounce her blessing on the coffee cake.

"We're just finishing up here," Charlene assured her as she brushed stray hairs from Stella's neck and liberated her from her plastic cape. Elizabeth hated to be kept waiting, even when she was ten minutes early for her appointment.

"Elizabeth, you're just the person I want to see," Stella said. "I want your advice on something."

"What would you like to know?"

"I'm thinking of opening on Sundays, afternoons only of course. After all the church services are over. So people really can take a day of rest on Sunday."

"What about you?"

"Well, I've got it figured out how the cooking could all be done Saturday night: pot roast or oven-fried chicken, potato salad, coleslaw, Harvard beets. I'd stick with the simple things like that, and just stay open one to five. So I could still get to church myself, and have the evening off, too. And I've already talked to Nita Rosen about waiting on the tables for me. You know they go up to Fort Wayne for their services on Saturday, so working on Sunday doesn't violate their rules. All I'd have to do is warm things up and put them on plates, and a person'd have to do that anyway, no matter what day of the week it is. Folks have to eat."

"That's true enough. Who have you asked about it?"

"Only you, so far." Stella knew how to flatter, and she knew how to plant an idea. "I was thinking I could start with opening the place up for the tornado victims benefit committee meetings. Maybe it would get more people out to participate if they didn't have to juggle making Sunday dinner with getting to the meetings."

"Well, the ladies would have more of a chance to take part, that's for sure."

"To tell you the truth"—Stella lowered her voice even though there was no one other than the three of them to hear—"I thought it might get Walter off his toot about setting foot in St. Sebastian's. You know, with rotating the meetings between all the churches, all that happens is a bunch of separate planning meetings." Stella knew for a fact that Frederick Tipton felt the same way, and that Frederick liked to take charge.

"Good morning." Ida arrived a full forty-five minutes early for her appointment, as was her habit. She liked to catch up on her magazine reading and listen in on the conversations. "My goodness, it's crowded in here!"

"Well," Stella announced, "I have to get back to work. I hope you ladies will come in tomorrow for my grand opening. Free rhubarb coffee cake for all. And I'll think about what you said, Elizabeth. About the ladies being involved more." With that, Stella made her exit, allowing Elizabeth to bring Ida in on the idea of Sundays at Clara's Kitchen. Before Elizabeth had finished her turn in Charlene's chair, Ida was convinced that it was all Elizabeth's excellent idea. All Stella would have to do is wait for the news to be spread that Frederick and Elizabeth had talked her into offering her newly acquired business in the service of soothing interfaith tensions and allowing the planning committee, with its members from each of Heaven's four congregations, the opportunity to come up with the biggest, best ice cream social to raise money for tornado victims that Hutter County had ever seen.

Heaven had a peculiar relationship to tornadoes. Five times in the town's history devastating tornadoes had swept into Hutter

County and stopped just short of where the Breck farm met the Burney farm. When they got there, they just dissipated. Went poof. Disappeared. All their rage deflated, their purpose lost. Was it something in the landscape? The hills so subtle you'd swear they weren't there at all? The vast open quiet of the fields, maybe. Who knows? Maybe the magnetic force of Heaven did it. Whatever it was, tornadoes had five times threatened Heaven and five times spared it, while devastating communities just next door. Proud barns reduced to rubble and splinters. Tidy hardwood houses broken as if built of balsa. Trees tossed like carelessly abandoned toothpicks. None of this ever happened in Heaven, so during tornado season they always did some kind of fundraiser for tornado victims elsewhere in the county and state. This year, the entire state had been spared, but folks in Kansas had lost lives and homes. Heaven would do what it could to help.

For the most part, it was a friendly competition among Heaven's congregations to see which could raise the most money at the ice cream social by hosting games or events. St. Sebastian's would be running a roulette table. Prince of Peace Lutheran would conduct cakewalks, while Mount Olive Presby planned a dunking stool. First Christian was hoping to entice everyone, including the losers at the roulette wheel and the children too young to gamble or toss balls to dunk the mayor, to comfort themselves with pie and coffee or—for the children—the freshest milk you could find short of sitting in the barn and getting the milk directly from the cow. After all, what goes better with ice cream than pie? A few First Christian congregants allowed as how they didn't really think gambling was an appropriate activity, but, they would shrug and say with a tinge of regret, "we don't control what others do."

Notwithstanding this lament, some people did the best they could to at least influence others, especially when it came to matchmaking. And what better place to matchmake than at an ice cream social?

The day of the event dawned as perfectly as a day can do. A bright blue sky, not a cloud in sight, the temperature in the seventies during church services climbing to a comfortable eighty-two by the time people arrived to eat ice cream and spend a little money helping the less fortunate. The courthouse lawn was festooned with balloons and banners, and thanks to the diplomatic efforts of Stella, the planning had gone exceptionally well this year. As a result, the place was crowded not only with Heaven's denizens, but friends and relatives from several nearby towns.

"Charlene, have you met Mr. Harris yet?" Elizabeth grabbed Charlene's hand and pulled her near.

"No, I don't believe I have."

"Let me introduce you," she said, then changed her tone to one of conspiracy. "He's the first eligible bachelor to come our way in a long time. Just took a job at Hoosier Chemicals, up from Muncie."

It was the day Charlene had dreaded. Till now, she'd been unusually safe in this small town where the bachelors, what few there were, were beyond any reasonable woman's consideration as a marriage partner. The eligible ones had already married, long since, already had family responsibilities: bringing home the bacon, refereeing Little League games, mowing lawns. The unmarried ones still lived with their mothers, or they drank too much, or they had embarrassing personal habits that no woman, no matter how skilled in the art of making over a husband, could ever hope to sufficiently influence. Or worse yet, they didn't even go to church, preferring instead to read books by philosophers who thought nothing really existed.

So for thirteen years, Charlene had been left alone. At first the ladies of Heaven presumed she was getting over a love affair gone bad. Besides, if there had been a marriageable fellow around they would have considered him Minnie's first. Poor Minnie—waited faithfully for Warren to come back from the war and then he left her in the lurch. Those four years she waited were the ones during which she went from young and fresh to not quite so young and just a little bit too anxious.

The next most likely candidate might be Alma Porter, but Alma, widowed in 1944, had told people in no uncertain terms that she had not one iota of interest in ever being married again.

That left Charlene. Charlene was older than Minnie and Alma. It would take a very particular kind of bachelor to be a good prospect for Charlene. He'd have to be older himself, perhaps a widower rather than a man who'd never married. Because you had to watch out for a man in his fifties or sixties who'd never yet married. But you also had to watch out for a divorced man because you had to wonder what he'd done to have a person leave him. Could be he drank, or was mean, or just couldn't hold a job.

The married ladies of Heaven had been through all these conversations, not in front of their single friends, of course, but in the spirit of wanting them to be happy and settled. Being settled was important, and everyone knew you couldn't really settle in until you found your partner for life.

So the ladies were tickled pink when Mr. Harris came to town. His wife and one of two daughters had been killed in a terrible auto accident some fifteen years back and he'd managed his grief by throwing himself into work. The other daughter had married a man from Kentucky and moved to Louisville. Mr. Harris was alone, but for exceptionally respectable reasons. And he seemed like a modern man who wouldn't object to a wife with a career.

Charlene knew she was in trouble. She'd already heard the gossip. Mr. Harris was a charming fellow. He was gentlemanly. He was trim, in good health, had a fine sense of humor. He was someone Charlene might love to have as a friend, someone to go fishing with maybe. But . . .

Elizabeth steered her relentlessly toward Mr. Harris, deftly managed the introduction, and slipped off to join Minnie, Ida, Thelma, and Stella to keep a covert eye on how Charlene and Mr. Harris might seem to be getting along.

From what the ladies of First Christian could see, their hairdresser and the new man in town were hitting it off. They watched from afar while Donald Harris gestured and Charlene laughed, while he walked her to the dunking stool, where the gesticulating made it clear that he was paying for her to take a shot at dumping Mayor Dumbauld. Charlene, they could see, was trying to demur but Mr. Harris was insistent. Finally, she took aim with the baseball and hit the target. The mayor went down, and Mr. Harris led everyone within sight in a round of applause. All the ladies watching were delighted.

Except Minnie.

Minnie couldn't believe what was happening to her. Seeing Charlene across the courthouse lawn laughing with Mr. Harris caused a knot to form in Minnie's stomach that was worse than the one she'd felt the day she got the phone call telling her Warren had jilted her for that French girl. What upset her so was that it was not Charlene she was jealous of, but Mr. Harris. She should be happy for Charlene if her friend was finding pleasure in male companionship. She should be, but she wasn't. Minnie was appalled to realize that what it came down to was this: she wanted Charlene for herself.

The ice cream social was turning out to be, beyond a doubt, the best ever. So many cakes had gone in the cakewalk that some of the Lutheran women had run home to get the extras they'd kept back for family use, and those were going fast too. At First Christian's pie and coffee booth, the same thing was happening. The pies were all eaten, and even Stella's stash of Monday morning coffee cake was disappearing down happy Sunday afternoon gullets. St. Sebastian's roulette wheel set an all-time record for gambling proceeds in Heaven, and the mayor got dunked so many times at Mount Olive Presby's booth that they had to send in their next two most prominent members to give him some relief. By the end of the day, Vern Culpepper of Culpepper

Insurance had been doused at least a dozen times and Marty French, the principal at the high school, had drawn so much fire—especially from the young people—that he alone had raised more money than any other single event since the inception of the Heaven, Indiana, Ice Cream Social to Benefit Tornado Victims.

Just about everybody headed home happy as pigs in a mud puddle. Everybody except Charlene and Minnie. Charlene had been unable to persuade the gallant Mr. Harris that she did not need a companion to see her home, though at least she knew she was well within her rights to say goodbye at her door without inviting him in. "Perhaps we can see each other again sometime," he'd offered.

"Perhaps we can," she'd responded as she smiled a good afternoon to him and slipped inside.

Meanwhile, as Minnie drove her folks home she couldn't help stewing. Something was fluttering in her chest. No, deeper than her chest. Somewhere things had never fluttered before. As she drove, she prayed. Prayed for it to stop. Prayed that her God would not give her such a capacity for love only to stand idly by and let it lead her to adore her hairdresser.

13

HEAVEN, 1960

For two long years, Donald Harris had pursued Charlene, while Minnie had agonized from afar. For two long years, Charlene had meted out the tiniest of responses. She'd let him walk her home from church because to have declined his offers would have been unacceptably rude, but she'd implied, in the most careful and vague way imaginable, that she might have a romantic interest in Chicago. To strengthen that impression, one Saturday every three months she designated a "manicures only" day, left her shop in the care of Amy, and drove north for the weekend. Donald was the only one privy to Charlene's hints of a Chicago romance (Charlene having let Elizabeth, Ida, and Minnie know that she had business affairs to attend to there) and he decided to bide his time, hopeful that the implied engagement might break off and that his dignified and respectful cultivation of this relationship might finally bear fruit.

Charlene's women friends were fit to be tied. It drove Ida nearly crazy, it perplexed Elizabeth beyond reason, and Thelma was simply beside herself. "When is he actually going to ask her out on a date?" she asked one day when the three of them happened to meet at Herman's Market.

"It's almost as if there's something funny about him," Elizabeth ventured.

"You don't mean . . ." Ida blushed, unable to even finish the sentence.

"It's just that you'd think a man would have made more of a move by now," Elizabeth mused.

"Does Frederick notice anything funny about him at work?" Thelma wanted to know.

Elizabeth stiffened. "Frederick would hardly pay attention to anything like that."

Minnie, for her part, had been contriving drives to Indianapolis, where she visited the library. There she sought furtively, feverishly, to find something that would explain her unconquerable infatuation. Wearing a scarf, skulking through the rows like a fugitive from justice, she would sidle up to the shelves and browse the books that purported to explain her strange and awful attraction.

She took to borrowing volumes without checking them out, as if, somehow, her library records were likely to be broadcast on the evening news. Stealing, some would say, but she always took them back. At night, after Laura and Paul were settled down for the night, she would read and reread the theories, and try to make sense of it all.

There was a word for it. Lesbianism. It sounded alien and dangerous. Psychoanalytic theories of it confounded her. They didn't feel true, and that made her worry that she was losing her grip on reality, that she was in denial, that she had repressed something terrible and was now paying the price. But for what? What could possess her to fall in love—because that's what it was, pure and simple—with another woman?

One writer spoke of the importance of not giving in to unnatural urges. Minnie canceled her appointment at Charlene's Beauty Shop that week, and prayed nightly for guidance, but she was so miserable she had to give in and call for an appointment the next week to reinstitute her regular Saturday morning shampoo and set.

Another said she was undeveloped as a woman, that she needed internal stimulation. Oh my lord, she thought, how would I ever get that? I'm not married! Her imagination would take her no further.

A third actually suggested that she was possessed. It was the closest Minnie ever came to considering Catholicism. She'd heard a story once of a priest in Marion performing an exorcism. Would she dare seek him out? What would people say if they heard about it? But no, she couldn't stand the idea of Heaven's Catholics looking at her, knowing something that shameful and personal about her. Having been raised in a community of solid Protestantism on the religious side and solid gossip on the secular side, she did not for a second think that secrets really could be kept, even between a priest and a parishioner.

Charlene sensed something terribly amiss, though she had no insight into what it might be. She could feel it in the tension in Minnie's neck during shampoos, so Charlene would linger on the sudsing, massaging gently, and take extra care with the rinsing to support Minnie's head while she sprayed the warm water along the nape. Sometimes it seemed that Minnie allowed herself to relax a tiny bit; more often it seemed that she locked her muscles tight against any attempts by Charlene to soothe her.

Charlene listened carefully to the small talk Minnie made for clues, but none were forthcoming. She attended to the chatting of her other customers with special care, hoping to hear something that would explain Minnie's unhappy state, but no one other than her seemed to have even noticed it. Once, as Minnie put her hand on the doorknob to leave the shop, Charlene blurted out, "Is anything the matter?" Minnie shook her head like she'd seen a ghost and hurried out.

Sometimes at night, Charlene's ache for Minnie called forth Charlie, confined to dream space. Charlene dreamt of Minnie, and when she did, Charlie's maleness asserted itself and lingered in the morning. It added yet another layer of preparation to Charlene's day, as she had to put those feelings back off limits before she dared open her door and walk to her shop. On her occasional trips to stay with

Joanne and visit with the remaining Full Self Sisterhood members, she shared her predicament of her unwanted suitor and picked up tips from Jacquie on how to tuck and wrap so well that her anatomical secrets remained suppressed and hidden even during the longest, most ardent shampooing sessions.

It was Easter 1960 before the gentlemanly Mr. Harris insisted on an answer from Charlene. Would she allow him to take her for a ride in his new Ford Falcon? She managed to hold him off another few weeks, but finally consented to a tour of some of the interesting sites in nearby Grant County. They drove into Marion, where he showed her the very spot where James Dean had been born, and through Fairmount where Dean lived as a teenager. They stopped at Wiley's in Upland for hamburgers and French fries, and drove past an old farm that was still maintained in its Civil War–era condition. As they drove, the talk turned to Indiana's recent primary. That is where Charlene finally found the wherewithal to thank Donald Harris politely and tell him firmly, as he said goodbye at her doorstep, that though she liked him, there were irreconcilable differences in their worldviews, and perhaps it would be better if they didn't spend so much time together.

His absence at church the next day did not go unnoticed. Ida simply couldn't contain her curiosity, and when they saw Ida heading in Charlene's direction, Elizabeth, Thelma, and Stella followed suit. Minnie joined the cluster too, but tried to seem as if she just happened to be walking that way.

Ida got right to the point. "Charlene, how did your date with Donald go?"

"It wasn't really a date."

"Am I being too nosy? I'm sorry."

None of the other women present were sorry. Ida had done precisely what they had neither the nerve nor the bad manners to do themselves. They were all anxious to find out if a new match had been made in Heaven. Minnie alone dreaded what they would hear when and if Charlene deigned to answer Ida's probe. It made her ill to contemplate Charlene in love with this man—or any man—and it made her ill to realize she was consumed with jealousy. Maybe instead of haunting the library when she got to Indy, she should find a psychotherapist. Someone who could help her figure out why she found herself so smitten with another woman. And more importantly, maybe this psychotherapist could help her figure out how to get over it.

"Don is a very nice, very intelligent man," Charlene finally said. "But . . ."

"But what?" Ida coaxed.

"I don't think we see eye to eye on some things."

The collective breath so subtly held by the group of lady listeners was equally so subtly let go.

"Oh?" Elizabeth was surprised. She'd figured the worldliness of Don Harris meant he'd not object to a business-owning, working woman. As far as she could tell, since that seemed to be Charlene's entire life, that should have made them compatible.

"Well, for one thing, he voted for Kennedy in the primary."

A tiny shock wave traveled through the assembled.

"You don't say!"

"But he's not Catholic!"

"I know. But he's a Democrat. I don't think I could ever develop much of a relationship with a Democrat."

"Oh, I don't know," Thelma piped up. "Democrats are people too."

"Well," said Elizabeth, "they say politics and money are the two biggest sources of conflict in a marriage."

"Who says that?" Ida challenged.

"They."

"Who are they?"

"The people who keep track of these kinds of things." Elizabeth let a slightly exasperated sigh accompany this, clearly her final words on the matter.

"I heard Lester say he did, too," Thelma said.

"Lester voted for Kennedy? You don't say!" Ida was aghast.

"You sure he wasn't pulling your leg?" Elizabeth frowned.

"I think he was serious," Thelma said.

"When did he say that?" Elizabeth couldn't believe it.

"At Clara's Kitchen. Talking to Maurice and Bobby."

"Well, you don't say. I never figured Lester for a Democrat." Ida shook her head to clear it of the foreign notion.

"He voted for FDR," Minnie reminded her.

"Well, that's different. Everybody was a Democrat back then," Elizabeth countered.

"Not my folks. They've voted Republican their whole lives," Minnie said. "How about you, Thelma? Would you ever vote for a Democrat?"

"I might," Thelma allowed.

"But not for Kennedy." Ida was adamant.

Thelma loved to tease Ida. "Well, he does seem to have some good ideas."

"But who would be calling the shots?" Ida couldn't believe her ears. "You want the pope running the country?"

"Didn't he say his religion was a private thing?"

"You believe that?"

"Why shouldn't I?"

"Well, I just think we have to be careful."

"We've got laws here you know. Separation of church and state."

"That's exactly why I don't trust a Catholic in the White House."

Charlene seized her chance to put an end to all speculation about her love life and, while she was at it, her political preferences. "That's what I told Donald," she said. "We've had eight good years with Ike. Let's keep it going with Nixon. I think I disappointed him, but that's the way it is."

On that note, the women said goodbye to one another and went their separate ways: Elizabeth to report to Frederick, Minnie to collect her parents for the ride home, Ida and Thelma to walk with their husbands to Sunday dinner at Clara's Kitchen, and Charlene to walk unaccompanied again and at last, up the brick walkway to her cottage.

Minnie's head was lifting right up off her shoulders and heading for the clouds. She was so distracted that she almost ran off the road, till a sharp comment from her father about watching where she was going brought her back to earth. The rest of the drive home she thought it over. Maybe with Don Harris out of the picture, her own feelings would settle down and she could get back to enjoying her weekly shampoo and set without getting all tied up in knots about it. Maybe what she'd been feeling wasn't unnatural jealousy, but just the instinct a person has to look out for the welfare of a good friend. That could be it. Yes, that could be it. In fact, that had to be it.

* * *

On a day in mid-August Lester took Minnie aside after church to explain that Helen had experienced a little "episode." Ever since Melinda's death, Helen had been obsessed with finding a fortune-teller who could tell her what had become of Melinda's baby. The one they'd seen the day before, up in Huntington, had somehow set her off to the point where she'd gotten confused and thought it was Lester who had died, not Melinda. "Land sakes," Minnie said, "then who does she think you are?"

"When I told her I was hardly dead, she took it as the name Harley Dade. So she's calling me Harley now, and letting me stay on to help around the place." Seeing Minnie's astonished look, he hastened to add, "I don't want her upset with people questioning her sanity. I'd appreciate it if everyone just treated her normal and went along with it. She'll snap out of it sooner or later."

Ida noticed the exchange and plied Minnie with questions, so in spite of her promise to Lester that she'd keep this extraordinary story to herself while Lester gave Helen a day or two to recover her wits, she had to say something to get Ida to stop pestering her. In the end, it didn't matter, because Helen clung to the notion that her husband was a hired hand named Harley and soon the entire town knew.

It gave everyone something to talk about other than Charlene's dating life or lack thereof.

* * *

They called it "the river" but it wasn't much bigger than the creek that had run near the Bader house in Kirbyville. It harbored many of the same creatures: minnows, tadpoles, Jesus bugs, dragonflies. The river had leeches, something Charlene didn't recall seeing in the Kirbyville creek.

She'd asked Minnie once if it had a name, and Minnie, bless her soul, blushed. "Not that you'd want to repeat," she'd said. "Goes back to slavery days when the runaways would come up by night from Kentucky. If you follow it far enough south, it'll take you all the way to the Ohio River. They'd lie down in the bottom of a rowboat, hide by day under the brush and overhang, then row by night till they got to Heaven. This was an Underground Railroad station."

Charlene's blank look had prompted Minnie to explain. "That's what they called the places that would hide the slaves till they got on further north. The bounty hunters had an ugly name for the river. The locals never called it anything but just 'the river.' See, they actually kept it off the maps at first so they could use it as an escape route without everyone and his uncle knowing about it."

Charlene loved the story of the river, and she loved the way the breeze blew ripples on the surface of the water. She loved the life in the water, at the water's edge, in the trees and grasses and shrubs along the riverbank. The chorus of peepers and the tadpoles in the spring, the percussive song of woodpeckers, the crickets' chirping on hot summer nights, the frogs emerging from the water and the minnows who stayed behind in the shallows.

No part of it was private, though, in this flat and farmed landscape. There were no hidden curves tucked behind impenetrable thickets, nowhere she would even dare dangle her toes, let alone strip down to indulge in a full-body mud bath. The river ran on the other side of an invisible inviolable barrier that kept Charlene from any direct connection with the water flowing within its muddy banks. If she caught herself wishing it were more like her secret creek bank in Kirbyville, she admonished herself. *It's better than no river at all. Be thankful for it as it is.*

14

CHICAGO, 1962

The voice on the phone was one she hadn't heard in years. Jacquie was back in town. Chi-town, as she called it. After a sojourn of several years in Manhattan. "I'm back," she announced, "and I've got fabulous news. I'm going to have the operation."

"Are you sick?" Charlene asked, trying to match the news with the celebratory tone of voice.

"Oh, no, darling. I'm making the change."

Charlene was suddenly aware of a click on the party line. Or did she imagine it?

"A hysterectomy is a major procedure," Charlene rushed to say, imagining Eunice listening in. "It sounds like someone's waiting to use the party line," she added. "Maybe I should call you back later?"

"Will you be up for the Sisterhood this month?"

"Yes, I do get up there on business every quarter. Perhaps we can get together then. Will you be . . . out of the hospital?"

"Not going in until December, darling. Listen, I can tell you're busy so I'll make it short and sweet. We're planning to celebrate my fiftieth, so come Friday night and plan to stay the weekend. Bring a party dress. We'll talk in Chi-town."

She would have to reschedule her Saturday morning customers, and that meant, most importantly, calling Minnie.

"Can I put you off till Tuesday? I'm going to be out of town for the weekend."

"Business trip?" Minnie asked, and wanted to bite her tongue. It surely was no business of hers, yet she'd felt the claws of the green-eyed monster and needed to know. She'd chatted up Donald Harris about his sense of why Charlene never warmed up to him, and now she was stricken with the certainty that there was a love interest in Chicago. One that might even cause Charlene to leave Heaven some dreadful day to move back there.

"I'm going up for a few days to celebrate a friend's birthday."

"Oh."

"I don't really want to go, you know, but she wouldn't take no for an answer. Jacquie—that's the birthday girl—just insisted. She recently moved back to Chicago from New York City and I haven't seen her since before the w—" Charlene caught herself. "—in ages. Before I moved here. She's got a whole weekend of shopping and sightseeing planned for us. Just a group of girlfriends."

"Well, of course you should go!" Minnie had finally recovered a modicum of equilibrium. A sedate group of lady friends. That made it less distressing. Maybe Donald was wrong. Maybe it really was about politics, and he just wasn't willing to accept that.

"So I'll put you down for Tuesday, first thing in the morning?"

"First thing."

* * *

"Oh, come with us, Charlene. It'll be fun," Jacquie urged. Except for Charlene, the aging eclectic band of cross-dressers enjoying their dessert and tea in the Walnut Room in Marshall Field's had been convinced by their prodigal, their youngest, most daring member—the only Sister who really wanted to be a woman, rather than just dress as one—to go on a tour of Chicago nightspots. "You have to kick up your heels once in a while."

Charlene protested. "I'm getting well past the age where heel kicking is of much interest. I live a very quiet life. I'll stay at Joanne's and watch *Gunsmoke*."

"For old times' sake, then," Jacquie wheedled.

"I'll think about it."

"Thank you. What are friends for, if not to help you celebrate?" Darla signaled for their check. "And to give you advice."

"I don't need advice. I've decided."

"That's why you need advice."

"You're really going to make it permanent?" Luella frowned.

"Most definitely. I've been thinking about this for a decade, ever since Christine, and it's time I actually do it. Ask not what you can do for your country, but what Sweden can do for your identity. I've booked passage in December."

"Christine?" Charlene asked.

"Jorgensen."

"Well, it's not for me," Theresa said. "My wife would never forgive me."

"That, darling, is how we differ. You want to have your wife. I want to be a wife. Don't you feel that way sometimes, Joanne?"

"I can't say that I do."

"What about you, Charlene? You could come with."

"Oh my, no."

"That's because she's sweet on that customer of hers," Theresa teased.

"But she is in a state of denial about it," Luella added.

"I'm in the state of Indiana," Charlene countered.

"But tonight," Jacquie said as the check arrived, "you are in Chi-town."

"Yes, but then I will go back home again."

They settled the check and exited into the warmth of a spring evening. "Tell me more about your friend," Jacquie said as they walked to Grant Park to take in the fresh air and do a little people watching before heading to a club that Darla had assured them was friendly to all. "She doesn't suspect? After all these years you've been there?"

"Oh, dear God, no."

"What's she like?"

"Full of life. Friendly. Caring. And," Charlene added with a smile, "she keeps her appearance up. She's my best customer."

"What do you think she'd do," Luella asked, "if she knew?"

"I can't imagine. I don't want to imagine."

"I'm so lucky," Theresa reflected. "Martha has always been my best friend. And she doesn't mind when I take off for a day or two when I just have to dress or go crazy."

"What's her name?" Jacquie asked.

"Minnie."

"And she's single?"

"She lives with her folks. They depend on her to keep their dairy farm going."

"I wouldn't have the nerve," Jacquie said.

"To do what? Milk a cow?"

"Live where I couldn't let my hair down once in a while. Do you ever think of moving back to Chi-town?"

"Never."

They walked on in silence for a few minutes. "What do you know about this club that Darla is taking us to?" Charlene asked Luella and Theresa. The three of them had fallen behind Darla, Jacquie, and Joanne.

"Not much. Just that it's friendly and lively. I'm not a club-going person. To tell you the truth, I prefer quiet get-togethers, like we have at Joanne's."

"I agree with Luella," Charlene said.

"It should be fun, though," Theresa said. "Someplace no one knows us."

"Isn't that everywhere?" Luella asked. "And what if things get out of hand? You hear about that sort of thing from time to time in these sorts of places. Bashers. Brawls. Police."

Darla, having overheard them, turned back to issue an assurance. "The bouncer is my next-door neighbor," she said. "His name is Felix Castorbach, and if it sounds familiar to you it's because he was a linebacker before he hurt his knee. He keeps it calm. And he pays the police."

*   *   *

Charlene nursed her Tom Collins and eased her feet out of her shoes to discreetly rub the emerging bunion on her left foot with the big toe of her right. It had been an exhausting day of shopping and sightseeing, and she was beginning to wish she had just gotten a cab and gone back to Joanne's while the others went out for drinks. Darla interrupted her thoughts by proposing a birthday toast to Jacquie, and they all held their drinks aloft, clinking them together and expressing their hopes that Jacquie would celebrate many more.

"Hello, ladies. Out for a little fun? Leave the hubbies behind? Or am I going to be lucky beyond my wildest dreams and hear somebody tell me you are all single? I would love to buy some beautiful woman a drink tonight." A lanky man with a touch of gray in his hair, sporting faded jeans, a Western-style shirt, and a longhorn steer bolero tie stopped at their table on his way back from the bar and flashed a smile all around.

"Sorry," Theresa said. "I'm happily married."

"Me too," Luella hastened to add.

"Thanks, but I'm waiting for someone," Darla said.

"I am," Charlene finally said, "in a committed relationship."

"As am I," Joanne demurred.

Jacquie said nothing.

"Well, Miss . . . ?" The fellow focused a dazzling, questioning smile on Jacquie.

"Jacquie. Nothing for me, thank you."

"Well, Miss Jacquie, in that case, would you care to dance?"

"I'd love to." Jacquie smiled as she stood to join the man on the dance floor.

"My name is Rod."

"Hello, Rod." Jacquie moved into his arms and waltzed away.

"I don't think that was such a good idea." Luella was still watching them. Out on the dance floor, Jacquie was throwing back her head and laughing. Rod guided her expertly through the crowd of couples and she followed, graceful and light on her feet.

"What are you worried about?" Darla sucked the maraschino cherry off the end of the tiny plastic sword that had pinned it into her drink and savored its artificial sweetness and unnatural texture.

"It's dangerous to deceive a man in a bar. Especially one on the prowl," Luella fretted.

"I told you this is a friendly club."

"To the gay boys," Luella frowned. "Not necessarily to us."

"Besides, is it a deception when she's scheduled to make it real?" Darla asked.

"Well, what do you think Mr. Rod out there would say to that? Would he feel deceived, even with the trip to Stockholm?" Theresa was worried too.

"I bet he'd be pretty mad," Luella said.

"Maybe," Darla allowed.

"Or maybe you think he'd be delighted to be able to say he knew her when." Joanne turned her attention to finding the couple on the dance floor. The others followed suit. Darla saw it first: all was not well. Jacquie was fending off some serious advances, twisting to get away from Rod, who wore the pleased smirk of a housecat with its paw on a cornered mouse.

Darla jumped to her feet, frantically searching for Felix. But Felix was already on the way over. He threaded through the crowded floor quietly, unobtrusively, and tapped Rod on the shoulder.

"Excuse me, sir, may I cut in?"

Rod turned to see who had the nerve. "Sorry, partner. This gal's mine." He grabbed Jacquie around the waist and held her fast.

"Is this fellow bothering you?"

"I would rather dance with you, if you don't mind."

"You heard the lady." Felix was skilled at defusing situations. He didn't touch Rod or try to physically separate him from Jacquie, but shrugged apologetically.

Rod considered his options. The man who was gently facing him down stood several inches taller and was heavily muscled.

"Rod!" Another voice entered the conversation. At a nearby table, two men were watching the unfolding scene. One of them raised his beer bottle and pointed with it to Felix. "He's the bouncer, buddy. Don't mess with him. No bitch is worth it."

Rod released his grip and shoved Jacquie toward Felix. "Scum," he snarled at her.

"Come on, boys, let's go." The third man at the table stood, but Rod gestured for him to sit down again.

"Naw. Let's stay for a while and keep an eye on things." He sauntered to the table, turned his chair around, and straddled it, resting his arms on the back, staring at Felix and Jacquie as they finished the dance. When the music ended Felix escorted Jacquie back to her seat. Rod waited till the bouncer was out of earshot, then stood to lead his friends to the exit, passing behind her on the way. "You think you're fooling me? I can tell sissy men a mile away," he hissed. "You don't even say 'Ow' when your titty gets pinched." He punctuated his remarks by grabbing her breast from behind and squeezing hard. "You think any self-respecting man would want something as ugly and old as you anyway?" He leaned in and growled directly into her ear. "You're a disgusting sack of shit. You want a cunt? Maybe I'll cut one for you."

If the incident sobered the ordinarily ebullient Jacquie, it positively unnerved Luella, Joanne, and Charlene. Darla and Theresa were rattled too. "Let's go home," Jacquie said, her voice shaking. "We can sing church songs and have tea. Like the old days."

"Like the old days," Luella whimpered. "Sounds good to me. I'm way too old for this kind of excitement."

"I'll ask Felix to call us a cab," Darla said, and they were glad she did, because when it came to pick them up, the three men from the club were still standing across the street.

* * *

"How was your trip?" Minnie shook out her umbrella at the door before entering, propped it against the wall, and headed directly to the shampooing sink.

"It was all right."

"I've never been to Chicago. What's it like?"

"Big. Busy."

"Was it a nice party?"

"It was . . . a little noisy for my tastes." *How soon can I change the subject without seeming rude or abrupt?*

"Were there a lot of people, then?"

"Uh hum."

"You must be tired from all that driving." Minnie was sensing the reluctance in Charlene, the edginess. She was writing it off to fatigue. "How many miles is it?"

"Around two hundred."

"Round trip?"

"Each way."

"Well," Minnie laughed, "you can see I was never much good at geography."

"Me neither. In any case, I'm glad to be back home."

Mollified by Charlene's apparent lack of enthusiasm for her Chicago trip, Minnie nestled her neck in the pink sink and closed her eyes.

"Is the water too hot?"

"It's just right. Just right." Minnie finally allowed herself to relax and let Charlene's strong fingers do their magic. If there was one place she had to stay for eternity, she thought, it would be in the shampooing chair. She couldn't decide, though, whether she would choose the moments of Charlene scrubbing the suds through her hair, or the moments of Charlene lifting her locks to flood hot rinse water across her scalp.

15

HEAVEN, 1963

The phone was ringing, refusing to stop. Charlene was trying to ignore it, since it was already 7:20 in the evening, twenty minutes after closing. She'd been there since 5:00 AM, sterilizing rollers, checking her supplies of papers and chemicals, then clipping, curling, and combing her way through the day. She dumped the dustpan full of hairs she'd swept from under the front edge of her supply cabinets where they always collected during the day when she was too busy to sweep thoroughly between customers, and told herself she'd let it ring while she put the broom away. If it was still ringing when she was done, she'd answer it.

Charlene had counted fifteen rings by the time she finally lifted the phone to her ear. It was her assistant, Amy, saying she had to come by first thing in the morning, as early as possible, before anyone else was there. She needed to get her hair done right away. She knew that she was scheduled to work that very afternoon, had three shampoos and two manicures lined up, but she'd have to take the day off. She'd explain when she came in at . . . yes, five thirty would be great.

Charlene could hear in her voice a trembling, and noticed that Amy was talking more softly than usual. And another thing Amy was telling her: Charlene shouldn't mention to anyone that she was coming in.

Amy lived on Gilman Street. Charlene could see her front door as she stood near the window of her shop the next morning. At 5:25 AM, she watched Amy ease the door open, step onto her porch, and ease the door shut. She had a scarf pulled down over her forehead and ducked her head as she walked the block to Charlene's Beauty Shop, so even as she stepped into the shop, Charlene didn't see her face at first.

"What'll it be today? Do you want to freshen your perm or just get a wash and trim?"

"I want it different," Amy said, locking the door again behind her.

"How different?"

"I want it a different color. A different style. I need it to travel well."

"Are you and Norm going somewhere?"

"I am. I'm sorry, Charlene. I know you have me on the schedule to work today. You know I'd give you more notice if I could. But I gotta quit. Quit and get out of here." Amy took off the scarf to punctuate her words.

Charlene gasped. Amy's face was a mess. She had makeup on, but nothing could hide the big purple bruise and the bloodshot eye. "What happened to you?" As Amy started to cry, Charlene apologized. "I'm sorry. It's none of my business."

"Everything in Heaven is everybody's business." Amy hurried to sit in the chair at the sink and put her head back. "Go easy on the left side," she said. "It's a little tender. My ear is still ringing." Another large bruise on her temple and a gash where her earring used to hang made it clear why.

Charlene worked silently, ministering with suds to her assistant's pain. She took a little longer than usual with the rinse, because she could see Amy relax just a tiny bit under the influence of the warm shower of water.

"Something with bangs," Amy said as soon as she faced herself in the mirror. "Like Mamie Eisenhower had but without those things at the side." With a few deft snips, Charlene clipped the modified Monroe look into oblivion.

"Like that?"

Amy approved. "Now brown. I don't want to be a blonde any-more. Whoever said they have more fun was a big fat liar. I'm going to stay with a friend from high school," she blurted. "She has a guest room. She lives in Akron. There's a bus at 7:29. I don't want Norman to know."

Charlene nodded. "Your secret's safe with me."

"I know."

They both fell silent while Charlene worked on the task of trans-forming a thirty-one-year-old glamour girl into a study of nonde-scriptness. Average brown hair, average-length cut, average style. Only when Charlene had finished trimming, coloring, and drying and was doing the final comb-out did Amy finally speak again.

"D'ya ever want to leave this place?"

"Oh, I like it pretty well here. But I might like to take a long vaca-tion somewhere. Maybe if my sweepstakes ticket wins. I usually only have time for a few days up in Chicago."

"Where would you go?"

"Someplace on the ocean."

"You been to the ocean before?"

"Once."

"I bet it's pretty."

"How's this?" Charlene gave the hand mirror to Amy and spun her around in the chair so she could see the back.

"That's good. Thank you, Charlene." She began to take money from her purse, but Charlene shook her head no.

"This is on me."

Amy began to cry. "Thank you," she said again. "Please don't tell anyone you saw me this morning. Especially Norman." Then she ar-ranged her scarf to cover the worst of the bruise and took a handful of Kleenex from the box Charlene offered.

"If you go out the back," Charlene advised, "you can take a short-cut through the alley and you won't have to walk by Clara's Kitchen on your way to the bus stop. You could even wait at the end of the alley till you see the bus coming if you don't want Herman to see you. He's usually getting ready to open the market by now."

Amy grabbed Charlene's hand in hers. "Thank you," she said yet again, choking back another spate of tears, and followed Charlene through her storeroom. "I want a new life," she added, as she stepped through the back door.

"Good luck." Charlene watched down the alleyway until she saw Amy flag down the Greyhound.

She was refilling her shampoo bottle when she heard the crash. At first she thought there must have been an accident. Maybe the milkman's truck hitting a post and breaking a headlight. . . . But as she came back out to the front of her shop she saw her own door, the window glass shattered, and Norman just outside, fist streaming with blood, bellowing. "Where is she?"

"Norman, what's the matter?"

"She's here, isn't she?" He was trying to reach through the broken glass to unlock the door, but couldn't let go of his bleeding fist.

Charlene hurried over, opened the door. "Oh my God, Norman, look at your hand! Why didn't you just knock? Here, come over to the sink and let's get a look at that."

Norman was sobbing. "Amy!" he screamed. "I know you're here. Where is she, in the bathroom?"

"She's not here, Norman. She's not on the schedule till this afternoon."

"Where is she?"

"What happened, Norman? Keep your hand still. Here." Charlene ran cold water over the wound and wrapped his hand tightly in a small white towel. "Hold it up in the air," she commanded, "to stop the bleeding. Sit down." Norman obeyed, slumping into the very seat Amy had occupied minutes before, taking great gulps of air as his convulsive sobbing subsided.

"I hit her," he confessed.

Charlene set about the task of sweeping the glass and wiping up the trail of blood.

"She makes me so mad sometimes," Norman added, then lapsed into silence. Finally, he got up. "I'll bring the towel back to you."

"No need. I've got plenty. But you might want to see the doc about that hand. You might need some stitches."

"You tell Amy when you see her to get her ass back home. Tell her I'm sorry."

"I'll tell her what you said if I see her."

"If? I thought you said she's coming in to work today."

"I said she's on the schedule. I have to ask you not to come in here, though, if she's here. I don't want my customers brought into the middle of anyone's personal problems. That's not good for business. Norman, do me a favor and just leave the door open on your way out. I'll get it fixed later."

"You got customers coming now?"

When Charlene nodded, he hurried out.

Charlene took the bloody towels to the back room, and got back to the front of her shop just as Minnie walked in.

"Isn't this just the most beautiful day?" Minnie loved May. Everything always seemed to be possible in May. The hens started laying well again. The cows, bred the previous August, calved. The fruit trees converted their fragrant blossoms to the hard green pea-sized buttons that would become peaches, pears, and apples. The black locust trees scented the air, more intense than honeysuckle, and you could make fritters with the blossoms that were absolutely delicious.

Charlene was glad that Minnie had bustled right by the broken door pane and not noticed it. She preferred Minnie's litany of what she loved about summer to having to answer questions about what had just happened.

*   *   *

In June, it was the June bugs Minnie loved: their raucous buzzing and bumping against the screen door, and the newly furrowed fields waiting to be fed seeds, and the mellow warmth of summer nights.

July would bring the knee-high corn and festivities on the Fourth, and this year the carnival was coming to town again the same week as the county fair. For a week, the housewives would have their wares on proud display, competing for purple ribbons that evidenced the true champions of quilting, canning, preserving, stitching, and gardening. For a week, the men would gather to contemplate the livestock, and see whose steer would win the judges' approval, whose hog would top the scales. And next door at the carnival, the Ten in One tent would astonish people with the human oddities housed within, while the children of Heaven would make themselves sick on cotton candy and spinning rides, balk at going home, and beg for more. For a week, young men would throw balls to try to win garish teddy bears for their sweethearts, and young women would press their bodies against their boyfriends and scream on the roller coaster, allowing the fellows to put protective arms around them. For a week, people would stand in line to see the fortune-teller, to have her look at their palms and tell them the answers to whatever was on their minds. Minnie wasn't sure yet what she was going to ask, except it wasn't going to be what was truly bothering her. She'd have to figure out how to ask indirectly.

"Are you going?" Minnie asked Charlene. "Or will you be out of town on business?" It drove her mad with curiosity to know what business it was that took Charlene to Chicago four times a year, but Charlene deflected the unasked question with practiced skill.

"I'll make sure I'm here," Charlene said. "I wouldn't want to miss it."

*   *   *

"You've come about your sweepstakes ticket?"

"How did you know?" Charlene was astonished.

Madame Gajikanes smiled. Her nine-year-old adopted grand-daughter was skilled at overhearing people in the waiting line. The girl had peeked in the back of the tent and told the fortune-teller of a stocky, nervous man who would want to know if someone named Amy was coming back, and behind him a tall woman with a sweep-stakes ticket. But there was something more. Something authentic. She hadn't remembered at first, but as soon as she'd held the hand, it had come back to her. She'd held this same hand nine years before. In this same town. The fortune-teller had wondered a time or two during the intervening years what had become of her.

"I know the ticket isn't going to hit," Charlene continued, as she held out her palm to be read. "I'm here because of what you said the last time. You said there was love in my life line."

"Yes. There still is. See where the lines intersect?"

"You said it would last a long time."

"And has it?" The fortune-teller was watching the face of her cli-ent, gauging how much to probe. Though the love line was long, as long as the life line, the life line itself wasn't exceptional. There was a problem with this client's heart. It didn't always do to tell that sort of thing. It depended on what a person was able to hear.

"For me, yes. For the other person, I don't know."

"But it has been there for a time?"

"I don't know."

"What would you like me to tell you?"

"What happens if I tell someone how I feel?" Charlene leaned in, the question almost inaudible.

Madame Gajikanes spoke as if offering a wild creature food from her hand. "You find out how that person feels in return."

"Will it turn out well?"

"How important is it for you to know?"

"I've been afraid to know for a long time."

Madame Gajikanes made a little intuitive leap. "Since you have lived here in Heaven."

The truth of the statement took Charlene by surprise, and she had to admit it, though she was realizing it for the first time. "Yes. Since 1945."

"That's a very long time to keep something to yourself."

"Eighteen years."

"Will you wait another eighteen years?"

"Do I have another eighteen years?"

The fortune-teller took a moment to answer.

"What does my palm say?" Charlene persisted.

"In eighteen years, you will be. . . ?"

"Eighty."

Madame Gajikanes smiled gently and shook her head. "I think it would be prudent to suppose you may not have quite that long."

Charlene nodded. "How long do I have?"

"What is in your future are possibilities, not foregone conclusions. You carry an enormous burden. It almost always improves matters to share enormous burdens."

"It is easier said than done."

"So many things are."

"It's dangerous for me."

"Yet you've survived dangers before."

"I was in the war."

"Yes."

"That was nothing compared to this. There I had nothing to lose. Here I have everything I have made for myself."

"When you came to see me before, was my reading helpful?"

"It's difficult to say. You told me I wouldn't win the Irish Sweepstakes."

"And was I right?"

Charlene smiled. Madame Gajikanes smiled. "Absolutely. I buy a ticket every year, and every year I lose. I bought one this year."

"And it, too, is not a winner." Madame Gajikanes ran the tip of her finger over the lines in Charlene's right hand. "You are still a hairdresser?" she asked.

Charlene felt a bit of a flutter. She hadn't told the fortune-teller this. But the woman had a way of knowing things, whether by the lines in a person's hand or who knows what, that was unnerving. She'd guessed Charlene's secret right off the bat, too. At least, Charlene guessed that she'd guessed it.

"The love I saw nine years ago—it has grown stronger." Madame Gajikanes watched Charlene's face, reading the struggle it masked. "But you are very afraid of something."

"Yes."

"Afraid it is one-sided?"

"Afraid it would be. If everything were known."

Most of what the fortune-teller did was skill, pure and simple, with a healthy spicing of subterfuge. There was a piece of it, though, that even Madame Gajikanes didn't understand. She didn't understand, for example, why every now and then she would be overwhelmed with an insight. Would feel an electricity that made her whole body vibrate, and feel as trapped by it as if she'd flung herself against a high-voltage fence. It's not that Madame Gajikanes thought about what to do next. At moments like this, she operated on pure instinct.

Here today was a woman whose hand told of love and who was afraid because she wasn't really a woman. She'd loved someone for a long time. Yesterday had been the woman who came in desperately in love and deeply ashamed. The puzzle was solving itself in her subconscious.

The words came to her and she spoke them aloud. "You must let her know."

"Who?" Charlene startled and barked it out like she'd been caught stealing from the offering basket at church.

And in that next moment, Madame Gajikanes put the pieces together on the conscious level. The woman who'd seen her the day before had impeccably styled hair, a strong love line in her hand, yet no ring on her finger. She asked at first about a lost kitten, but finally wanted to know if the fortune-teller could give her advice on behalf of a theoretical friend who feared she was not entirely right in the head. Who had what she felt were abnormal urges. Was there a place in her friend's palm she could look to see something like that? The answer was plain as day. As clear as the hairdresser's heart problems.

"Is there someone you see very frequently?" the fortune-teller asked Charlene. "Perhaps a customer? Perhaps she makes more appointments with you than she needs to? I'm seeing something about a small animal, also, but it's not important now. Now what is important is that you trust this person. Trust her with what you know I know."

"And if she despises me for it?"

"She won't."

"You know that from my palm?"

"From your palm. And from my heart."

As she left the tent, Charlene hoped she wouldn't see anyone she knew, but there was Norman, Amy's Norman, who had apparently been waiting for her. He fell in beside her as she walked toward the end of the midway. "Did she tell you anything useful?"

"My sweepstakes ticket is a loser," Charlene told him, mentally willing him to leave her alone. He kept in step with her, obviously needing more conversation. "What about you?"

"I don't know if it's useful or not," Norman said. "It's not what I wanted to hear."

Charlene gave him time to continue.

"She said Amy's back. Which I actually knew already. She's staying with the sister that lives out at the end of Elm Street."

"She told you that?"

"Well, you know how they do. She confirmed it. Charlene, tell me the truth. Has Amy called you?"

"No, I haven't heard from her since the day she left town."

"Cross your heart and hope to die?"

Charlene glanced at the man walking next to her. *Cross your heart?* He was talking like a seven-year-old girl instead of a thirty-five-year-old man.

"Cross my heart and hope to die," she assured him.

Norman was struggling to hold back tears. "Can I tell you a secret, Charlene?"

"Sure, Norman."

"We was never married. That's what the fight was about. She wanted to get married and I . . . I didn't want to . . . and one thing led to another, and now she won't come home."

"You hit her because she wanted to get married?"

"She made me do it, Charlene. She just wouldn't understand. And now"—he lowered his voice, signaling an even deeper secret—"her goddamn sister's took out a goddamn restraining order against me! Says I threatened her property. Like her goddamn property is worth more'n my rights. Kyle Johnson served it this morning. Told me Amy's afraid of me, and to keep away from her. Sonofabitch." Norman spit the words out and began to cry in earnest.

"Who raised the fist, Norman?"

Norman's tears stopped in their tracks, and his mouth took on an ugly snarl. "You women," he hissed. "You're all alike. You stick together like shit and lie like rugs." And he stormed off.

Charlene made her escape from the fairgrounds and walked the river route back to her house. Norman's insult was the last thing on her mind, but Amy's return was important news. She might want to make a trip to Chicago to try to sort out her feelings, and reinstating "manicures only" days would make that easier to plan.

Monday morning, Amy was waiting at the door when Charlene arrived to open the shop. "I hope my job's still open."

"As a matter of fact, it is," Charlene said. "Can you come in tomorrow afternoon?"

"I can. We have to change the paperwork, though. My name's Amy Bickford. Norm and I was never married. I just used his name so people wouldn't talk."

*   *   *

Minnie lay awake watching lightning split the sky. A sudden summer storm was rolling across the fields, heading Heaven's way. She counted the seconds till the thunder rumbled, something she'd done since childhood. From this long practice, she knew the worst of it would hit the Kelso farm in another ten minutes or so. She probably should check to make sure all the windows were shut. Maybe have a cup of tea, get it going quick before she didn't dare have the electric stove on. She got up, pulled the window down by her bed, then stepped into her slippers and pulled on her housecoat. No need to wake her parents. Their bedroom faced the front of the house, so the rain would be blowing away from their open window. She went downstairs and, while the water heated, secured the kitchen and dining room against the coming onslaught. Forty-five years she'd been in this house. Forty-five years, it seemed to her, with the feeling that a storm was coming.

It always felt like it would be the end of the world when it came, but she always woke up the next morning anyway. Like she'd awakened every morning for the past week since she'd visited the palm reader at the carnival. The fortune-teller had read her well. Told her something was troubling her, twisting her insides into knots. Said something was passing her by, and that she had to reach out and grab it. Warned her not to wait any longer.

"Easy for you to say," Minnie muttered to herself as she poured the water into the cup and turned the burner off. "You don't have to do it," she continued, addressing the absent carnival woman as she dunked the tea bag into her cup.

"I thought I better get up and shut the windows." Minnie's mother appeared at the bottom of the steps.

"It's okay, Mom. I got them already."

"What about the living room?"

"It's blowing the other way. It'll get too hot if we close all the windows."

"Is Gabe home yet?"

"He lives in California, Mom. Remember? He married Sheila when he was stationed out west."

"Oh."

"Do you want some tea?"

"Don't put the stove on during a storm."

"It's okay. The water is already hot. I'll make you mint so it won't keep you awake."

"That's all right. I have to stay up anyway until your brother gets home."

"Gabe lives in California, Mom."

"Oh. You just told me that, didn't you?"

"It's all right. Here's your tea."

The crack of a lightning strike made them both jump. "My goodness." Laura was wide-eyed and worried. "That was close."

"Yes. It sounds like it might have hit one of the poplars. I'm surprised Dad isn't up. He usually can't sleep through a storm."

A look of consternation took over Laura Kelso's face. "Oh my! I forgot about Daddy!"

Minnie reached over and patted her hand. "It's all right, Mom."

"No, it isn't. Something's wrong with Daddy. I came downstairs to tell you and I forgot." Agitated, she pushed herself up, knocking her chair over in the process. "We've got to get upstairs!"

"What is it, Mom?"

"He's not himself."

Minnie was already halfway up the stairs. "You stay there," she commanded her addled mother. "I'll check on him."

Mrs. Kelso moved to the bottom of the stairs and called up after her, "Maybe we should wait until Gabriel gets home."

Minnie found her father staring at nothing, a blank panic in his eyes. "Dad?" Minnie stopped halfway into the room, an instinct telling her to give him space. He'd always been a reserved man.

Her father shifted his gaze to her, fully intending to demand an answer to "Who are you?" But when he spoke, neither he nor his daughter could understand what he was saying.

*   *   *

Helen knew something was up when Minnie missed her regular Monday morning egg-and-butter-trading time, so she called to find out what was wrong. Minnie apologized for not letting her know sooner and filled her in. Doctor Brubecker, bless his heart, had come out of semiretirement to make a house call. He'd arrived in the middle of the storm to confirm that Minnie's dad appeared to have suffered a stroke. He'd stayed the rest of the night till he was assured that Paul's condition was stable and he was finally asleep and resting comfortably. They would take him over to the hospital in Marion to confirm the diagnosis later in the day. The doc had packed up his old black bag and headed to his office only moments before. Minnie was still awake, finally on her way out to milk Bossy Flossie, who was two hours overdue for relief and bellowing to beat the band. Helen put her eggs in the Kaiser and headed off to sit for a while in the Kelso kitchen so Minnie could tell her the full story and then go up to bed to catch a nap without having to worry about her mother waking and wandering off.

*   *   *

"Well, poor soul, she hasn't been out of the house except to go to the barn in two weeks." Ida talked to Charlene's reflection while Charlene combed through Ida's newly permed hair, coaxing the curls to loosen just the tiniest bit. "Helen goes over on Mondays, Wednesdays, and Fridays; I've been taking Tuesdays, Thursdays, and Saturdays; and Thelma goes Sundays so she can at least get the milking done without having to worry. They've got Paul set up in a hospital bed downstairs so she doesn't have to run up and down the stairs all day. Minnie's moved a daybed into the kitchen so she can head off Laura if she starts to go for one of her midnight walks. I told her she should have sold all the cows, but she's a stubborn one, you know. She said she wants to keep the one because she always knows what to expect from Bossy Flossie, and with her mom and dad she never knows.

"Paul's gotten more crotchety than ever, if you can imagine. Just growls and grunts. And Laura is pleasant, thank goodness for that, but she's going downhill awfully fast. I think the shock of Paul's stroke has set her back."

Charlene handed Ida the mirror and turned the chair so she could see the back. Ida frowned.

"Do you want it combed out differently?"

"Oh, no. Goodness. No, the perm is perfect. It's just that I saw a gray hair. See right here?"

"Would you like a touch-up with a little color?"

"No, I'm going to go home and pull it out."

"Well, if you get to the point where there are too many to pull, let me know. I can blend them back in next time you come in for a perm."

"To tell you the truth, I already color my hair. I just missed this one somehow."

Charlene knew Ida colored her hair. She could tell from the uniform hue, the way the roots were just the slightest bit less reddish in tone. "Well, I surely never would have guessed. It looks so natural!"

Ida laughed, pleased, affirmed. "It's not that you wouldn't do it better, but you never know who's going to stop by while you're here. It's like the town square. You'll keep my secret, won't you?"

"Of course." Charlene undid the clasp at the back of the plastic apron, shook it out, and swept up the hair clippings while Ida climbed out of the chair, retrieved her purse, and put cash on the counter.

Charlene watched her go and wanted to weep. That's why Minnie hadn't been in for two weeks and hadn't even been in touch. She couldn't believe it had taken two weeks for her to find out. Perhaps if she had asked earlier she'd have found out earlier.

The first few days after her visit to the fortune-teller she'd worked herself up to figuring out how she might broach the subject to Minnie when she next came in. Which she always did first thing on Saturday mornings. But Helen had called that Thursday and canceled Minnie's appointment. Helen wasn't a chatty woman, and she gave Charlene no opportunity to ask the cause. Then Thelma called, aware of the opening in the schedule, to ask if she could come in instead. Charlene was tongue-tied, afraid to ask for information about the cancellation. Afraid it would give her away. It was better not to ask anything at all, at least not until Ida came in for her appointment the following week. She knew Ida would have made it her business to know about anything unusual going on in Heaven, and would volunteer as many details as possible.

It was all the more frustrating that Minnie's appointment had been canceled because Charlene, riding a small wave of courage from the fortune-teller's counsel, had been mulling over just how to broach her subject. Minnie, she would say, you are my closest friend here in Heaven. I hope that will never change, because I have something very important to tell you. She had practiced it every morning between the palm reading and the cancellation as she tweezed eyebrows, rubbed creams and lotions into her skin, curled eyelashes, applied lipstick. *You are my closest friend. I hope that will never change. You are my closest friend.* At the end of the entire process, she would mouth the words she dared not yet say aloud, even to herself. *Minnie, I'm a man. I'm a man and I love you.*

When Helen called to cancel the appointment, Charlene's resolve began to unravel. In her imagined confession to Minnie, she began to wrestle with whether that was the best way to say it. Should she go first with her declaration of love? *I love you and I'm a man.* Let one idea sink in fully before broaching the other? *I'm a man . . .* but what if that was the end of it? What if Minnie right there ran screaming to the police, or perhaps even worse, to the other regular customers, some of whom had husbands who served on the town council? Alma Porter even served on the council herself.

At any rate, it seemed risky to begin by revealing her sex. On the other hand, beginning with a declaration of love (*Minnie, I love you. I want to spend my life with you*) could as easily lead to mayhem as the first option. This line of thinking always led to the memory of Anne's shoulder blades, her scorn. She made herself so sick with worry she even missed church—the one place where she'd certainly have heard the news sooner—due to a raging headache.

Hearing the reason for Minnie's absence finally redirected Charlene's thoughts. She forgot, just for a moment, her own consternation and thought instead of how to be a good friend. She could make a house call.

* * *

The sun was sitting low in the sky when Charlene pulled up the Kelso driveway. She sat for a minute in the car, taking deep breaths, trying to quiet her racing heart. She'd lived in Heaven for eighteen years. Eighteen years. And in all that time, she'd never been to Minnie's house. In fact, she'd only been in one house other than her own during all those years.

Once, when she had first come to town, Charlene had stepped out of the post office to discover a flat tire on her car. Alma, the postmistress, had invited her into the cottage next door where she and her daughter Wilma lived to use the phone to call Bobby at the service station and wait for his arrival. Bobby was out on a call, so Alma changed the tire. Charlene could have helped: she knew perfectly well how to change a tire, but she didn't dare. Every impression she made had to be carefully planned and cultivated.

It was a deliberate tactic, avoiding ever going to anyone's home in Heaven. Going to someone else's home would mean the obligation of inviting that person to her own home, would mean having to hide the plethora of personal care products she relied upon to maintain her mask. You just never know when someone is going to need to use the powder room. And decides to snoop in the medicine cabinet for good measure. And comes to wonder about the shaving cream and razors, the tweezers and depilatories. Church socials she attended, and once in a while she took a meal at Clara's Kitchen, but by and large, her life consisted of long hours in her beauty shop and shorter hours in her little house. And aside from the day Minnie brought her the welcome basket, no one other than Charlene had set foot in that house. Charlene's social life in Heaven, such as it was, happened at work, where Minnie came once a week, Ida every two weeks, Helen every month, Elizabeth, Wilma, Stella, Thelma, and Katie less predictably, but often enough that Charlene considered them friends as well as customers.

Of course, too, there were the Full Self Sisters, or what was left of them. Of the group, Charlene felt closest to Joanne. But in spite of the many years she'd known her Chicago friends, Charlene felt apart from them. Sitting in her car in the Kelso driveway, Charlene felt a surge of loneliness, and wondered what it would be like to have someone to come home to.

Then the ancient collie that had been asleep on the front porch roused himself and announced to those within that a visitor had arrived, and the door opened. Minnie stood at the threshold. Charlene had no way to know Minnie was every bit as heartachy and flustered as Charlene, trying to look as normal as possible as she waved her friend in out of the car. "Come in, come in. Don't mind Sidney. He's too old to hurt anyone. Hardly has any teeth left even if he wanted to. You are so kind to come out to the house like this. It's just so hard for me to get away these days, even to get out to the barn to milk Bossy Flossie. I surely don't know what I'd do without all the good friends who are helping out sitting with Mom and Dad so I can at least do that."

"Minnie, who is that? Who's in our kitchen? Have you offered her a cup of coffee and a piece of pie? Do I know you?" Laura shuffled into the room and peered at Charlene.

"Yes, ma'am. We've met at church. I sit two rows behind you every Sunday."

"Oh, I haven't been to church in such a long time! You know since Paul had his stroke we can't get out much."

"Yes, I know."

"I hope you don't think I just stopped going because I felt like it. We just can't leave him alone, you know. And then the truth is, I don't drive anymore, and it's such a long walk. Now when I was a girl we walked all the way into town and never thought twice about it. Well, we didn't own a car. No one did in those days. Oh, where are my manners? Would you like a cup of coffee? There's a cherry pie, too—let me get you a piece."

"No, thank you, Mrs. Kelso. I'm just here to fix Minnie's hair for her."

"What's wrong with her hair?"

"We're just going to do a shampoo and set."

"Well, now I've seen everything. Have you always done house calls? You know Agnes Siebold always did my hair but I had to go to her. She never came to me! Oh yes, I had to go to her. If I'da known you did house calls, I would've called you up. Well, if I'da known who you were. What did you say your name was again?"

"Charlene Bader."

"Bader. That's a German name, isn't it?"

"Yes, ma'am."

"And you do shampoos and sets?"

"Yes, ma'am."

"Well, all right then. Where would you like me to sit? I guess over there by the sink. There's more room here in the kitchen than in the bathroom."

Minnie started to interrupt, but Charlene caught her eye and winked. "So we'll do you first and then Minnie?"

"Why yes, that would be fine. Now tell me when you came to Heaven. I don't remember meeting you before."

"1945."

"Oh, that was a terrible time, wasn't it? We lost our son in that war."

"I'm sorry."

"Mom, it was *after* the war we lost him, and he's still alive. He just doesn't visit much," Minnie explained to Charlene, "because he lives in California and his wife's family is all out there."

"I thought he ran off with some French woman."

"That was Warren. Remember Warren, Mom? The fellow I was going to marry?"

Laura Kelso thought for a moment. "Good-looking boy. What ever happened to him?"

"He stayed in France."

"Where?"

"France. The country."

"Was he from France?"

"No, Mom, he was from Gas City."

"Well he certainly turned out to be a no-good bum, that Warren. I don't know why the good Lord took our Gabriel and left Warren to break your heart."

"He didn't take Gabe, Mom. Gabe's alive in California."

"Oh. You just told me that, didn't you?"

"Yes, I did. They have that little bakery that they send us cookies from every year at Christmas, remember? You love those Christmas cookies."

"Oh, those are such wonderful cookies. Have you ever tasted their cookies, Miss . . . Miss . . . oh, I forgot your name again."

"Bader."

"Bader. It's terrible when you can't remember things, take it from me."

Charlene waited a second, busying herself with running the water, checking the temperature, rolling up a towel to make a head and neck rest. And sure enough, the question about marrying and cookies seemed to have evaporated from Laura Kelso's consciousness. She returned to her earlier theme.

"I don't believe I've ever heard of a hairdresser making a house call before. Doctors used to do it, come out when a body was sick, and Dr. Brubecker still does. That Dr. Hansen makes you come all the way into town. You know that doesn't make any sense, to bring all those germs into the doctor's office. That's why I won't go to him. Only to Dr. Brubecker. A doctor's office is supposed to be clean. But you make house calls to cut hair?"

"Well, not many. Actually, this is the first time."

"What in the world for?"

"I thought you might like to get your hair washed, Mom." Charlene was noticing how gracefully Minnie worked to spare her mother's feelings. No subtle complaints here about how Laura's condition kept Minnie tethered to the house. No wisecracks about it being *her* appointment and not Laura's. "And I know you don't like to leave Dad alone so I asked Charlene if she'd stop by after her regular hours and give you a shampoo."

Laura Kelso was confused, but delighted with the attention. "Now who did you say you are?" She opened her eyes to peer at the woman who stood over her.

"Better keep your eyes closed, Mrs. Kelso, so the soap doesn't get in and sting them. I'm Charlene Bader. I have the beauty shop in town."

"I thought that was Agnes Siebold."

"She retired."

"Now did you work for her? I don't remember seeing you before."

"I came after she closed her shop."

"But she didn't really close her shop, did she? She always had that little room at the back of her house."

Minnie left her mother in Charlene's hands while she went to check on her father. Since his stroke, he hadn't left his bed. Though no longer able to speak, he was as querulous as ever, except when he was asleep, which was an increasingly large portion of the day as well as the night. He was sleeping when she looked in on him. She opened the window a little wider to let in some breeze. She could hear her mother and Charlene talking out in the kitchen. It was all welling up in her, all the feelings she'd so carefully contained, stashed away, buried. She'd tried to put them at the bottom of her hope chest, and locked the chest in a closet, but now it was more like her feelings were a jack-in-the-box popping up to frighten her when she wasn't expecting it.

Yet the fortune-teller said she was normal. Charlene's voice in her house, talking to her mother. This is the way it would sound if Charlene were part of Minnie's family. Maybe she could allow herself to crave Charlene as a sister. Instead of a brother who abandoned the family, an older sister who would always listen and would help. Now that would be normal, wouldn't it? A normal thing to want?

Minnie sat by her once stern, strong father, who lay reduced to an inarticulate, quarrelsome, snoring man, and cried. She didn't cry often. In fact, perhaps five times in her adult life. Once when her fiancé went off to war, once when he called to say he wasn't coming back, once when Melinda Breck died, once when she thought Don Harris was going to take Charlene away from her, and this evening. Unlike the other times, this time she couldn't stop. Every heartache she'd ever felt, every one of life's unfairnesses, every slight, every insult, every sling and arrow came back to pierce her heart and she gave in to the profound fatigue of having held so much in and so much together for so long. She wanted to wail aloud, to scream and even curse, but she dared not wake her father. Nor alarm her mother and Charlene.

She choked that urge back. It made her throat hurt, not to scream. She buried her face in a sofa pillow to muffle her sobs. When she heard the hair dryer start and saw the light of the floor lamp flicker because the wiring was not up to such fancy new gadgets, she knew it was time to marshal all her forces to collect herself. She dried her tears on the corner of her apron, and blew her nose on one of her dad's handkerchiefs that she kept next to his bed so she could wipe the spittle that insisted on escaping from the corner of his mouth when he slept. Then she went to the bathroom and splashed cold water on her face until the redness subsided.

"Minnie?" Her mother was calling from the kitchen.

"Be right there." One final check in the mirror to make sure she was presentable.

"How does it look?" Laura was obviously pleased with her hair, but midwestern protocol called for her to hear it from someone else.

"It looks great, Mom."

"Did you know this lady makes house calls? I'm sorry," she said, turning to Charlene, "I've forgotten your name."

"Charlene Bader."

"That's a German name, isn't it?"

"Yes." Charlene caught Minnie's eye and smiled to let her know it was okay. Minnie's mom could repeat herself as often as she liked. Charlene was feeling as happy and at home as she'd felt since the days when she was Charlie, five years old with his mother Ilsa sitting by the bed telling stories of life in Bremen or chatting about the ladies at church.

"Mom, would you like to sit with Dad for a bit while Charlene does my hair?"

"Is he asleep?"

"Yes."

"Well, I guess I might could do that. Do you think it will wake him up if I turn the radio on?"

"Not if you keep it low."

Laura picked up the hand mirror and took one more look at her freshly washed and styled hair.

"It looks fantastic, Mom. Maybe if we get someone to sit with Dad Sunday morning you could go to church and show it off."

"I could do that," Charlene volunteered.

"You would?" Laura jumped at the offer.

"I'd be happy to."

"Well, that's very nice of you." Laura was beaming. She hadn't been out of the house for three weeks, even to help with the milking or get the mail from the mailbox, and she could hardly wait to see what Alice Siebold would say. And the minister, whose name she couldn't quite bring to mind. She knew he would compliment her. She headed to the living room to keep an eye on Paul and was asleep in the rocking chair within three minutes.

In the kitchen, Minnie let her head drop back against the towel roll and felt the hot water cascade through her hair and over her scalp. She felt her eyes start to tear up again, and spoke to keep her emotions in check.

"That feels so good."

"Not too hot?"

"No, it's just right. It is very kind of you to offer to sit with Dad Sunday morning."

"I'm glad to do it."

"You don't have to, you know. By now she's already forgotten you said it."

"That's all right. She'll still enjoy getting out and seeing people."

"I wish I knew how to thank you."

Charlene was scrubbing Minnie's scalp; Minnie's eyes were closed against the suds and water. Maybe that's what gave Charlene the courage.

"You're my best friend in Heaven, Minnie."

A pause. Charlene scrubbed. Minnie thrilled, but relaxed under the touch.

It's now or never, Charlene thought, suddenly remembering one of her mother's sayings: you say A, you got to say B. I've said A, she thought. Here goes B. "There's something I've wanted to tell you . . ."

Another pause. This wasn't easy. Wasn't easy at all.

Minnie considered opening her eyes and decided against it. "What?" she finally prompted.

"I hope it won't change our friendship . . ."

"How could anything do that?"

"I want to tell you something no one in Heaven knows."

Minnie felt a flutter of excitement.

"And no one must ever know. Except you."

And fear. Minnie felt fear. And monstrous curiosity.

Another pause. Charlene was still scrubbing, stalling for time.

"You can tell me," Minnie assured her.

Charlene pulled the sprayer out, tested the rinse water. "Is that all right?"

"Perfect. You know just how I like it."

Charlene rinsed, Minnie waited. The tension was glorious and awful. Minnie wanted the moment to last forever, and couldn't stand for it to last another single second. "What do you want to tell me?"

Charlene turned the water off, wrapped a towel around Minnie's head, and helped her sit up straight. Suddenly, this had to be face to face, eye to eye. Charlene pulled a chair out from the table for Minnie to sit in, and sat across from her dear, dear friend. She took a deep breath and blurted it out. "I'm a man."

Minnie stared, her face and mind great blank expanses.

"I'm a man," Charlene repeated before her nerve could fail her, letting her voice deepen to its natural pitch.

Minnie blinked. There she was still, still sitting there. Charlene. In front of her. Telling her things that didn't make sense and made everything make sense.

"I don't understand," she finally managed to say.

"I don't either," said Charlene. "But it's true."

It might have been a minute, it might have been five. Finally, Minnie spoke again.

"You're a man?" She was reconsidering every aspect of the person who sat facing her. The angles of the face, the sinews of the arms, the long strong fingers, the voice, husky for a woman. The eyebrows, the nose, the lips. She could sort of see it. Sort of. "You aren't one of those ones who had that operation, are you?"

"No, no operation. I'm just a man."

"Why . . . ?"

"It's a long story. A very long story. There came a time in my life when I wanted nothing to do with what had happened before. And I . . ." Charlene rested her hands on the table and stared at them.

There was another painfully awkward pause.

"Go on."

"I had done some of this. Dressing like this. But I'm not . . . I'm not, you know. I'm a man. I'm not attracted to other men. Never have been."

"Oh my Lord, and I thought . . . I thought. . ." Minnie was too embarrassed to go on.

"What?"

"I thought . . . I wasn't normal. Because I had feelings for you. I thought I was one of those women who . . . but I was never attracted to any other woman, just you."

"You were . . . you had feelings for me?"

Minnie blushed and for the second time that evening felt tears coming on.

Charlene managed a wry smile. "And you thought you weren't normal? I'm the one most people would say isn't normal."

Minnie snuffled into a paper napkin. "Are you sure you're a man?"

"Oh yes, I'm sure."

"Why . . . why did you . . . why don't you. . ."

"Act like one?"

"Yes."

"That's a fair question. I guess I got to a point where I decided I didn't like a lot of what men do to each other." Memories flashed through like bullets.

Minnie was still studying Charlene's facial structure. Yes, she could see it. She could see a man's face, if she blurred her eyes a little so she could ignore the carefully tweezed eyebrows, the precisely applied lipstick. It was too strange. Too strange. She held to the table edge to steady herself.

Finally Charlene spoke again. "I was in the war. I was a dentist. We would fix a man's teeth so he could go out and get killed by or kill someone who probably had a dentist too. My assistant Tommy had a girl waiting for him in Iowa. I met her after V-E Day when I went to tell her about how much she'd meant to Tommy. I think that was when I snapped. The army said I was dead anyway. They thought Charlie Bader was killed in action in Belgium. It was really a German boy less than half my age who'd stolen my uniform and tags, but try telling anything to an army bureaucrat. They brought me home, at least. At least they didn't try to bury me in Belgium! But they never got the paperwork straightened out.

"Anyway, I used to dress up now and then, just once in a while when the feeling came over me too strong to ignore. I lost my wife over it. She didn't know and found me . . . came home early one day and there I was. She didn't understand, she thought I was a homo, a guy who likes guys. But I don't. I like women. I just figured I'd never meet one who could understand that a man can have these needs once in a while. I only know one fellow like me lucky enough to have a wife who knows and doesn't care."

"How many fellows like you do you know?" The world was suddenly, alarmingly, far larger than Heaven, Indiana.

"A few. Up in Chicago, where I lived before the war. They get together now and then so they have an outlet. Six left now, including me. Two of the others are married, and all one of them ever does is worry about getting caught."

"So that's why you go to Chicago. To see your ... men friends ... who wear dresses."

Charlene nodded. "And to be a man, too, once in a while. Kind of crazy sounding, I know. But sometimes I like to go for a whole two days without having to shave and put on makeup. I just have to keep a hat on so my hair doesn't give me away."

"So you never can just be you?"

"I'm always just me."

"I mean, you never can stop thinking about hiding something."

"I've gotten used to it."

"Don't you ever want to not have to think about it at all?"

"I think it's dangerous to want things you can't have."

"Maybe so ... but it's so sad."

"I'm not sad, Minnie. I have a good life."

"Would you want a life like your friend? The one whose wife knows and doesn't care?"

"Like I said, it's dangerous to want things you can't have."

"Maybe you can have that." Minnie held out a hand.

"You have been such a friend to me." Charlene saw her own hands already on the table. She looked at the distance of three or so inches between hers and Minnie's, her heart beating wildly. She wanted to take Minnie's hand. She wanted to say all the things she hadn't said since Anne left. But the fear wouldn't let go. The fortune-teller's words. Anne's shoulder blades. Minnie's hand, waiting. Anne's contempt.

"Would you like a wife? One who knows and understands? I would like to understand."

Charlene dared to touch Minnie's fingertips. "Do you know," she said, "that I have been in love with you for most of the eighteen years I've known you?"

Minnie bit her lower lip to hold back her tears. "Most?" she managed to say. Then suddenly she got up and shoved the daybed against the door. "I forgot. So if Mom wanders at night, she doesn't get outside."

To Charlene, it was a slap, bringing her to her senses. Minnie was not barricading her mother in. She was keeping the rest of the world out. The world that would never understand. The world that loved nothing better than a scandalous story. The world of Rod and his friends. The grown-up Scootches and Taylors, always ready to mock. The pious churchgoers like Anne. The busybodies like Elizabeth, the gossips like Ida. Men like Norman, ready to hate and blame. She looked at Minnie, tears spilling down her cheeks. "I realize I'll have to leave Heaven now."

"Why?" A wild look in Minnie's eye, panic in her voice.

"I'll be run out on a rail if I'm lucky," Charlene said. "There's probably quite a few around here that would do far worse. You know they would. I have to be gone before anyone else finds out."

"How is anyone going to find out?"

"Things in a small town have a way of getting around. You surely know that. No one here can keep a secret."

Minnie sat back at the table, pulling her chair closer to Charlene's, watching her face.

"I'm the only one who knows?"

Charlene nodded her head yes. "So far. The only one in Heaven."

"Well, then." Minnie reached again to take Charlene's hand, and this time, Charlene allowed her fingers to interlace with Minnie's. "I have loved you," Minnie realized as she said it, "since the day I brought that basket to your house. And you cannot"—she choked the words out through her own tears—"absolutely cannot leave. No one else will ever know."

Then Minnie, who was never at a loss for words, had nothing more to say. They stayed that way without speaking, but great waves of silent communication crashed between them as each thought back on all those years, reviewing moment after moment in this new light of mutually declared love, until Laura Kelso appeared at the door between the living room and the kitchen.

"I'm going up now," she announced to Minnie. "Daddy's asleep."

"Okay, Mom." Minnie dropped Charlene's hand.

Laura peered at Charlene. "What did you say your name was?"

"Charlene."

"Did Minnie offer you coffee?"

"Yes, thanks."

"Would you like a piece of cherry pie?"

"No, thank you. I'm sure it is delicious. Maybe another time."

"All right, then. Good night."

"Good night, Mrs. Kelso."

"Good night, Mom."

Minnie watched in the direction of the stairs until she heard her mother get to the top and start down the hallway to her bedroom. Then she turned to Charlene and smiled flirtatiously. "What did you say your name was? Before it was Charlene?"

"Charlie."

"Charlie. I'm very pleased to meet you."

"And I am delighted to meet you."

Minnie sat down again next to Charlie and took him by the hand. "Charlie, we aren't getting any younger. We'd best start courting."

And then a second wave of shyness came over both of them and they sat quietly, side by side, just holding hands until it was time for Charlie to drive home to become Charlene before the first rooster crowed and his comings and goings might be noted by Heaven's early risers. Minnie stood at the door and looked at the taillights of the Ford receding down the driveway. She stayed there till the sun peeked over the horizon of an amazing new day, milked Bossy Flossie, then crawled into the daybed for a nap before her parents would wake up and need her help. She pulled her pillow into an embrace and fell asleep imagining what it would be like to sleep in a double bed with her beloved. She still couldn't quite imagine Charlie as Charlie, not the whole person who sported skirts and had breasts and wore makeup, but with eyes closed she could remember every shampoo, and imagine his strong hands in hers, her hands in his. Charlie's hands.

* * *

After that first house call, everyone in Heaven seemed to think that it just made sense for Charlene to go out to the Kelso farm once a week on Friday afternoon to wash and set Minnie's hair and Laura's too. Anyone would do whatever they could to help a neighbor out in a time of need, and with Paul an invalid and Laura losing her wits, this surely was a time of need for Minnie. Helen continued bringing eggs on Mondays for their weekly trade of eggs for milk. Ida started her day there Tuesday mornings and Thelma came in the afternoons to sit with Paul while Minnie and Laura tended Bossy Flossie. Lester stopped by on Wednesday afternoons and Friday mornings at the crack of dawn to take a couple rounds of milking. Herman took to calling before he left the market to see if the Kelsos needed anything from his store. And if there was a prescription to fill, Evelyn Wasmuth at the pharmacy would drive it out to drop it off.

In their weekly visits, a routine quickly developed. Charlene would do Minnie's hair first, then Laura's. She'd pack up all her things while Minnie put her mother to bed and checked on her dad to make sure he was all right.

Then they'd make a pot of coffee and sit at the kitchen table telling each other lifetimes of stories. Charlie told Minnie about Kirbyville, Texas, and the creek where he watched tadpoles, took mud baths, and hid from bullies; Minnie told Charlie about the day her father taught her how to milk a cow, and surprised her by squirting a stream of hot fresh milk right into her mouth. Charlie told of his sister Hannah's antics; Minnie told of her brother Gabe's love of animals. She told him that she'd known Warren from before they could walk. He told her about going to dental school in Dallas and meeting Anne at church.

"I know it's selfish of me," she confessed, "but I'm glad you didn't live happily ever after in Dallas. When Don Harris came to town I got so jealous, and I thought there was something wrong with me. It was that carnival lady—the one who reads palms—who knew. She said things to, well, to reassure me I guess."

"What did she tell you?"

"That my love was natural." Minnie blushed. Charlie took her hands and cradled them in his own. He traced along the backs of her fingers, outlining the shape of each fingernail while he thought a little about what to say next.

"She told me," he finally said, "that the love in my life would last."

"You know the train from Louisville up to Chicago used to come right by our house. Now it's just the ten forty-five freight, but there used to be passenger trains. My bedroom window looks right out onto the tracks. Some nights I'd wake up or couldn't sleep in the first place, and I'd sit in bed and wait for that Louisville train to come by. It generally was on time, came through at one forty-two in the morning. Sometimes I'd see things, you know. People in sleepers doing all kinds of things like they had their curtains shut but they didn't. One time there was a full moon, and something must've been on the tracks. Maybe they hit a cow, or just had some mechanical trouble that delayed them. So there that train sat, more or less right outside my window, the light of that full moon shining right into the train. And there were two women in one of the sleeper cars . . ." Minnie blushed again. "Well, kissing and . . . whatnot. It didn't look natural to me."

"Do I seem unnatural to you?"

"Land sakes, no. You're just . . . Charlene . . . and Charlie. No, I can understand you wanting to be like a woman. Well, not like those women I saw on the train. It seems to me God made men and women to be with each other."

"Maybe God gets a little confused sometimes and isn't real clear about which one He's made."

"You believe that?"

"I don't know what to believe. One of my friends in Chicago feels that way. He's getting an operation to change."

Minnie shook her head. "I just can't imagine that. Well, I don't suppose it's my right to judge. If I'd never found out you were a man, I'd still . . ." She trailed off, flustered. "Charlie?"

"Yes?"

"Now that I know, it feels funny to me that you wear a dress and have long hair. I know you have to. But maybe when we court you could bring some pants to wear. After my folks are asleep. Would that be all right?"

So Charlene shopped for a wig with a modified widow's peak and cut her hair. Everyone admired her new look, which wasn't a whole lot different from the old look. When she came out to the Kelso farm, she could make a fast change to Charlie once Laura and Paul were asleep. Only Minnie could see the gray hair growing in, accentuating the difference between Charlene and Charlie.

One unusually warm night they stood outside in nearly full moonlight. Charlie put his arm around Minnie and they stood in silence for a good long time, looking out into the night at a tiny point of light in the distance. "The ten forty-five'll be by here any minute," said Minnie.

"Did you ever imagine getting on one of those trains to see where it went?"

"No, I can't imagine leaving. Never could. I've never wanted to leave Heaven. No, that's not true. I wanted to go away to college but Dad said there was only enough money to send one to college and that was my brother. He went down to Bloomington. Dad wanted him to study animal husbandry so he could come back and help run the farm. But then the war came along and he enlisted. He and Warren and Lester Breck and Lester's cousin Will.

"Gabe had a sweetheart. Someone you know, in fact. He was dating Stella. And we would go out on double dates and talk about the way we'd have a double wedding when they got back from overseas and then build the houses. Then Gabe and Stella had a falling out, and she started dating Walter. Walter never went overseas because he had such flat feet the army rejected him. He worked at Hoosier Chemicals, though, so he did his part for the war effort. Warren and I were still engaged, though, and he bought me a ring and gave it to me just before they shipped out. And of course you know the rest. Gabe fell for Sheila out west, and Warren went for a French girl. At least Gabe brought his bride home to meet us that first Christmas. Warren never came back at all. Got as far as New York, or wherever it was they actually discharged him, turned around, and went right back to Paris."

"But if he'd have come back, you would have married him."

"Why, of course! We were engaged. We had set the date. I got my hair done."

"I remember." Charlie parted her hair in the middle with his finger. "You wanted something young, but not too young either. Not too fuddy-duddy. With bangs."

"I think I've become a fuddy-duddy."

"So have I. A gray-haired fuddy-duddy."

"I think I hear it." The long moan of a whistle sounded in the distance.

The train was visible now, a string of lights chugging its way across the horizon, heading their way. It slowed down as it approached the railroad crossing on Center Road, and followed the curve of the river as it rumbled on into and through Heaven, coming within a couple hundred feet of where they stood. And even though it was only a freight train, and Charlie was wearing pants, Minnie moved away.

"Afraid someone will see us?"

Minnie felt herself redden. "Yes," she confessed.

"I don't want you to be afraid all the time." His heart ached, seeing her in such distress. "Maybe I should leave. Go back to Chicago."

"Don't you dare!" She pulled Charlie back to her and planted a kiss. "It's time I stopped worrying."

*   *   *

Paul died in his sleep at the end of September.

"There you go, Mrs. Kelso. Do you want to see how it looks?" Charlene held a mirror up for Laura, who looked at her blankly.

"It looks great, Mom." Minnie watched them from across the room. "Thank you, Charlene—I know Mom would if she could." They were becoming quite practiced in switching from being female friends to being sweethearts and back again, depending upon the time, the place, and whether there were any witnesses.

"Don't mention it. I'll put a net on it so it doesn't get too mussed up when she sleeps."

"Okey-dokey, Mom, time for bed."

"Just keep the net on at night, and it'll comb out real nice in the morning."

"You need to tinkle before you go to sleep, Mom?"

"No, I don't believe I do."

"Why don't we go anyway. Just in case, like you always used to say."

*　*　*

Laura paced a two-step, dancing back and forth as she stared in agitation at the kitchen clock. "Oh my. I don't know where Daddy is and it's time to go to church." It was actually Saturday, but she knew that when she got dressed up, it was church time.

"Mom, it's okay. Dad isn't coming with us today."

"He isn't? He'd never miss church. Why isn't he coming?"

"He's meeting us there, okay?" Minnie steered her mother out the door and down the walk.

"Where is he?" Laura allowed herself to be led by her daughter, but she stopped suddenly, attacked by a thought. "Maybe we should wait here for him. If he comes home and we aren't here . . ."

"He'll be at the church, Mom. You'll see. Let's go now so we aren't late." Minnie opened the car door and stood ready to help Laura get situated.

"Do I look all right?"

"You look wonderful, Mom."

"Is my hair in place?"

"It's beautiful."

Laura furrowed her brow, trying to remember something, and Minnie took advantage of her distraction to gently guide her mother into the car, close and lock the door, and get herself into the driver's seat.

Laura touched her hair, noticing the unfamiliar sensation of a tight curl. "Did someone come to do my hair?"

"That was Charlene."

"Does she go to our church?"

"She sure does, Mom." Minnie started the car.

"Wait!"

"What, Mom?"

"Aren't we going to wait for Daddy?"

"Remember what I just told you?" Minnie asked and immediately wanted to bite her tongue. Of course Laura didn't remember. She barely remembered Minnie as her daughter, let alone an exchange of five minutes ago. Asking if she remembered only made her knot up in frustration.

"I forgot. I forget so much these days. I just don't know what's happening to my mind. I've got holes in my head. My stupid head." Laura started to cry.

"You're doing fine, Mom." Minnie patted Laura's hand, eased up on the clutch, and started down the driveway. The car wheels crushed the drifting leaves, releasing spicy fall smells into the air to mix with the exhaust.

Laura liked riding in the car. She rolled her window down and let the breeze bring her the scents of autumn, smiling until she smelled, then saw, a leaf pile burning as they drove past. Minnie did her best to head off Laura's anxiety. "Brush pile, Mom," she said. "It's still enough to burn today. Maybe I should do something with our leaf pile when we get back."

"I don't think it's a good idea to burn leaves," Laura fretted.

"I'll walk the mower over them and chop them up," Minnie promised, "then put them on the garden. They'll be good mulch for the brussels sprouts."

Conversation about the garden carried them to the little church, where Herman Hess was ushering. He'd put a "Reserved for Kelso Family" sign on a sawhorse by the street just in front of the entrance.

"Isn't that nice, Mom? We don't have to walk far at all. Good morning, Herman."

"Good morning, Minnie, Mrs. Kelso," Herman nodded.

Laura stood uncertainly, peering at Herman, unable to make his face into a meaningful image.

"Are you ready to go in?" Herman asked.

"Give us just a minute," Minnie said.

As Herman turned to welcome others who had just arrived, Minnie took Laura's hand, holding it firmly while she looked into her mother's restless eyes. "Mom, I know it's hard for you to remember some things, and especially what I'm going to tell you now. We're here at the church for Dad's funeral."

"Funeral?"

"Yes. Dad died."

"Daddy died?"

"Yes, Mom. Four days ago."

Laura worked hard to understand the words.

"We're going into the church now for the funeral service, and afterward we'll ride to the cemetery for the burial."

"Oh, look! There's that woman who came to our house."

Minnie turned to see Charlene walking up Church Street.

"Charlene," she called. "She's the one who fixed your hair so nice," she told Laura, who put a hand to her hair and smiled at the return of a sliver of memory and the feel of the curls. She loved having her hair curled, but Paul had forbidden paying anyone to do it, even Agnes Siebold in the old days, so even after Laura's hands had gotten too arthritic to manage the do-it-yourself perms she had to sneak out to see Agnes. Then a magical woman had arrived to make her feel like a queen in her own kitchen.

Laura reached out to take Charlene's hand as they entered the church, and insisted Charlene sit next to her in the family section. There was room, because Gabe had called to say he'd used all his vacation time and besides he wasn't sure but what it might upset Laura more to see him and then have to say goodbye again than it was worth. The friends and neighbors around them all took in the scene and were relieved that Laura wasn't going to latch on to them, with her lost urgent eyes. They had no problem with Charlene sitting in the family section.

Throughout the short service, Laura clutched Charlene's hand in her own, and with her other hand she touched her perm. Afterward, she agreed to ride in the hearse only if Charlene would ride next to her. Wild wings beat in Minnie's chest. This is what it would be like to have a real husband. Someone who would be the pillar of strength for her mother to lean on. Someone who would soothe by virtue of his very presence.

At the graveside, as the casket was lowered, Laura smiled, still clutching Charlene and patting her hair every once in a while. Charlene caught Minnie's eye and Minnie felt her chest crack open. Great wracking sobs exploded. In a move imperceptible to all but the two of them, Charlene started to pull away from Laura and move to Minnie and Minnie shook her head no, warning Charlene away. It was Helen who saved the day. She made her way through the cluster of mourners to stand by Minnie's side. Stoic, sensible, reserved Helen put a hand on Minnie's back. "You go ahead and cry all you want," she told her, and that's just what Minnie did. Helen just kept patting her back and telling her it was okay. And even Helen shed a few tears.

Pastor Van Pelt had seen this sort of thing before. The opening of emotional floodgates, the way folks who held everything together fell apart and the way friends rallied to their support, and the way, once it was over, no one would ever mention it again. He kept preaching.

It didn't do to stop and let undue attention be called to people who were suddenly showing private emotions in public.

By the time he finished, Minnie composed herself. In fact, he timed his remarks to go on precisely as long as she needed in order to do so. When she was calm again, he invited the assembled to join him in the Lord's Prayer. And then, concluding his remarks in the name of the Father, the Son, and the Holy Ghost, he commended Paul's spirit to heaven and gestured to the pallbearers. They each shook a shovel of dirt into the grave and then the gravediggers took over the rest of the burial while those who'd come to see Paul off stepped out of mourner formation and transformed into informal, quietly buzzing clusters. In twos and threes, they came by to touch Minnie's hand and gaze briefly and mutter their condolences. "So sorry for your loss." "He was a good man, your father." In lower voices they would lean in and say, "It's a blessing your mother doesn't understand."

Charlene appeared, Laura still attached. "I'll take her home," she offered, "and sit with her until you get back if you want. Unless you think she'd rather go over to Lester and Helen's for a bite of supper first."

"I want to go home," Laura announced before Minnie had a chance to respond. Laura turned to Charlene and tugged on her arm. "Take me home now."

"Okay." Minnie had to work to keep from dissolving again. "I'll bring some leftovers from the buffet. I won't be long."

At Lester and Helen's, where everyone gathered for ham, scalloped potatoes, green beans, peas, macaroni salad, Jell-O laced with fruit cocktail, and angel food cake, Minnie stayed close to Helen. She drew strength from her friend's almost military bearing.

Ida was solicitous, but when she began to enthuse about how helpful Charlene had turned out to be, Minnie excused herself and went to the bathroom. In another world, she would reward Ida's faithful friendship by confiding in her. In this one, she screamed silently until she felt like she was in control again.

She pulled into her driveway with two plates piled high and wrapped tightly in aluminum foil, the ritual "life goes on" comfort food that seems to follow all funerals. Charlene met her at the door and took the plates to the refrigerator. "Tomorrow's dinner," she said. "Laura was hungry and tired, so we had cream of wheat for supper and I helped her get into bed. She's sound asleep now, but she wouldn't close her eyes until I promised to come next week to do a shampoo and set." Charlene smiled and leaned forward to place a kiss on Minnie's lips. "I told her I'd be happy to."

Minnie pulled the curtains shut.

"I want you to look like a man when you do that."

Charlene pulled the careful blonde curls from her head and Charlie stood now, wearing a dress, but Charlie to be sure. "Come here so you don't see what I'm wearing." He pulled Minnie to him and kissed her all over her face so she had to close her eyes.

"If you want to, we'll leave Heaven," he murmured to her. "Charlene will close up shop and Charlie will wait for you and your mother wherever you want to go."

"I couldn't ask you to . . ."

Charlie put a manicured finger to Minnie's lips. "You can ask me to do anything. You can ask me to go jump in the lake. You can ask me to be a dentist again. Anything. I'll do whatever you want me to do."

And then Minnie collapsed against Charlene's chest, Charlie's chest, Charlie's chest feeling like Charlene's chest, but Charlie's chest, and the next thing you know it was just Charlie and Minnie clinging to each other as if their lives depended on it.

Minnie had thought about this moment. She'd worried that her body, though virginal, was not the way it was when she was eighteen and imagined a wedding night. She had worried that she wouldn't know what to do. Worried that her increasingly erratic periods would interfere, or worse yet, that when this moment happened it would happen when she would be fertile. Charlie, too, had worried. Worried that so many years—decades even—of celibacy would take their toll: that his body would not remember what to do. Worried that it would be difficult for Minnie physically. Worried that it would hurt her.

But here it was: the moment. And in this moment, everything was instinct and nothing was worry. It was perhaps not surprising that his hands found her hair first. Instead of putting every hair in place, though, he mussed it, kissed it, buried his face in it. And while he, who had so often seen his beloved from the very circumscribed point of view of the hairdresser, got to know her now in this entirely new way, she learned who he was underneath all his superb artifice.

Her fingers found the buttons and hooks, opened the clothing. Her nose found the hair on his chest, and nuzzled it. Her hands found the muscles of his back. And then Minnie took his hand and led him ever so quietly to the bottom of the stairs, where without a word they left their shoes, then tiptoed up the stairs past the bedroom where Laura lay sleeping into Minnie's own room.

The need to not wake Laura imposed exquisite limits. Soundlessly, Minnie closed the door, and for the first time since she'd been a teenager, turned the iron key that had rested forever in the lock. Charlie hadn't seen a key like that since Mrs. Hesher's rooming house in Dallas.

A current ran between them; their fingers interlaced, melded together.

If there had ever been a question of Charlie's maleness, there wasn't one now. Pain and pleasure mingled as his free hand fumbled with the urgency to step out of the skirt, the slip, the panties, and most excruciatingly, the wraps. The long, binding cloth that kept him under cover.

Minnie realized his predicament. She dropped his hand and took the end of the wrap, uncoiling it. *Is this real? Am I really doing this?*

Charlie watched as she sat down on the edge of the bed next to where he stood. He could see the part in her hair, and he reached to touch it. To touch her silky curls.

A rush of relief as she pulled the last of the cloth away, and now he sat next to her and tried to control his trembling fingers as he worked her buttons one by one.

Clothes on the floor now. Nothing tidy like his wedding night, cautious, half-clothed and in the dark, but everything tumbled and out in the open, in the light. Nothing hiding them. They fell on top of the sheets. Nothing between them. No nightgown. Just his skin and hers. Her skin so soft! Nothing between them. Nothing at all. And all in silence. Exquisite silence.

"I wish I could marry you," Charlie whispered afterward.

"Why can't you?" Minnie lifted her head to watch his response.

"I'm dead, remember?"

"That's what the army says."

"Yes, that's what the army says."

"But you're not dead."

"No. No, I'm not. I've never felt more alive."

Minnie sat up, pulling the sheet around herself, suddenly modest again. "I would rather we be married if we're going to . . . do this again." And, turning red but forging on, she added, "And I do want to do this again. Let's go to Chicago and get married. We don't need the army's permission. We wouldn't even have to wait if we go to Las Vegas. Or Mexico."

"I don't have anything that proves I'm Charlie."

"Can't you get your birth certificate?"

"I don't know. Maybe. What about your mom?"

"We'll take her along. If she talks back home here about that nice man I married people will just figure her mind is totally gone."

"Back home? How could we come back home here if I'm Charlie?"

Minnie's eyes filled. "I don't know, Charlie. I don't know."

Charlie pulled her to him. "I think we'll have to just go along the way we have been. At least for now. And think about something like marriage later. Unless you want to either leave Heaven or give Ida and Elizabeth and all the other good ladies a heart attack and risk their husbands stringing me up."

"Don't say that!"

"But that's the way it is."

"I suppose."

"Minnie, listen, dearest Minnie. Tonight's not a night to make any more decisions. We'll see each other once a week like we always have and I'll think of you every day in between like I always have and we'll take some time to figure it out."

"I love you, Charlie."

"I love you, Minnie."

"Now you better get out of here before the roosters wake up the neighborhood."

*   *   *

What would they have done without Laura as a cover? Everyone at the funeral had seen how much Laura took to Charlene, and how good Charlene was with Laura. How patient, how reassuring, how kind. No one seemed to ask whether it was really necessary for Charlene to continue to make house calls, now that Paul was dead and in his grave. In fact, they all kept their contributions going.

Charlene started closing her shop an hour early on Fridays and opening two hours later on Saturdays so she had at least a little time to sleep after she got home from the Kelsos before it was time to begin her daily transformation.

Laura was increasingly unable to remember much of anything, but she did retain her fondness for watching Bob Hope's show, and like as not would insist on it before Friday bedtime. It helped to settle her down so that when she went to bed at nine thirty, there'd be three hours that Charlie could spend with Minnie before it was time for a quick shave, costume change, and drive back home.

At first they made plans for a wedding in Chicago. But the more they tried to envision it, the more complicated it became. It wasn't just a matter of taking Laura along. There was the question of who would milk Bossy Flossie, and what tale each would have to tell to convince everyone in Heaven that they just happened to be going out of town during the same week, and how long they'd have to be there to get a license, and before that, even, how long it would take Charlie to be able to get his birth certificate from Kirbyville because his driver's license said "Charlene" on it, and how they'd manage afterward to find married time together and where they would go to live, and well, it just got so impossible to sort out that Charlie finally found himself quoting Ilsa. "Minnie," he said, "maybe we should just be thankful for what we got."

Because when it came right down to it, neither one of them wanted to leave Heaven. Charlie said he was too old to start over, notwithstanding the declaration he'd made to Minnie on the night of Paul's funeral. Heaven was where he'd finally found happiness, so why leave it? And Minnie had never wanted to leave in the first place, couldn't imagine anywhere else on this earth she'd rather be. There was yet another consideration. Though Laura no longer recognized the people who greeted her at church, she did know her house and her routines. It was impossible to imagine her adjusting to life anywhere else.

So they developed rituals and found ways. Minnie started taking Laura to Sunday dinner at Clara's Kitchen, and Laura would demand that Charlene accompany them. So much of their relationship had already been expressed as female friendship that it was not difficult at all to maintain those roles and that relationship in public.

Minnie got a private line, telling the folks at the phone company that she wanted to be sure that if Laura needed an ambulance, she could get through right away. Though Charlene still had a party line at her house, she already had a private line at her shop, so they could talk on the phone first thing in the morning after Charlene got to work, and last thing in the afternoon before she closed up shop. Charlene had never been one to gossip, but she did enjoy calling one day to tell Minnie that Stella had been in for a trim and had opined that Minnie looked wonderful these days. No doubt, Stella had conjectured, it was a result of not having the burden of caring for Paul all the time. Everyone knew how difficult he had always been.

* * *

Charlene could tell right away that something was wrong. She could feel it in the urgency of the little bell over her door ringing as someone pushed it open. Katie Denson was due, but not for another ten minutes. The woman hurrying through the door was Alma Porter. Alma didn't have an appointment, almost never made an appointment. She came in four times a year to get her hair cut as short as fashion and reason would allow, and that was generally it. Not only that, but it was still lunch hour, and people generally went home for lunch, or else stopped in at Clara's Kitchen. They didn't come to the beauty shop over lunch.

Charlene fought a sudden panic that something had happened to Minnie. "Alma, what is it?"

"They shot him." Alma, who never cried, looked like she was about to cry.

"Who? Who got shot?" Charlene's mind raced. "Him" meant Minnie was safe. But what "him" would Alma be talking about? Her husband had long since died. She had no brothers, no sons.

"The president."

"What? Who? What president?"

"The president. They shot Kennedy! He's in surgery. Do you have a radio? He was in a parade in Dallas. The governor was shot too."

Charlene ducked in the back of the shop and grabbed the little transistor she kept there to keep her company in the morning before she opened and in the evening while she cleaned up.

"Did you hear?" The door jangled again as Katie Denson rushed in. Then, registering Alma and Charlene focused on the radio, she asked, "Anything new? Is he going to be all right? Mother of God keep him alive." She could see as Alma looked up at her that the news was not what she prayed to hear.

"They just pronounced him dead."

Katie sagged into the waiting-area chair. "Oh dear Jesus," she gasped. "Oh my dear God, don't tell me they killed him. Oh no!"

They sat in stunned silence for several seconds. Finally Katie spoke again. "He was the first president I ever voted for. With Ike it wasn't going to make a difference anyway. Everybody was voting for him, so I knew my poor little vote wouldn't make a difference. But John Kennedy. Such a handsome man. Much better-looking than Nixon, and smarter by far, too. Oh, those poor children! To have a father killed like that."

"Who would do such a thing?"

Katie bowed her head. "Hail Mary, full of grace," she murmured, fingers grasping for a rosary that wasn't there, choking on words from her childhood. "The Lord is with thee. Blessed art thou amongst women, and blessed is the fruit of thy womb, Jesus. Holy Mary, Mother of God, pray for us sinners, now and at the hour of our death. Amen." She raised a tear-stained face to Charlene. "I'll have to cancel my appointment today. I can't . . . I just couldn't . . . I think I need to go to church."

"That's fine, Katie. Just call me when you want to reschedule."

"I have to get back to the post office," Alma said as they watched through the window while Katie hurried down the street in front of the shop.

"I'll see you later, then."

"Charlene . . ."

"Yes?"

"What's the world coming to?"

Charlene shook her head. "I don't know, Alma. I don't know. I didn't vote for him, but this . . . this is unthinkable. This is. . ."

"A tragedy," Alma finished.

They looked at each other, longer than people in Heaven usually did, until Alma broke the mood of communion.

"Well, I have to get back."

Charlene checked her appointment book. There were two more appointments scheduled, both from Hartford City. She turned off the radio and closed her eyes. Dallas. The entire plaza was new since she'd lived there, finished a few years after she moved to Chicago, though the old buildings around it were ones she'd passed on her way to her dental school classes all those years ago. Fear came over her, tightening her chest. Too much hate in the world. Too much disorder. Opening her eyes, she shook it off and made herself get up. She didn't want to hear any more news. It would arrive soon enough. Someone would burst through the door with the latest. If no one else, Mabel Swanson of Hartford City, due to arrive at two thirty. Later she'd call Minnie. For now, Charlene preferred to fill her mind with ordering and reordering the bottles, brushes, combs, and clips on the counter beneath the mirror. It was something she could control.

It was unusually crowded that Sunday at church, and crowded too at Clara's Kitchen afterward. Evelyn and Herb Wasmuth joined Minnie, Laura, and Charlene at their table. Herb's interest in how the autopsy would have been performed, combined with Laura's incomprehension, gave the conversation a surreal quality. Nonetheless, both Charlene and Minnie felt comforted by being able to sit together in public and share the shock and grief.

*   *   *

Maybe it was that sense of shared tragedy, or maybe it was just that Stella couldn't help herself as a hostess. She loved to serve people food. She loved to serve good people good food. She hated to see anyone feel lonesome, especially herself. So she decided to launch an annual tradition. She made a list of the folks she knew who were single, or couples who were childless, who didn't have a family to gather with on that somber Thanksgiving, and she invited them to Clara's Kitchen for a turkey dinner with all the trimmings. She pressed her husband Walter into service as her waiter, and she did all the cooking. Alma and her daughter Wilma came, Donald Harris was there, Maurice from up the alley, Minnie and Laura, Charlene, Amy, Helen, and Lester, though in deference to his wife, everyone called him Harley when they were within earshot of Helen.

And then, because it had been too sad a week to celebrate so soon after the president's death, she launched another annual tradition and invited them all back on Christmas Day.

No one batted an eye when Charlene started to spend Sunday evenings out at the Kelsos' too. No one would begrudge Minnie some respite from being the only caregiver. So by the time the week of Christmas and New Year's came around, Minnie and Charlene had several opportunities each week to see each other as good friends, and Minnie and Charlie had two nights a week to see each other as lovers.

Christmas Eve, after Laura had been tucked in bed and topped with a feather comforter, Charlie and Minnie sat by the little Christmas tree to exchange gifts. Minnie went first. She could hardly contain her glee as Charlie worked the bow off the package and loosened the paper at its taped joints. Seeing her anticipation, he slowed the process down, the better to enjoy it himself. He carefully folded the paper covered in Santas and sleighs, so it might be used again. He opened the box slowly, and put the lid aside before peeling back the layers of tissue one at a time. The smile on Minnie's face was uncontrollably broad. He paused before opening the final fold and looked at her. Had he ever known such happiness? Finally, because she was bursting with eagerness for him to see his gift and he was so full of feeling that he had to move, to discharge some of the energy, he folded back the last layer. There, nestled in rustling gold paper, was a curled-up pile of fur. At the top end, a tiny face with black beady eyes rested its chin on its glossy brown body. Charlie clapped his hands and Minnie laughed out loud. He pulled the fox fur neckpiece from its nest, and marveled anew at his beloved.

She took it from his hands, draped it around his neck, and pulled the head and tail gently toward her, leaning forward to plant a kiss and say softly, "Merry Christmas."

His voice was thick as he whispered back in her ear, "Now it's my turn. I know we decided it wouldn't be practical, but—" He reached into his pocket. Charlie dropped to one knee as he held out a tiny square of a box and flipped it open with his thumbnail. "Minnie, will you marry me?"

The next day at Clara's Kitchen, they sat in the daze and glow of it all. Minnie's ring was tucked into a pocket where she could, from time to time, slip her finger inside it and sneak a smile across the table. The fox fur spent the day dozing on Minnie's pillow. Everyone around them was so full of Christmas cheer that no one noticed they were particularly bedazzled.

The following week, they rang the new year in together. It was a perfect night. Laura went to bed early, and slept through the night. Charlie and Minnie sat up late, planning a secret wedding. Charlie showed Minnie the birth certificate he'd managed to track down by writing to the county clerk in Jasper County, Texas. New Year's Day all the shops were closed, so Charlene wasn't expected to see anyone until Thursday. They had waffles and sausages for breakfast, and played Scrabble with Laura. That afternoon, they lingered on a goodbye kiss at the door while Laura napped in front of the television.

16

HEAVEN, 1964

The door swung open and a blast of frigid air entered, along with Alma Porter.

"Charlene, do you have room for a walk-in? Just a shampoo."

"If you can wait about twenty minutes. I'm just finishing up here with Sue Ellen Sue. And then I have to put the neutralizer on Evelyn. How do you like the birthday girl's 'do?"

Charlene spun Sue Ellen Sue around in her chair to show Alma the soft curls that framed her nearly ten-year-old face.

"Is today your birthday?"

Sue Ellen Sue was pleased to be able to respond to Alma's question. Now that she was almost ten, a double-digiter, as her father called it, she was eager to develop the social skill of conversing with grown-ups in a way that let them know she was no silly little child.

"No, my actual birthday is Sunday, but I'm having my party tomorrow night. I wanted to get my hair done today so the curls would have a day to relax. I read in *Seventeen* to do that. I showed my dad a picture from the magazine of how I'm getting it done and he said it looks perfect for a double-digiter."

"And how old will you be?" Alma asked.

"Ten." Sue Ellen Sue hoped Alma would notice that it was precocious for a ten-year-old to read *Seventeen* magazine. She was really seven years ahead of her time.

"So you are having a party?" While Charlene rinsed Evelyn's rollers with neutralizer to stop the chemical curling process, Sue Ellen Sue happily filled Alma in on who was invited. Though since Alma had sorted the mail, she already knew who'd gotten invitations, at least the ones sent courtesy of Uncle Sam's delivery service.

"Ellie, Kenny, Sarah, Melanie, Sam, Melissa, George, my aunt Twyla and uncle Rob, Grandma and Grandpa Tipton, and Grandma Rockwell. We're going to have a bunch of stuff to eat."

"What are you serving?"

"Pigs in a blanket, potato chips, coleslaw, soda pop, ice cream, and cake."

"Sounds delish."

Another arctic air blast signaled that Elizabeth Tipton was back from Herman's to pick up her daughter.

"Ready to go?"

"As soon as I get my coat on and pack up my Toni twins."

Sue Ellen Sue ran to the coat tree like someone who had read tips about how a young girl should run, lightly on her feet, her head cocked ever so slightly to the side. She put her coat on, tossed her curls a time or two, just to feel their bounciness, and gathered up Christy and Misty.

"Have a wonderful party," Alma called as they bustled out the door.

"Yes, have a good party, and happy birthday," Charlene added. Ida, who was soaking her hands in lotion in preparation for a manicure with Amy, added her voice to the chorus, as did Amy. Katie, who had been under the dryer and consequently unable to hear the details, simply smiled and waved. Sue Ellen Sue, for all her determination to carry on like a grown-up, failed to acknowledge their good wishes. She was distracted, thinking about giving her Toni twins haircuts and permanent waves, so they'd look just like her. It made her silly with excitement, and she skipped along the street ahead of her mother, who warned her to watch out for ice.

By mid-afternoon a thick, blinding snow had begun to fall. Charlene locked the door to her shop and called Minnie to say she planned to spend the evening at home, as it looked like a bad night for driving. If it cleared by the next afternoon, she could come out Saturday instead. But Saturday, the snow was still falling, mixed with a freezing rain that encased all in a layer of ice. The television reported that businesses in a four-county area were closed, roads were closed, trees and telephone wires in some areas were snapping from the weight of ice and snow. Charlene chipped and shoveled the icy snow from her little walkway three times before acknowledging shortness of breath, a tightness in her chest, and fatigue in her muscles. When another two inches accumulated, she watched for a few minutes from her open front door, marveling at the beauty of streetlight-illumined flakes as they fell, then pulled the door shut. She'd just have to shovel the new stuff in the morning. She brewed a cup of tea and curled up to watch Saturday night television.

Something made her risk it. Sitting there in her house alone, with the snow piling up, thinking of Minnie and Laura so near, yet separated now not by a mile of country road but by a thick blanket of ice-encrusted snow. She didn't want to wait for the safety of her private line at the shop. She picked up the party-line phone and, miracle of miracles, it was still working. She dialed Minnie's number, thrilled like a teenager to hear the bleating signal that a mile away was being transformed into the ring Minnie heard. Minnie picked up on the second one.

"Minnie," Charlene said, always mindful of the possibility that nosy neighbors on the line were listening in, "how are you and Laura holding up? Do you have everything you need to get through this storm?"

"Oh yes." Minnie's voice made Charlene smile. Everything about Minnie made Charlene smile. "We were just watching Bing Crosby," Minnie said, "singing 'I've Got My Love to Keep Me Warm,' but then the power went out for just a minute and when it came back, the television reception was still out. Our transistor radio works, though."

Charlene ran a hand down her left shin and up her calf, feeling the stubble. "I've kept busy shoveling the walk," she said, "but I got tired of that after the third time. I've decided I'm just going to relax and enjoy myself since there's nothing else I can do anyway. I watched Lawrence Welk, and now I've got *The Hollywood Palace* on, too. My TV is still working."

At the other end of the phone line, Minnie settled into the corner of her sofa and leaned her head back, sandwiching the receiver between her ear and the pillow, imagining lying in her bed snuggled next to Charlie. "We made chocolate chip cookies," she said, "and hot cocoa with marshmallows on top, like Mom used to make for Gabe and me on nights like this. It's so funny, the way I'm more like the mom now and she's like the child. She wanted to know if we're going to Stella's for dinner tomorrow. Isn't that something? She's forgotten Dad and half the time doesn't remember my name, but she remembers where she gets a good meal!"

Charlene laughed. "No one ever forgets Stella's cooking. I'm surprised the phone lines are still working," she added. "The last time we had an ice storm like this, I remember my phone going out for almost two days."

"They say there's another three to four inches still headed our way," Minnie said. "I imagine by morning the lines may snap."

"I imagine so."

"I guess we'll just sit tight until it all melts," Minnie said. "They said on the weather report it might be Tuesday night or Wednesday morning."

"I wonder if Sue Ellen Sue had her party."

"Huh?"

"Sue Ellen Sue was telling us at the shop yesterday all about her tenth birthday party. It was supposed to be this afternoon, but I imagine they probably had to cancel it."

"Or postpone," Minnie suggested. "Elizabeth isn't one to just cancel something if she's put good money into setting it up."

They went on that way, luxuriating in small talk, remembering other snowstorms, concurring that snow was preferable to rain, except you need a certain amount of rain for crops to grow, of course; wondering how long this new show *Hollywood Palace* would be on ABC, now that *The Jerry Lewis Show* had been canceled; agreeing they preferred Bing Crosby to Jerry Lewis and wondering who the guest host would be next time. Minnie asked who had been in the shop Thursday and Friday besides Sue Ellen Sue, and Charlene caught her up on all the news she'd overheard.

"We sound like an old married couple," Minnie dared to say, "catching up on gossip at the end of the day."

Charlene, who had listened carefully throughout their conversation and heard no telltale clicks signifying eavesdroppers, dared drop into Charlie for a moment. "I can't imagine a better life than to be half of an old married couple with you. That's my idea of heaven on earth."

Minnie had time to echo Charlie's sentiments before she had to cut the conversation off. "Mom's ready to get off the pot and she's calling for me. Just a minute, Mom," she yelled away from the phone, and then spoke softly into it. "I love you, Charlie."

"And I love you," Charlie whispered back. "Till death do us part."

"I'll see you Friday." Minnie made a smooching sound and hung up the phone.

Bing was still crooning on ABC. Charlene was suddenly aware of feeling a little queasy, and her arms ached from all the shoveling she'd done. She decided a hot bath would feel good. Outside the ice was piling up on the tree limbs. The streetlight caught the crystals and made them glow. While the tub filled with hot water, Charlene sat at the front window and watched the cold clear coating of everything familiar, so that it was transformed into something that looked like a scene from *Fantasia*. She turned the TV off and got into a bathrobe while she waited for the tub to finish filling. When it was as high as it could get without wasting water in the overflow, she leaned over, turned the water off, and imagined Minnie climbing into a bath at the same time out at her house. Her very last thought, as she began to straighten up, was how good the hot water was going to feel.

*   *   *

Ida opened her door to see if the newspaper had been delivered just as Trey Shaw came running by. "Is school still closed?" Ida called to him.

"The hairdresser lady is dead," he yelled back, and then blushing ferociously, added, "and she's not a lady at all!"

"What are you talking about?"

"I was walking through the alley and heard a screaming and saw the cop car there and saw the door open and looked in to see if I could help and Mrs. Breck and Officer Hess was there so I just peeked in a little."

"I can't understand a word you're saying."

"The hairdresser lady."

"Charlene?"

"She's dead, but she's a man. I gotta go." With that, Trey took off down the street. Ida was fourth on the scene at Charlene's house, confirming Trey's account.

She went right to Clara's Kitchen with the news, and that's why Minnie was spared hearing from her first. Helen, bless her heart, had called the Kelso farm right there from Charlene's living room. She didn't tell Minnie directly what had happened, but she ordered her to take her phone off the hook until she could get out there. Minnie was puzzled, but did what Helen told her to do. When Ida called from the counter phone at Clara's Kitchen, she got a busy signal.

Helen arrived at the Kelso farm within minutes and was relieved to see Laura napping. She sat Minnie down at the kitchen table and told her straight out. "There's some terrible news and I didn't want you to be taken by surprise. Minnie, I know she meant a lot to you ..."

Minnie felt her stomach clench. She knew from the shift in Helen's voice that it was something to do with Charlene. It had to be. She'd managed not to worry all day Sunday and Monday, and even Tuesday, because the phone lines had indeed gone out sometime around midnight Saturday, and had not been repaired until late Tuesday night, but she'd expected a call Wednesday morning from the shop.

"You know me, Minnie. I'm not good at beating around the bush, much as I'd like to. Charlene is dead. I had an appointment at ten and she wasn't there—well you know she's always there for her appointments. I just had a bad feeling about it. I called information from Clara's and tried her phone but there was no answer so I went over to the police station and asked Harry to go with me to check in, make sure she was all right. She didn't answer when we knocked, so we went on in. Looked like she went suddenly, must have been a heart attack. Looked like she was about to take a bath. Minnie, are you all right?"

Minnie was staring wild-eyed at Helen.

"Minnie?"

"She's dead?"

"Yes. And there's something more."

"She was about to take a bath?"

"Yes, she was in her bathrobe."

The stunned shock on Minnie's face convinced Helen that the next news she delivered was beyond Minnie's ability to imagine.

Helen was still there when Ida arrived. Fortunately, Laura woke up at the same time and needed Minnie's attention, so Helen was able to deflect Ida, tell her Minnie already knew. Ida fretted and fussed, wondering who Minnie had been talking to on the phone, then saw that it was sitting off the hook. "Minnie?" she called into the living room, "do you know your phone is off the hook?"

"Oh my goodness, no. Hang it up for me, will you?"

Out in the living room, Minnie was relieved to have her mother awake, to help her to the toilet, to get her into clean clothes. In the kitchen, Helen suggested to Ida that since Minnie was so busy, they probably should be on their way. She popped her head into the living room and told Minnie as much, catching her eye, winking. Minnie returned the gesture with a grateful hint of a smile, but even from across the room, Helen could see the tears that were streaming down her face. "I'll call you later," she promised, and hustled Ida out before she could see Minnie's grief.

* * *

Herb Wasmuth had seen a lot in his day. He'd put pieces of Pops Breck's body back together after the combine accident so it could be tucked into a suit and put on display. He'd patched up Sonny Fleeson's mangled remains when the young prom king wrapped his car around the big oak out on River Road coming back from the party in Hartford City. He'd made Maude Colbert look pretty again when she'd finally given in to the cancer that ravaged her mouth and throat, and put twenty attractive pounds back on Mable Dumbauld when stomach cancer finally took her to the next world.

When they first brought Charlene in, they had her robe wrapped around her, and brought one of her Sunday outfits along. But before he left, Harry Hess motioned Herb to him away from the corpse, as if the dead hairdresser might somehow overhear. The men moved instinctively to confer across the room in low voices.

"I don't want you to be shocked, Herb."

"You know that's pretty hard to do."

"I know. You're gonna see something here that's gonna shock you. I just wanted you to be prepared."

What, Herb wondered, could he possibly see that he hadn't at some point or another already seen? Did she have some skin disease? Cut her wrists? Is she missing a breast? Are there boils or bruises?

"She's a he."

"She's what?"

"A he."

Herb looked Harry straight in the eye. He was known as a prankster, but if this was a prank, it surely was in bad taste. "Naw."

"Yeah." Harry wasn't kidding.

"Charlene is . . ."

"Yep."

Harry took deliberate steps back toward the stretcher that bore Charlene's body, and slowly peeled back first the sheet that covered her head to toe and then the bathrobe. Herb paled and turned away.

"I can't do this."

"Can't do what?"

"Prepare the body. I can't put that skirt on a man."

"I know what you mean. My stomach's turned too. But she—he don't have any appropriate clothes for a man. All's we found in the closet were informal clothes. Slacks, you know. For burial, it wouldn't be formal enough. So we—Claude and I—figured mebbe use the skirt and blouse and keep the coffin closed."

"I can't do it."

"I know what you mean."

"It's not Christian."

"Tell you what. Claude and I are gonna meet with some of the ladies that were customers, see if they know anything about a next of kin. We'll see if they agree it'd be best to keep it closed. Then you could put . . ." He couldn't quite come up with a pronoun. " . . . the body in the slacks. No one would ever have to know."

*   *   *

Claude Tipton cleared his throat and paced a little at the front of the meeting room at the police station. It was crowded, usually having to accommodate a half dozen people at most. Now twice as many were packed in. "First of all, I want to thank you for coming down to the station today. I know this is a difficult time for all you ladies, and we're going to make it as quick as we can. Anytime there's something comes out unusual like this at a person's deceasement . . ."

"Doncha mean death, Claude?" Harry Hess hated fancy language.

Claude ignored Harry and continued. "We have to do an investigation. Just to make sure, you know, that there's no foul play. Now as far as we can tell, the deceased didn't have family. We did find a birth certificate, so we know the real name was Charles Ernst Bader. We found copies of tax forms the deceased had filed. There were no dependents listed. Do any of you recall ever hearing the deceased talk about family?"

Minnie wondered if it was obvious to everyone that she had plenty to tell and was deliberately withholding it. Her ears burned and she knew from the fiery heat she felt that her face was bright red. But she couldn't bring herself to offer any information. She was afraid one thing would lead to another. That she'd spill the secrets that had just days ago filled her heart with unbearable love and now ripped it with unfathomable grief.

"I believe," Elizabeth offered, "the deceased had a sister named Hannah who lived in a nursing home in Indianapolis who died some years ago." Like Claude, Elizabeth couldn't quite yet resolve for herself whether to call Charlene "he" or "she." Ida concurred, and looked to Minnie to confirm the fact.

"Yes," Minnie managed to say, silently thanking them for taking the lead. "I believe Charlene did say something about a sister." She searched her memory. It was she who'd told others in Heaven about the dead sister, long years ago, when Charlene first had come to town.

"There's no one else in the family," Wilma reported. When everyone turned in surprise to hear her offer such a definitive bit of personal news about someone, she explained. "Charlene told me once when she first moved here that she was alone. Her folks died of the flu before her sister died."

The question of next of kin having been answered, Harry and Claude moved on to a short list of additional questions that drew clear and emphatic answers. Yes, Charlene did go to Chicago every now and then for business reasons. No, no one knew what the business was. They always assumed it had something to do with keeping up on the latest hairstyles and products. No, no one knew who she was in contact with in Chicago. No, she certainly didn't have any enemies. Land sakes, no!

When Harry broached the delicate question of whether the casket might be closed, to spare onlookers a spectacle (not to mention sparing Herb considerable discomfort), the response was immediate and fierce. Funerals at First Christian were always open casket. Folks wanted to be able to see a body looking natural, healthy, in peaceful repose, and thanks to Herb's skills, they always did.

Claude and Harry did their best to persuade the ladies that it just would be too upsetting to display, but to no avail. Not only that, but the women wanted Charlene buried just as they knew her. Take the news back to Herb, they told Claude and Harry, that we want the casket open and the body to be Charlene's.

Herb didn't like it. He didn't like preparing Charlene's body to look like a woman, even though it was no more preparation than Charlene had done every day of her life in Heaven. Herb worried that people would come just to gawk. He didn't think that would be dignified. So he took it upon himself to dress the body in slacks and close the casket before opening the doors to the viewing chapel.

It was Herb's own wife who sounded the alarm among the women. They wanted to pay their last respects, and if they gawked a little in the process, what of it? Weren't they entitled? They who'd been living their lives a story at a time, shared in Charlene's shop? They'd been open, trusting, honest (at least as far as any of them would admit) in that shop. They'd told Charlene just about anything that was on their minds, or ever had been, or ever might be. And she'd been faithful to them. No detail shared with her ever found its way back into the rumor mill. Charlene could keep a secret. They wanted her to be able to take her secret to the grave with her. Never mind that it was a secret now entirely in the open. So an unprecedented event took place at the Wasmuth Funeral Home.

Helen marched at the head of the line, followed by Evelyn, Alma, Wilma, Elizabeth, Stella, Ida, Katie, Eunice, Amy, and Minnie, with an uncomprehending Laura in tow. It was a parade of determination, a path of loyalty to Charlene, yes, but just as importantly it was an insistence on the principle of the thing. A person's secrets were a person's secrets, no matter how much they became public knowledge.

So a baffled and reluctant Herb closed the chapel, took the corpse back into his workroom, and changed its clothes. He put the wig back on. He removed the pants. He dressed Charlene in the light gray wool suit with a bright pink silk blouse. Given that there were mourners waiting to pay their respects, and he felt decidedly squeamish about touching the corpse too intimately, he chose not to bother with pantyhose, but to just slip the high heels on that would show by their shape under the velvet casket blanket that the outfit was complete. His hand shook as he tried to apply the lipstick, so he called Evelyn in to add the finishing touches.

* * *

Minnie came first thing the next morning in order to have some time alone with her beloved. She looked down at Charlene, laid out in that stylish gray wool suit with the cheerfully pink silk blouse, ruffled at the neck, hiding the collarbone and hint of an Adam's apple that Charlene had explained to her was how she could tell another man even if most would see a woman. She wished it could have been different: that they could have gotten married, lived in the open as man and wife. But how could it have been different? Charlie couldn't have come to Heaven, not as Charlie. Not as a hairdresser. If he'd have never come to Heaven, how empty would Minnie's heart have been all these years?

And if they'd dared discover each other earlier? Charlie had been right about that. A secret like that you just can't keep forever. They couldn't have stayed in Heaven. And neither of them wanted to live anywhere else.

So maybe it was best the way it had worked out, Minnie thought, clinging desperately to math to staunch her grief. They had each other to look forward to for nigh onto nineteen years once a week. How many times was that? Helen would know. She'd know without having to write it down. As many times as she'd stopped by to trade her eggs for Minnie's milk and butter during these same nearly nineteen years.

The chaotic emotion made her knees feel weak. She sat down, and pulled the chair close to the casket.

There was a time when Minnie expected to have not only a husband, but children. She indulged herself for a moment thinking of what children with Charlie would have been like. They might have had sons. At least two, to help out around the farm, to learn the ways of milking and churning, the business of selling milk and the importance of maintaining equipment.

If the timing was right, they might have avoided war. Minnie didn't think much of war, and what it did to men. Her own fiancé deserting her, Charlie so devastated by it he gave up his masculinity nearly altogether, her brother getting the notion that there was a better place to be than home helping on the farm. He even said once that San Luis Obispo was more heavenly than Heaven. What kind of a name was that for a town?

Maybe she and Charlie would have had girls. Of course, then you have to worry about someone taking advantage, like what happened to poor Melinda. What if she'd had a child like that?

Or they might have had one of each: a boy and a girl.

Gerbil-like, her thoughts raced in the cage of her mind, the what-ifs? and why-nots? They built to a crazy crescendo: *How can this be? How can I go on?*

Minnie was on the verge of losing any vestige of composure when she heard the chapel door behind her open. She resisted the urge to turn around until she sensed someone standing behind her to her right, then glanced back through the blur of tears to see Elizabeth. Minnie nodded hello and Elizabeth moved up to sit beside her.

"I still can't believe it." Elizabeth stared at the elegant corpse. "Can you?" Minnie dabbed at her tears with a hankie and watched Elizabeth from the corner of her eye. "Frederick said it was a disgrace to have an open casket like this but I told him it was a necessity. Especially after all those stories."

"Stories?"

"You know, just the stories about Charlene being—not really being a woman. Being a man."

"But the stories are true."

"I know they're true. But that's not how I want to remember her. I refuse to have my picture change to someone I can't trust. She looks wonderful, doesn't she? Just like she was in life. So elegant. She always did look good in pink. It sets off her blue eyes so beautifully. I'll tell you what, though. I would never want to go through this again. I don't like the idea of some man having his hands on me when I don't even know he's a man. So from now on, I'll go to Michael's up in Fort Wayne. At least I know what he is! I was trying to keep Sue Ellen Sue from knowing all the sordid details, but you know she overheard Frederick and me talking about the open casket thing and she just pestered me till I had to tell her. Well, I'd rather she heard it from me than from other kids. You know how they get things confused. How they exaggerate. Do you know she'd actually already heard? Trey Shaw told her. You know what she asked me? What's an erection! I said where did you hear anybody talk about that? She said she overheard Trey Shaw telling the boys at school that Charlene had the biggest erection you ever saw. I told her Trey Shaw had no business talking like that, and she should just put it out of her head."

"Is that true? Does a man . . . when he dies, does. . ."

"I don't know," Elizabeth pondered. "I expect I've got a fifty-fifty chance of finding out someday. If Frederick goes before I do."

Minnie felt a pang. Helen had seen her Charlie like that. In broad daylight. Harry had. Even the Shaw boy. It's not what Charlie would have wanted.

"The hair doesn't look quite the same," Elizabeth said.

"It's the same," Minnie said. She wished Elizabeth would go away. But it got worse. Elizabeth went on.

"Why would anyone do something like that? Frederick said if Charlene was younger he'd have guessed she was trying to get out of serving in the war, but they weren't drafting men that old."

"Maybe he did serve." Minnie couldn't abide this attack on Charlie's honor. "I believe they allowed doctors and dentists to volunteer even if they were above draft age. Maybe he was a doctor or a dentist." Lord, it was so galling to know all the details and not be able to say them right out!

Elizabeth laughed. "I doubt Charlene was a doctor," she said. "Though I guess she did make a few house calls, didn't she? When she came out to your place, did she act any different?"

"Than what?"

"Well, you know. Than she did in the shop."

"She was entirely herself," Minnie said.

"Sue Ellen Sue is so disappointed," Elizabeth prattled on. "She loved every minute she got to spend in Charlene's shop. She told me once she wanted to be Charlene when she grew up. Isn't that cute? She was just four then. You can be yourself and be like Charlene, I told her. Be a hairdresser and fix everyone's hair, but still be Sue Ellen Sue. Oh, she said, okay. Kids are something, aren't they?"

"I imagine they are," Minnie allowed. "I wouldn't know myself."

"They wear you out but they're a blessing." She stood and stepped up to the coffin. "Herb did a beautiful job," she said, "as usual. Look how the casket lining is just dark enough to set off the light gray of her suit. Who's with your mom?"

"Lester."

"Lester's a good man."

"Yes, yes he is."

"If you ask me, Helen got the cream of the crop with him," Elizabeth said.

"Yes, she did."

"Don't tell Frederick I said that." Elizabeth laughed a little self-conscious laugh, as if she'd betrayed something or someone, perhaps herself.

"And Lester got the smartest, prettiest woman in town," Minnie asserted.

Elizabeth flinched a bit inwardly, because it was true. If it hadn't been for her home ec grade, Helen would have been valedictorian the year Elizabeth was salutatorian. "Of course," she said, "it didn't save them from heartbreak, did it?"

"No, it surely didn't."

"You never know," pronounced Elizabeth.

"No, you never do," said Minnie.

They stayed for a few moments more in silence. Finally, Minnie stood again and stepped next to Elizabeth at the side of the coffin. She directed some silent thoughts to Charlie. To Charlene. To her friend. To the love of her life, to her secret admirer. To her secret heartthrob. To her confidante. To who would have been her husband in fact, who was her husband in spirit. To the whole complicated person who lay there, beyond the reach now of such mortal confusion and doubt.

"I'll miss her," Elizabeth said.

Minnie was surprised to hear a catch in Elizabeth's voice. It was all she could manage, her voice thick with the unsaid, to respond, "Yes, me too."

They walked to the parking lot together. If Elizabeth knew, Minnie thought, would she understand? Maybe, maybe not. But no one could ever know. How Heaven might respond to finding out that Charlie and Minnie had held out on the town, that Minnie had participated in Charlie's deception of them, well, that was a precipice over which she was unwilling to plunge. It would change too much. Most importantly, it would allow others into the world she and Charlie had kept exclusively their own. She'd be prodded with questions, be pitied perhaps, perhaps be censured. Most definitely, there would be plenty of talk, and most of it would be behind her back. No. She couldn't abide the thought that anyone would judge what she and Charlie had together. When they buried Charlene tomorrow they would bury Minnie's story right alongside and there it would stay.

Minnie sat in her Chevy and waited for Elizabeth to pull out of the parking lot. She had to be careful. She was raw, on the edge. She sucked in the winter air, crisp and biting in her lungs, and let it out with deep, wounded sighs. What was it Charlie's mom used to tell him? "You rest, you rust." She would rust quickly if she rested, she thought. Rivulets of rust would trace the tears that kept insisting on leaking out. Her face would crack apart, crumble to red dust. There would be no end to it. And who would care for Laura, affable and confused, who was waiting for her right now, even though she probably wasn't quite sure who it was she awaited? Who would milk Bossy Flossie? Who would manage leasing the fields? She had to go on. She couldn't pine and wallow in regret.

She started the engine and eased the car out of the lot onto the icy street. It came to her in a flash. There *was* something she could do, a covenant she could keep with herself and her dear Charlie. Next week, she would go up to Michael's in Fort Wayne and have her hair dyed black. That would be her widow's weeds. She'd wear that black till she was dead and six feet under in her own grave, and only she would ever know why.

* * *

The funeral was set for Sunday afternoon. On Friday, the ladies of Heaven and especially of First Christian turned out to clean Charlene's house and beauty shop, and to bundle up the clothes for charity.

Minnie chose to go to the shop with Helen. Ida and Thelma had declared their intention to go through the household items, and Minnie knew for a fact that it would be simply too much for her to bear, to watch her beloved's house ransacked and reduced to estate sale categories. *How much will you give me for this life?* In her mind, a macabre auctioneer wheedled his crowd. *Do I hear fifty? Fifty? Who will give me fifty?*

She looked around the little shop that had become the center of her life for close to two decades. Never again would she face the wall of mirrors to watch Charlene at work, catch her eye and feel the thrill of knowing she was loved. And though she would miss the intimacy they'd managed but a few times since their brief discovery of love, it would be the touch everyone knew that she would miss the most: the tingle of her scalp, the tickly feeling on her neck, the sweet sensation of Charlene's hands—her Charlie's hands—on her head.

Everyone would miss this touch, in fact. It was as if Charlene had been a healer, laying on hands. All her customers had experienced it, coming in with a headache, or a heavy heart, and leaving an hour later unburdened.

It was Minnie who'd suggested that the proceeds from selling Charlene's house, equipment, and inventory of supplies be used to establish a scholarship fund to send someone from Heaven to learn the trade. There would be enough to pay for the coursework and lodging at the Indianapolis Beauty College and enough to purchase new equipment when the time came.

She'd had the idea as she marched with the ad hoc committee that had insisted Herb Wasmuth put the skirt back on Charlene. She knew Elizabeth would take the idea back to Frederick, and that he'd bring it up as if it were his own. Meanwhile, she'd mentioned it to Alma, who served on the town council with Frederick, to be sure to let it come up. It passed unanimously in the ad hoc meeting they held at Clara's Kitchen.

In order to keep her feelings in check, Minnie mused about who might apply while she boxed curlers, combs, and brushes. The little bell ringing over the door startled her out of her reverie. Elizabeth and Sue Ellen Sue were bustling through, stomping snow off their boots and shaking their hands out of mittens and gloves.

Elizabeth launched right into her news. "Sue Ellen Sue heard us talking about the scholarship and says she wants us to wait for her to graduate from high school so she can get it."

"'Cause I want to be a beautician when I grow up," Sue Ellen Sue chimed in as she hung her coat on a hook by the door.

"That'll be a ways off." Minnie couldn't help but smile at the ten-year-old who stood so assuredly at the entrance of the shop.

"Only seven years if I go straight from high school."

"I sure will miss having Charlene till then," Elizabeth sighed. "I got pretty used to not having to drive for forty minutes to get my hair done."

"I know," said Minnie. "It sure was nice." Her voice threatened to break so she left it at that.

"Anyway," Elizabeth said, "we thought we'd come help you pack things up for the auction."

Sue Ellen Sue was in the chair, spinning around and around.

"Sue Ellen Sue," her mother admonished, "that is not helping. That is playing." She put Sue Ellen Sue to work boxing up unopened cans of hair spray and bottles of shampoo.

The bell over the door rang again, ushering Ida in. She'd found some things at Charlene's house, she announced. A lock of hair, and a name.

Minnie's heart leapt to her throat. What name had Ida found? Would it betray her?

"What color?" Elizabeth wondered.

"Blonde," said Ida, and pressed on. "Did any of you ever hear Charlene mention someone named Joanne Bailey?" she wanted to know.

Minnie let Elizabeth continue to do the talking. "No, never heard of her."

"Well," Ida said, "I found a little address book tucked into Charlene's underwear drawer so I looked through it to see if there was anything Harry and Claude should know."

Minnie had to turn away. Bad enough Ida and Thelma had pawed through Charlene's dishes, pots, pans, dresses, blouses, skirts, and shoes, but her most private things? She couldn't bear knowing how titillated Ida must have been to find the falsies and wraps. The hair only Minnie knew was Hannah's.

Ida continued. "But all it had in it was the phone number for a supply shop and the name and number for a Joanne Bailey. I thought, well, that's probably someone who would want to know what happened, so I dialed the number. It was in Chicago." She paused for dramatic effect.

Elizabeth was busy marveling at Ida's willingness to, as Frederick would have put it, butt into other people's business. Minnie was struggling to breathe. It was Sue Ellen Sue who urged Ida on. "What did you tell her?"

"Well, I asked if Charlene Bader was a friend of hers and she said yes, and I told her the sad news and then I asked her if she ever suspected anything unusual about Charlene and she said what did I mean, and I said well she isn't a she, you know, it turns out she's a he, passing as a woman, had everyone in Heaven fooled, but Charlene was really a man."

"What did she say when you told her that?" Sue Ellen Sue wanted to know.

"Hush!" Elizabeth commanded, but Ida answered anyway.

"She said, 'You don't say!' and I said, 'I do say! I saw it for myself.' And I told her about how Charlene must've had a heart attack, about to take a bath."

Elizabeth's voice was strained. "Don't you think you should have let Harry handle the call?"

Ida, rebuked, stood her ground. "And hear it from someone with no manners?"

Helen saw the suffering on Minnie's face. "I'm sure she appreciated your letting her know," she said to Ida. "Can you ladies finish up here? I need to go pick Harley up now from sitting with Laura, and that means Minnie has to go too."

They rode in silence back to the Kelso farm, Helen assiduously attending to the road, Minnie staring mournfully out from the passenger seat. When they got there, Lester reported that Laura was asleep.

"Let's go then, Harley." Helen cut off any impulse Lester might have had to chat.

"Thank you." Minnie managed to hold herself together until she saw them shut the car door and drive away. Then she went upstairs to her room, pulled out Charlie's fox fur from its resting place in her bottom bureau drawer, and clung to it as she sobbed herself to exhaustion and sleep.

*   *   *

Like Herb Wasmuth, Pastor Van Pelt at First Christian had also seen and heard a lot in his day. He'd married young couples who had their firstborn "premature" at nine pounds, he'd counseled wayward husbands and wives, he'd helped distraught parents, spouses, and children deal with the gruesome and untimely deaths of children, spouses, and parents. But he'd never before faced the challenge of what to say about the fact that a congregant among them had not only passed on, but had passed as a woman. Charlene had attended his church almost every Sunday for the entire eleven years he'd served, and seven and a half before that. Not once had he suspected. It shook him to his core—not that it was possible for a man to pass as a woman, or, for that matter, a woman to pass as a man, but that Charlene had seen fit to keep the secret. How it must have burdened her—him! Pastor Van Pelt wished Charlene had trusted him. He searched his memory for clues, and found none. How could he claim to shepherd his flock if he knew so little about the individuals who composed it?

By Sunday, he'd written and rewritten his remarks, but still wasn't sure what he had to say. He put aside his prepared text and looked out at the little church full of people.

"This past week, as you all know, one of the members of our congregation here was called home to God. I know you were all as shocked as I was to learn that the person we've known for all these years as Charlene was actually Charles. Charles Ernst Bader. I know many of you have prayed for guidance this week, as I have. Many of you have wondered as I have what drove our friend to live such a secret, solitary life. Perhaps you have felt betrayed and angry. Perhaps you have felt guilty. I know I have. I have felt the pain of knowing Charles Ernst Bader carried a heavy burden, and I was not discerning enough to help him sort it out. But for today, let us put aside our pain and confusion, our angry feelings, our should-haves. Let us put aside our burning curiosities and our scandalized sensibilities. Let us come together, yes, to bury our friend, but also to praise.

"Let us praise the steadfast confidence that our friend, as Charlene, maintained. She created a haven on this troubled earth. A place of safety and assurance. A place where each woman who visited was queen for an hour. As I've talked to you ladies these past few days, this is what you have told me. That in Charlene's Beauty Shop you felt beautiful. You felt honored. You felt secure.

"And let us forgive. Let us forgive our friend for keeping such an enormous secret. Let us forgive him for living among us in a lie. Let us forgive ourselves whatever uncharitable thoughts we may have had upon hearing about his true identity."

Some part of Minnie managed to split off, keep her ear on the words, nod her head when others did the same. Inside her heart, though, she raged. Beat her breast, tore at her hair, wailed.

"Let us pray. Let us pray that Charles Bader's soul will rest in peace. Let us pray that God will look with compassion upon his sins and with love upon his foibles."

After the minister's homily people didn't know what to say. Well, they never did know what to say about extremely personal matters, and this was a most unusual and extremely personal matter for everyone in Heaven whether they'd known Charlene personally or not. They were grateful that Pastor Van Pelt had spoken for them. The men could shake each other's hands in friendship and community and simply agree tersely that it was a good sermon. The women could embrace one another and say not a word, just separate from their hug and look each other in the eye for the briefest exchange of a slightly rueful smile. The kind of smile that only shows in the eyes, that says we have a little secret to share.

The secret the women of Heaven shared was the thrill of infidelity. Another man's hands had been on them, not their husband's hands, only on their heads of course, which is why no one could ever seriously question their faithfulness. Their husbands touched them other places, some roughly, some with consummate gentleness, some like a wicked and sly game, some like hesitant schoolboys, some like self-involved movie idols. But their husbands never worked fingers in little lathered circles around the base of the head, up by the ears and then to the front and back down to the base of the neck again, only this time scrubbing the top of the scalp on the way. This had been Charlene's province, solely hers. They felt their ears tickle and their scalp tingle when they looked at each other. They were a harem of sorts. The thought crossed the mind of Elizabeth and she suppressed a smile, knowing it would be impossible to explain to anyone the "hair-um" pun that was her private entertainment. She could tell Alma tomorrow. Alma would chuckle with her and that would be that.

The men of Heaven were particularly thankful this morning because they weren't quite letting themselves think about what they would have done, would have had to have done, if Charlene's Charlie-ness had come out before her death. Those notions just slipped back under the murky surface of the collective male consciousness of Heaven. No need now to stir it up. He's dead anyway. She's dead anyway. Whatever. The ladies want it to be she, that's okay with us. We don't want to dwell on Charlene's maleness anyway. Not when our wives went to see her week in and week out for nigh onto two decades. No sirree.

* * *

The respite in the weather had been brief, so the entire funeral ceremony was held at First Christian. The grave would be dug when there was another thaw, the casket stored at the cemetery till then.

Just about the whole town turned out. The women insisted on attending, and their husbands went along to humor them, but also because they felt a little unsettled. They were a bit jealous, though they didn't know it. Would they be this missed when their time came? Would their wives weep with contained grief and dignity the way they were weeping now, dabbing at their tears, looking into the middle distance, lost in their own private worlds?

Helen Breck sat slightly apart from Lester, at the end of the second row. Helen knew more than most in Heaven about secrets. She'd kept her own awful secret for a decade now—that she was the one who knew what had happened to her daughter's baby. She knew because she was the one who abandoned the newborn by a carnival fortune-teller's tent. And, too, as far as anyone knew, she still thought

her husband was a handyman named Harley Dade, a momentary confusion she pretended persisted. She felt closer to the dead hairdresser
now than she ever had in life.

Ida was on the other side of Helen, feeling more central to
Heaven's affairs than she ever had before. After all, she'd been almost
the first to know. And she alone had spoken to Charlene's friend in
Chicago.

Just behind her sat Frederick, Elizabeth, David, and Sue Ellen
Sue Tipton. Frederick had an arm around his son's shoulder as if to
protect him from the aberration about to be buried. Elizabeth held
Sue Ellen Sue's hand. The young girl was somber, thinking of how
Caroline and John John had stood at their father's funeral. Elizabeth,
a woman who always had a two cents' worth to add, or an "if you ask
me" to contribute, was speechless even in her own mind, aware only
of a void in her life now. Charlene's Beauty Shop had been a place of
respite for her, where she could go to assert her own individuality and
ideas. Where would she go now to be listened to?

Katie Denson sat with her parents, Reba and Lawrence, and her
daughter Ellie. (Robert, her husband, was at Pete's Gate, holding
forth on the injustices of the world to anyone drunk enough to be a
willing audience. That included Norman, who had convinced himself that the reason Amy left him all those years ago was obviously
because she'd been having an affair with—whatever they said his
name really was.) Unlike Sue Ellen Sue, Ellie had never been inside
Charlene's Beauty Shop, but she'd had a shock at the funeral home
looking into the casket. Charlene was the woman she'd seen at the
carnival the year before, standing in line waiting to have her palm
read. Alma and Wilma Porter were in the pew just behind Ellie. Alma
was thinking about making a quilt, maybe something that would
commemorate Charlene in some way. Wilma was thinking that it was
easier for a woman to dress—at least casually—in men's clothing and
get away with it. For once in her life, she felt lucky to be female. And

she could hardly wait till she would have enough money saved up to go far, far away to college.

At the very back of the church, unnoticed by the others, was a stranger in her sixties. The only one present who might have recognized Joanne Bailey was lying in the casket.

Minnie had positioned herself in the last row of pews. Because everyone was here, there was no one to sit with Laura, so Minnie had bundled her mother up and brought her along. Laura was confused, kept thinking it was her husband's funeral and commenting on how suddenly the weather had changed, because the morning Paul died it was a crisp fall day and now it was already bitter winter. Minnie was glad for the excuse to sit in the back, near the door, in case her mother got restless. It gave her comfort to see how beloved Charlene was, how people were sticking with her even after they'd found out. She was bursting with the love she felt for Charlie and for Charlene. For someone who loved to gossip, it was new territory to have such a spectacular secret that she knew she would never tell. At first it had made her ache, to be in the company of people who talked about Charlene, tried to figure her out, tried to understand why she'd done what she'd done. Minnie could have told them. Could have shared with them Charlie's pathway from Kirbyville to Heaven. Could have warmed them with anecdotes about his devotion to his sister, sobered them with accounts of his war service, and astonished them with tales of his friends in Chicago. All these things that she'd just learned herself in the past few months she could have parceled out to her friends in Heaven. But that would dilute them for her. She would hoard these memories. Heaven had plenty of stories to go around without her telling about Charlie. She was the only one in town who'd known Charlie. The only one.

"It's nice to see so many people come out for Paul," her mother beamed.

Minnie patted her hand. "Yes," she said. "Yes it is."

At the pulpit, Eunice Switzer had finished singing "His Eye Is on the Sparrow" and Pastor Van Pelt was inviting the assembled to conclude the service by joining him in the Lord's Prayer.

"Our Father, who art in Heaven, hallowed be thy name. Thy kingdom come, thy will be done, on earth as it is in heaven . . ." The congregation continued in its single, somber monotone, speaking of daily bread, trespasses, and temptation. Minnie thought about heaven. The other heaven. She wanted to believe in it. She wanted to believe that someday, she and Charlie would be together again.

The stranger who'd been standing in the back slid into the pew next to Minnie. She spoke softly in Minnie's ear. "I'll be slipping out now," she said as Minnie turned to see who it was, "before people start to leave and wonder who I am. But I wanted to let you know how very much he loved you. We could all tell from the moment he first met you. He loved you beyond measure." And when Minnie gaped, the stranger answered her silent question. "Joanne Bailey."

Minnie nodded, understanding now. "And I loved him," she said very quietly and close to collapse. "I will always love him." Joanne touched Minnie's arm in a brief gesture of empathy, and then was gone, just as the congregation voiced the last of the prayer.

"Forever and ever," said the good people of Heaven, and as the prayer ended Minnie joined in. "Amen," she whispered. "Amen."

Heaven, Indiana

JAN MAHER

DOG HOLLOW PRESS
PLATTSBURGH, NY

1954

Elephants paced restlessly, their immense feet beating slow syncopations. Monkeys gossiped nervously of fearsome and forbidden places. Chameleons flicked their quick tongues and tasted the August air. An unblinking boa curled around the single rock that graced its cage; the tiger mother bared her teeth and readied her claws.

Out on Millstone Road, up in Lester and Helen Breck's barn, daughter Melinda howled in surprise, then roared in rage. Pain had taken her past exhaustion to a point of pure compelling necessity. Angry at the wrenching labor, this betrayal by nature, she took a great gulp of air and finally expelled her squalling daughter. Rough hands guided the infant upwards to her mother's belly, placed her at the breast. The anonymous babe turned her lips, seeking the nipple, and laid claim to her first meal.

Around the corner and down the road, the Wild Animal Caravan of the Hoosier Midways Carnival, mysteriously persuaded that the worst of some invisible storm was now over, finally settled down to sleep at the Heaven, Indiana 4-H and Fair Grounds.

* * *

There was a distracted air about this new mother. She was the farmer's daughter immortalized in bad jokes about traveling salesmen. Her own bad joke had passed through a little over eight months earlier, leaving samples all over central Indiana. One grew in the belly of Melinda—not a particularly bright girl, but a pleasant and obedient one. She'd been instructed by her father to make up the extra bed for the Fuller Brush man. "I'd like the gentleman to feel at home," he'd said.

The peddler knew an opportunity when he saw one. "You know what would make me feel most at home?" he asked the innocent Melinda. "I've got a pretty little wife there, and she keeps me warm at night. If you really want to make me feel at home, you could come back later, after your folks is asleep, and cuddle up here with me for a bit, so's I'm not so lonesome."

Melinda enjoyed this seduction. It was different, doing it in a bed. The brush man was a far more accomplished lover than Cedric Burney, her classmate across the border of the back forty. She didn't think to consider what might happen next.

By the time Melinda's surprised roar pushed her infant into the Midwest world, she'd been sequestered for fully four months—kept in the barn by her mother, who told friends and neighbors that Melinda had gone to Iowa to help an ailing great aunt. Seventeen weeks in the barn had changed the farmer's daughter. She'd grown more and more to trust the ways of cows and pigs, less and less to expect anything of mothers.

It was her father who attended the birth.

Helen Breck did come out to take a look at the newborn, and found her worst fears confirmed. So when Lester came to tell her that Melinda had developed a fierce fever in the predawn hours of her second day postpartum, Helen did what had to be done. A woman no longer given to tears, having long ago learned that they got her nothing but more grief, she was determined not to cry. She wrapped the infant in a clean piece of flannel, put it in a picnic basket and put the basket in the Kaiser. "Bring Melinda in the house," she told Lester, "and give her as much hot chamomile tea as she can take. I'll be back in a bit." And she drove off to town.

Lester was afraid to ask his wife where she was intending to go. These past many months, he'd felt unable to ask her about anything she was planning, had preferred instead to wait and see. The tortured determination on Helen's face the day she sent Melinda to the barn had chilled him, made him suddenly fearful of something he couldn't name. The keen intelligence and wry wit he loved in her had given way to humorless hypervigilance. Now she carried herself coiled, ready to spring, and it kept him in a state of constant, unfamiliar anxiety.

He protested at first. "Don't you think she'd be better off in one of those homes, Mother?"

But Helen would hear none of it. "How will she take care of herself? No stranger is going to look after her as well as we can."

"Couldn't she just stay in the house, then?"

"Now how long do you think it would be till the whole town knew? She has enough trouble with people taking advantage without these young fellows around here getting the idea they can have their way with her."

Lester had to admit that she had a point. Helen had always been fiercely protective of Melinda, and Melinda was pretty dependent on them. This did seem to be a way to manage the situation without getting all of Heaven in an uproar over it.

So instead of arguing further with Helen's decision, he'd done his best to make the girl comfortable in her exile. He set up the rollaway bed for her, built a little table and bench, brought out an extension cord to run off the light in the chicken coop so she could see after the sun went down, hauled up the old platform rocker so he could sit sometimes and keep her company. He brought her books to look at, quilt patches to work on, and a Ball jar full of fireflies with holes poked in the lid—hoping it would amuse her as much as it had years before, when she had tried to read by their light.

They didn't talk much about her situation. She never questioned the appropriateness of her punishment. There had been rumors at school the year before about Gloria Montgomery, a girl over in Montpelier, who graduated from high school and went off to social work school in June. Everyone seemed to know that girls didn't go to college and even if they did, no one went in June. It was pretty clear that Gloria had made a big mistake, was "p-g," would be gone for a few months, and would reappear later, slimmer, without a whit more education. Perhaps, Melinda reasoned, Gloria had been sent to a barn, too.

Melinda and her father sat quietly most of the time, or Lester read a bit from the Bible or from Volume D-E-F of the Wonderbook Encyclopedia, which Melinda had bought some years back at an estate sale.

As close as they got to be, though, it embarrassed Lester to be the one she hollered for when her water broke. He had to keep reminding himself that he'd delivered dozens of calves, and this was surely no different.

* * *

At the midway, there was still a hint of dew on the grass, and everyone was sleeping in. The night had been still and hot; sleep hadn't even been an option till well after midnight. Helen took care that no one saw her stop near the tent of Madame Gajikanes, the Gypsy fortune-teller, nor saw her place the basket at the door. Then she got back into the Kaiser and drove on.

She made a stop at Clara's Kitchen, parking up the street so her footpath to Clara's would take her by early-riser Ida Mueller's yard. There, Helen stopped to compliment Ida on her beautiful flowerbeds, and stayed to chat a full fifteen minutes about the winning lima beans at the Centennial Fair. "Fordhooks," Ida said in summary, "are always the best bet."

"That's a fact," Helen agreed. "You can always count on Fordhooks."

At Clara's, she discussed the new elementary school principal with June Wade, who took her order for black coffee and white toast. June had heard he was a young fellow, not much more than thirty. "He'll have his hands full with all those Bickle children running around the hallway," Helen opined.

After breakfast, she strolled up the street to Herman's Market and picked up a loaf of Korn Krust bread. On the way back to the car, she waved through the window of Charlene's Beauty Shop to Minnie, helmeted in the dryer, first customer of the day.

At home again, she checked on Melinda, who was inside now, tossing in her sleep. She sponged the girl's forehead, and cleared away the teacup. Then she went out to the barn, to make sure there were no obvious signs of its having been used as an inn. Lester had put the bed away, moved the rocker back to the porch and brought the books and sewing projects inside. Helen dismantled the extension-cord lighting system and liberated what were left of the lightning bugs. Next, she went to the summer kitchen, where a peck of Kentucky Wonders Lester had picked that morning waited. He had already fired up the old woodstove and started water heating in the canner. She slid the pot aside, lifted the burner, and looked once over her shoulder to make sure he wasn't around to watch. Then she pulled an old photograph from her apron pocket and tossed it onto the bed of burning coals. She watched till flames crawled completely across the image before replacing the burner. Only then did she allow two or three tears to surface before drying her eyes on her apron hem and turning her attention to stringing the beans.

The next day at church she bubbled with news. "Melinda called from the bus station in Marion late last night, back from Sioux City. When we picked her up, she was so tuckered out from traveling that she went right to sleep in the car, hardly even woke up to go to bed, and was still sleeping when we got up for church this morning. Well, we decided to let her just rest up a bit." She dropped her voice and confided, as if telling secrets of state. "You know, it's a two-day trip on the Greyhound. The poor thing is just exhausted."

"Your Aunt Doris is feeling better, then?"

"Oh, yes," Helen said. "Melinda says she's fit as a fiddle now."

"It's a blessing to have family to help you out when you need it."

"Yes, it sure is."

*   *   *

There's a particular kind of haze that hangs over an Indiana town on a hot August day. It isn't really bright golden, at least not in Heaven. It's almost white.

The fortune-teller slept in her tent that Friday night. Something she rarely did, but there was more air there than in the trailer, and the August heat was so still and pressing that those with any options to do so bedded down where there was at least hope of a bit of breeze.

John and Maggie Quinn Fletcher fled with their chubby, but not yet giant infant to the Riverside, where they sat far enough apart to let any wayward breeze circulate freely between them. The baby, a girl, was colicky. Maggie let her suck a finger dipped in whiskey before handing the pint bottle to her husband. Then she raised her skirt over her immense knees and fanned herself with it. John settled his bulk on the bank of the river and sipped the whiskey. Between them, they weighed well over half a ton, and August heat was one of their greatest occupational discomforts, if not outright hazards. The baby was, as yet, in the normal weight range, but it, too, was suffering from the heat.

The less kind among their audiences declared it a miracle that John and Maggie were ever able to get near enough to each other to accomplish pregnancy in the first place. But somehow they had, though Maggie had been unaware of her condition until the night of the Memorial Day parade. She had eaten heavily that evening, her value to the carnival dependent on her ability to top the scales at more than five hundred pounds. An illness earlier that spring had caused her weight to dip precipitously to four hundred eighty-one, and she needed to gain back the lost twenty pounds. Her part of the sideshow involved stepping onto elephant scales for a weigh-in. The scales had initially been altered to keep her above five hundred, but a rare inspection from Weights and Measures that day had required Mr. Coleson, the carnival manager, to correct the "error."

The night of the parade, Maggie thought she had heartburn. When she began to have cramps, John sent for Granny, as everyone called Madame Gajikanes. Granny was known, in addition to her fortune-telling, for having a few tricks up her sleeve: old Gypsy cures, it was said. The carny people were generally willing to put much more trust in their own Granny than in any of the small-town doctors who practiced along the carnival routes.

Maggie's water broke just as Granny arrived, and it hadn't taken her psychic powers to note that Maggie's problem would be fully apparent in a moment and far more chronic than heartburn.

So when Granny awoke from the mugginess and stepped outside her tent that August morning to catch a breath of air, she thought at first that John and Maggie had left their daughter Lenore at the door. It took only a moment to realize, however, that the infant at her feet was entirely new, no more than a day or two old.

Granny didn't hesitate. She brought the basketed baby in. "And who are you?" she crooned to it, as she peeled back the bits of blanket and clothing to see if it was a boy or girl who had come visiting. "A little girl? That nobody wants? And nothing to your name. Nada en todos. Rien de tout. But that's all right. That's the best way to be. Nothing to hold you down, nothing to keep you back. Let me see your hand, little one." Gently, she pried the tiny fist open. "A strong heart line," she assured the infant. "That's good. You'll need it in this world. And you've got a good long life coming, too." She touched the life line and the baby closed her fist again, holding tightly to Granny's finger. But what struck Granny most about this newcomer wasn't her life line. It was her eyes. They seemed to take in everything.

Madame Gajikanes laid her plans. Old Man Coleson wouldn't want to deal with another infant. He was already in an uproar about John and Maggie, although he grudgingly acknowledged that the child was indeed adding to the value of the sideshow. Not that children were forbidden or even discouraged. They were doted upon by most of the regulars. It's just that Coleson hated surprises and he abhorred scandals.

And Granny knew for a fact that an abandoned baby was somebody's scandal; especially one abandoned at a Gypsy's tent. No matter that Madame Gajikanes wasn't a real Gypsy. The myths were as pervasive as they were fallacious, and Old Man Coleson was obsessive about avoiding trouble. His was a Sunday-school carnival of the first degree. He wouldn't want any headlines about baby-stealing to sully his reputation.

She had, of course, no bottles with which to feed a baby. Maggie did, but Granny couldn't trust her to keep a confidence. Some who knew Maggie best said her mouth was the very biggest thing about her. There was Lillian, on the other hand, whose prize Bengal had just given birth. Granny went to Lillian and told her a child had arrived from heaven.

She left with two bottles and a three-day supply of baby tiger formula. She mixed the formula with one of her own that kept the infant safely quiet in the back room of her tent. Her customers on Saturday and Sunday never guessed that while their secrets were being discovered in the wrinkles of their palms, Granny kept one of her own just a few feet away. And when the photographer from the Heaven Historical Society took a human-interest photo of the town's new babies at the gate to the fairgrounds, with the Centennial Fair and Hoosier Midways forming the backdrop, only two infants were featured: Eleanor Alice, born the tenth of June to Robert and Katherine Denson, and Sue Ellen Sue, born the fifth of January to Frederick and Elizabeth Tipton. The unnamed baby found the twenty-first of August by Nancy White (known to her clients as Madame Gajikanes) went entirely unremarked.

* * *

The sun came up Monday morning on a day that promised little relief from the heat. At the Breck farm, Melinda was too feverish to articulate her consternation. She was fairly sure she'd had a baby, but she couldn't seem to find it. Fitful sleep, strange dreams, flames, images of her skin like parchment paper catching fire at the edge, then wafting up in ghostly white ash. "Mother," Lester called out from Melinda's bedside, where he had relieved Helen of the watch at four o'clock, when it was time to feed the chickens and milk the cows. "I think she's taking a turn for the worse."

Helen Breck finally admitted she was out of her league. She called Dr. Brubecker then, and reached his nurse, who told her the doctor was on vacation for another four days. Relieved, she called his backup, who arrived from Hartford City just in time to watch Melinda draw her last breath. Helen professed astonishment when the doctor declared that Melinda appeared to have given birth very recently, and that under the circumstances he'd probably have to order an autopsy. She broke down and sobbed, beat her fists upon her stolid husband's chest and wondered aloud and copiously how Melinda could have done this to them; wondered, moreover, what could have happened to the baby. Even insisted that the Chicago Greyhound station be searched for what would be their first and only grandchild, their only hope of an heir.

* * *

Monday was strike day for the carnival. While the rest of the folks finished folding their tents and packing up their props, Granny announced that she was off for a minute or two to coax her old '38 Chevy to the gas station, fill the tank. And it was as easy as that to slip out of Heaven, go off to find another carnival where no one would question the sudden appearance of a new granddaughter. Later, Lillian, thinking quickly, told a furious Coleson that Granny had gotten an urgent letter from her estranged daughter Peggy on Saturday, and after a long distance call on Sunday night, had felt compelled to make the trip to Ohio, where her help was needed.

On her way out of town, Granny passed by Sheriff Johnson, headed out to the Breck farm to see what all the fuss up there was about.

1960

She wasn't what you'd call a well-behaved child. For one thing, she changed form constantly. Sometimes she was an infant, sometimes a toddler, sometimes big enough for kindergarten or even first grade. Sometimes she chattered, sometimes she was sullen and mute. Sometimes she looked like Lester's side of the family, blond and blue-eyed; sometimes she favored her hazel-eyed mother; sometimes her eyes darkened more like Helen's and her hair showed hints of being naturally curly. And she drove Helen crazy the way she'd just sit in the corner of the kitchen and stare at her, or worse yet, chant a barely coherent scrap of childhood rhyme. Eeny, meeny, miney, moe, she droned over and over, till Helen thought she would scream.

"Hush, now," Helen would admonish, but the child refused to hush, except when any of Helen's egg customers dropped in. At those times, she disappeared altogether.

And then Lester, who had at least tried to be helpful at the beginning of this nightmare, up and died in an accident exactly six years after Melinda's return from Sioux City. Lucky for Helen that fellow Harley came along looking for work just about the same time, so at least the farm was still operating at full efficiency.

She met him at the cemetery where she'd gone to visit Melinda's grave. She bent down to put some flowers by the headstone and when she straightened up again, it was Lester's name she saw at her feet. She turned to the kind-looking stranger nearby and announced, shocked by the suddenness of fate into an uncharacteristically quavering voice, "My husband's dead."

"Not hardly," Lester assured her.

"Harley," Helen repeated, trying to remember if she'd ever met this fellow before.

"Hardly dead," Lester said. "Why, I'm standing right here, Mother."

Helen stared a moment, then looked around wildly. Lester could tell something was very wrong.

"Are you all right?"

"I'm a little nervous, to tell you the truth."

"Can I do something to help?"

She looked at the grave. It looked back at her.

"I wonder if you wouldn't mind giving me a ride home," she said, surprising herself with the boldness of it. It wasn't like her to ask anyone for favors, let alone perfect strangers. "I don't know if I ought to drive right now." She looked up at the sky, as if she expected lightning to strike. And if she wondered why this man had no car of his own, she kept it to herself.

As Lester held the car door open for her, she managed to remember her manners and thanked him. "Harley Dade? You must not be from around here. I never heard of any Dades in Hutter County."

Lester wasn't sure what to say. They rode in silence to the main road.

"It's up left about two mile," Helen directed him.

He ventured to ask how her husband had died, and listened while Helen filled him in on the details of his own presumed death. They coincided precisely with the particulars of Omar Breck's death, Lester's father. Pops had died back in '49 in a grim combine accident.

When they turned up the driveway, Helen sighed. "I don't know what I'm going to do now. That hay needs baling."

Lester glanced across at her. He decided to play along for the time being. "I reckon I could get that done for you."

"You know how to run a baler?"

"Yes, ma'am."

"I don't have a lot to pay."

"Well, I don't really need a lot. Just a place to put my head at night and meals is all. Maybe a little bit of cash for my Mail Pouch and a cuppa coffee in town now and then." It was the same compensation he'd always worked for.

She hired him on.

Lester thought about it while he chewed a comfrey leaf and rode the John Deere through the rows. Seemed to him like this was how Helen had decided to deal with guilt. Like someplace deep inside her, she believed she was being punished for abandoning the little baby girl, and she'd translated that into some kind of figuring that she didn't deserve happiness, or a husband, or much of anything. Lester hoped that if he just humored her, she'd come back to herself. Maybe then she'd laugh, thinking about how she mistook his reassurance for the name Harley Dade. It surely had been a long time since he'd heard her laugh.

In the meantime, he accepted the situation as his own punishment. He didn't want to let himself expect too much, or want too much. He too had sinned, and it was fitting, even necessary, that he pay for it.

Helen, he knew, had been haunted about her choices almost from the beginning. Within days of her impulsive decision to drop the child at the tent stoop of the Gypsy fortune-teller, she'd started looking for Hoosier Midways. But in the whole long six years, that particular carnival had not returned to Heaven, nor had it appeared in any other nearby community.

The first week after Melinda died, the doctor, as obligated by law, had filed a death certificate at the Hutter County seat. The Brecks, mindful of this requirement, had done their own reporting, calling the local sheriff to ask aid in contacting agencies and officials in Chicago and Sioux City. Lester Breck suffered for these deceits, but he'd long ago relinquished all decisions related to child-rearing and business to his wife. Now was certainly no time to question her wisdom. Besides, he knew enough to figure that since he had tended Melinda's labor, and hadn't insisted on medical attention for her when she started to fail, he was probably guilty of something under the law, not just in his own conscience. And he wasn't prepared to live as an outright criminal either in or out of jail. He valued his acreage and his camaraderie at the Grange. He valued hot breakfasts at Clara's Kitchen before sunup. He valued Indiana sunsets and a plug of Mail Pouch while riding the tractor.

So cooperating authorities searched the Chicago and Sioux City bus stations, and interviewed Helen's Aunt Doris. When Doris said no, she'd never even seen Melinda, Helen fainted so convincingly that the sheriff figured the girl had deliberately deceived her mother to hide her shame. For Helen had shown him letters the girl had written. And they were in her handwriting (the conscientious sheriff had checked, even though he regarded the Brecks as salt-of-the-earth citizens). Once a week, Helen had dictated to her barnbound daughter what to write about life in Sioux City, and had shared those letters with enough people that it was generally accepted as true that they were written and mailed from there. Eunice Switzer even remembered a Sioux City postmark, although she'd actually never seen an envelope.

When the official investigation died down, Helen set about her own discreet mission to locate the infant. "Our only hope," she told folks, "is to take it to God." She went to church each week and asked Him, but said that in the meantime, while she waited for His answer, she wanted to consult that fortune-teller as well. "I heard that the one with the carnival this year really has a gift. Didn't she tell Eunice

Switzer exactly where to find her lost ring?" But no one seemed to know for sure where the carnival had gone.

Ida said she thought there was usually a carnival in Muncie by Labor Day, but Helen made the drive in vain. No one she talked to in Muncie could remember a carnival having been there for at least three or four years. Of course, Helen didn't want to seem to be too fixated on that particular fortune-teller, so throughout that winter she consulted palm readers in Fort Wayne and Richmond, an astrologer in Indianapolis, and a numerologist in Marion. The next summer, and for five summers thereafter, Lester dutifully drove her to visit every fortune-teller at every county fair or carnival within a hundred miles of Heaven. None of them was named Gajikanes. Helen asked each of them, nonetheless, about the lost child. All of them spoke in soothing generalities. Helen regarded them all, to a woman, as fakes.

On the twenty-first of August, they visited the Huntington Fairgrounds and spoke with a crystal-ball-gazer whose sole insight was "Sometimes, near is far and far is near." Something in Helen snapped. She sat silent all the way from Huntington through Marion. When they passed the farm stand in Gas City she told Lester to back up and get some flowers, she wanted to visit Melinda's grave. Lester might have been worried right then, if he had been a worrying man. She hadn't been to the cemetery since the funeral.

Of course, after Helen announced Lester's death to Minnie, there was some talk. Lester took Minnie aside and explained, as much as he was willing to, what had happened. "I'd appreciate it," he said, "if you kept it to yourself for now. Just in case she snaps out of it, you know, I don't want her to feel embarrassed."

"Oh, you can count on me," Minnie said, and when she confided in Ida she asked for the same assurances.

Ida didn't tell a single person, other than just to mention it to Eunice. "Poor soul," she said, and Eunice nodded. Maybe it was her husband Earnest who overheard and didn't have the sense to keep it quiet. However it happened, it wasn't long till most of the town knew. But when they saw Helen in church, she looked so normal. She sang the way she always sang, she put two dollars in the collection tray the way she always did. And back on the farm, she continued to function in all the various ways she had over the years. The eggs she traded were just as fresh, the bills paid just as promptly. So no one felt it necessary to interfere with this insistence on treating Lester as her hired hand. As long as her husband was willing to put up with her, they figured, it wasn't for them to get involved.

Except, of course, they did keep an eye on the situation, just in case. After all, what are neighbors for, if not to keep an eye out? "You never know," Minnie would say to Ida.

"That's right," Ida would reply. "You never do."

Even Eunice, who usually did all her shopping at Herman's, started buying eggs from Helen, so she could check on her at least once a week. She tried to find ways to linger and look around on her egg days, but Helen had a way of discouraging that.

She tolerated the hovering of her friends, but Helen was happiest when she was alone. She even managed to discourage the little ghost of a girl, who, as the months went by, grew dimmer, but never older now.

Sometimes Helen stood at the kitchen window and watched Harley on the tractor. She liked to watch him because he walked like Lester, talked like Lester, used the same gestures, even sounded the same when he sneezed during hay-fever season. She kept those observations to herself, however, not wishing Harley to get any improper ideas. He was, she was relieved to note, a gentleman. Once in a while, he'd overstep his boundaries and ask about something he had no business asking about, or tell her she was looking particularly attractive that day, but he always backed right off when she let him know he'd crossed the line.

*   *   *

Hanging on the wall of the one restaurant in Heaven is an embroidered sampler that reads:

> *Monday's soup is full of peas*
> *Tuesday's soup contains some cheese*
> *Wednesday's soup has lots of tomatoes*
> *Thursday's soup has beets and potatoes*
> *Friday's soup is minestrone*
> *Saturday's soup has macaroni*
> *Sunday's soup's the very best*
> *'Cause Sunday is our day of rest*
> *See you in church!*

At the bottom, the needle artist had cross-stitched a little white church with a steeple and a wisp of smoke coming from the chimney. Beneath the sampler, in careful block lettering on a piece of stiff shirt cardboard, hung another, somewhat more recent message:

> *Now open on Sundays—*
> *Serving Chicken Noodle Soup with All Dinners.*

Clara's Kitchen hadn't been run by Clara for a couple of years, but when Stella took over she thought it wouldn't really be respectful to change the name. After all, Clara had put her life into the little cafe, doing all the cooking and serving at first, and setting her hours to accommodate everyone possible. If she had given it up due to death, maybe Stella would have called it Stella's Place, but Clara was just retired. So to honor her, Stella kept the name and menu as they'd always been.

Most of Stella's customers were regulars. She had some ideas for building up the business—bringing in more customers from nearby towns and getting more of Heaven's families to eat dinner out once in a while. But she didn't mind that breakfast was usually slow. She enjoyed having the time to sit sometimes and chat with the fellows who came in faithfully for their morning coffee and sweet rolls. The home-baked sweet rolls were one of the two specialties Stella had added to the menu, the other being rhubarb coffee cake when rhubarb was in season. Stella had a huge patch of rhubarb.

This morning, Lester was holding forth for her benefit and that of Maurice Wilson and Bobby Bennett. Away from home, Lester was a gregarious, garrulous man, and Clara's Kitchen was for him a lifeline. Helen never liked people "poking around" her house, as she put it. If she had something to say, she'd come to you. And she didn't have a whole lot to say these days. What she did have, she saved for her once-a-month visit to Charlene, her hairdresser. Then too, she certainly didn't expect a hired hand would have the audacity to invite people to her house. No, he could just go on down to Clara's if he wanted to set around shooting the breeze with a bunch of fools.

Lester was nostalgic today, and feeling philosophical. The conversation had somehow turned to fireflies, and everyone had a story to tell about how, as kids, they had collected them. Maurice remembered the mysterious glow it made when you stepped on one and smeared it across a patch of concrete.

When it came to Lester's turn, he settled back in the booth and shook his head at the preciousness of his memory.

"There's a way of watching lightning bugs takes you right out of this world. You set on your porch, or out in a lawn chair, and begin to pick 'em up just about a half hour after sunset. By ten or so they're all over the place. One here, then it goes out and the next thing you know it's over there. Or maybe it's a different one this time. It takes your mind right out watchin' 'em. They're like stars. Like they say about stars, being born and dying all the time all through the ages, only lightning bugs are right in your own yard.

"When Melinda was just a little thing I remember taking her to the county library once. There was this fellow—well, I suppose he must've been a librarian—asked the kids what they were curious about. Well sir, I didn't wait for the kids to answer. I just piped right up and said lightning bugs. What about 'em, he says. Well, how they do that, I says. How they light up. So he looked it up right on the spot. Now I don't remember what the explanation was. But I remember he said folks down in the jungle in South America got lightning bugs so big they strap 'em on their shoes so they can see at night." He paused, and got a distant look in his eye. "When Melinda heard that story about lightning bugs as big as flashlights, her eyes got just about that big too and she wanted some on her own shoes. Wondered why we couldn't just hop on down to South America and get a few."

Stella wasn't sure it was a good idea for Lester to get started on Melinda stories. She'd seen him before like this. He'd start with what seemed like a happy memory of his daughter, and before you knew it, he'd get a dark look in his eyes and settle into silence. And silence was not Lester's natural, healthy state. She asked, "Warm your coffee, boys?" and filled all the cups, then announced that she had to get the soup started for lunch.

That galvanized everyone. They stood, downed their last cups in a few long swigs, and headed out the door—Lester to harrow his winter wheat field, Maurice to ready Heaven's Bread for the day's business, and Bobby to open his service station. ("If you don't like the service in Heaven," the motto on his custom-printed wall calendars said, "you can go to Hell." Some folks thought it was sacrilegious to have a motto like that, but Bobby kept his own copy of the calendar in his jumbled and greasy shop area where customers weren't allowed and women preferred not to set foot anyway. He mailed the others out in plain brown wrappers to his best customers, and they kept them tucked away in garages and workrooms.)

"Bye, fellows," Stella called after them as they banged through the screen door. Stella exhaled, and headed to the kitchen to chop up the onions. Clara's Kitchen was momentarily empty.

Later that night, Lester dared to reminisce again. "Remember that time when Melinda was little and I took her to hear about the lightning bugs?" he asked Helen.

"What are you talking about," she snapped. "You never took her anywhere when she was little. Why, I never even met you till she was twenty-two and six years dead."

Lester nodded. "Well, I reckon I ought to get on to bed."

"Don't forget to turn the light out." Helen gathered her mending and headed upstairs.

"No, ma'am."

BOOK CLUB GUIDE

1. What does the title *Earth As It Is* mean to you?

2. What stays with you most about the book? Which character(s) and/or situation(s) do you identify with most?

3. How do the characters—both major and minor—negotiate the interplay between identity and society? Do any of their experiences feel familiar to you?

4. As Charlie/Charlene comes into a clearer sense of his/her identity, what does s/he gain? What does s/he lose?

5. The scenes in Chicago, in Europe during World War II, and in Heaven show characters who are sometimes brought together by circumstances or interests but who would not otherwise necessarily encounter one another. How do we move through different identities as we move in different groups or have intense experiences with people whom we ordinarily might never meet?

6. How do Charlie's war experiences prompt his decision to present and identify as a woman in day-to-day life?

7. What role do church and religion play in Charlie/Charlene's life? In Minnie's life? In the lives of the various communities in the novel? How is this similar to or different from the roles played by religions and centers of worship over the past century in the social life of our nation's various communities?

8. How do Charlie/Charlene and Minnie each experience the ways in which community both supports and limits their lives?

9. How does Heaven change Charlene? How does Charlene change Heaven?

10. Charlene is a listener. How does the power of listening serve her? How does it serve her customers?

11. How is Charlie—as Charlie—different at the end of his life than he was as a young man?

12. How has Minnie been changed by the end of the book? What might be the effects of these changes in her future?

13. What varieties of gender identities are expressed by the characters in the novel?

14. How does fear of gender variance shape the lives of the characters, both in terms of each character's inner life and in terms of the social pressures each faces?

15. How have attitudes about gender variance in the world of 1933–1964, as portrayed in the novel, changed in the twenty-first century? Are there ways in which they have not changed? Places where they have not changed?

16. What familiar worlds were made unfamiliar to you in this novel? What unfamiliar worlds were made familiar?

JAN MAHER's writing credits include a novel, *Heaven, Indiana*; plays *Ismene, Intruders, Widow's Walk,* and *Most Dangerous Women*; and books for educators *Most Dangerous Women: Bringing History to Life through Readers' Theater* and *History in the Present Tense: Engaging Students through Inquiry and Action* (co-authored with Douglas Selwyn). She holds a doctorate in interdisciplinary studies and has taught interdisciplinary seminars, education-related courses, writing, and documentary studies at colleges in New York, Vermont, and Washington State. She is a senior scholar at the Institute for Ethics in Public Life, State University of New York at Plattsburgh.

CPSIA information can be obtained
at www.ICGtesting.com
Printed in the USA
FSOW01n1646010217
30295FS

9 780253 024046